Homici ___
Hampshire

A Cleo Marjoribanks Murder Mystery

Barbara Bothwell

Cleo Marjoribanks moves into her new home in the New Forest and one evening finds the body of her housekeeper in the swimming pool. The lady's husband and one of Cleo's cars is missing. Paula (lady of the manor) befriends Cleo, an outspoken Londoner who clashes with the spoiled brat daughter. Between mysterious happenings, help from her crime report friend, Primrose, and a very strange car chase, the women help DCI David 'Steaming' Kettle solve the crimes.

Except where actual historical events and characters are being described for the storyline of this novel, all situations in this publication are fictitious and any resemblance to living persons is purely coincidental.

For more information about Barbara Bothwell:
www.barbarabothwell.blogspot.com
www.auntiestravels.blogspot.com

Barbara Bothwell has always written, no matter what other work she has been doing. She began as a secretary and ended her working life as a secretary but, in between, she worked in advertising, public relations, travel courier, gift shop manager on cruise ships. An Essex girl she became a 'gypsy' living in Mallorca, California and Florida.

In her teens she began writing romantic short stories which became crime novels when her heroine found a body. Now she writes cosy crime starting with the Cleo Marjoribanks series. Another series in the South Downs Murder Mysteries based in West Sussex and involving more police action.

'Cleo Marjoribanks' series:

Homicide in Hampshire
Dirty Deeds in Downdene
Ghosts in the Guest House
Murder in Mitcham Parva
Trouble in Trewith Green

South Downs Murder Mysteries:

Antiques in the Attic
Model Murder

Stand alone:

Rock'n'Roll Murders
Death of a Copycat

Chapter 1

I snatched up the phone in the pool room (using me skirt to hold it, of course. No point in reading mystery novels and doing it all wrong), all the while staring at the thing in the pool. It had to be Janet Spencer. It was wearing her dress. And there was red in the water. I knew she was dead and, while talking to the police, I wondered how I was so sure she was dead. I know I should have jumped into the pool to get her out and begin resuscitation but... The thought of what I might see made me gaga, so I scarpered, at least as best me high-heels would let me! (As I can't swim, it probably wouldn't have been a good idea anyway.)

I shot off straight down the hall, grabbed handbag and keys from the table near the door then scrabbled with the door locks. Why are they always a problem when you're in a hurry? At last I was out in the night air and could take deep breaths.

And don't ask me why I was in the pool room when I'd just come home. If you walk indoors and see lights on that shouldn't be on what would you do? No, not what I should have done – panicked. I went to investigate. Course it wasn't until later that I realised I'd been stupid.

It felt like I was standing outside for ages before I heard the cops arrive. Blue light flashing and siren moaning, just like a sick cow.

The car pulled up in front where I was leaning against the wall by the open front door.

One of the coppers eased his bulk from the car "Constable Brown," was the terse introduction. "Are you alright, madam? Are you Mrs. Marj-or-ibanks?"

"Pronounced Marchbanks," I corrected automatically. "I think I'm alright. Yeah, I called." I moved away from the wall and pointed into the house. "Down there, all the way to the end is the pool room. She's in the pool."

He went in, at the same time indicating to the other – younger - man who was also now out of the car, to stay with me. Did they think that if they left me there alone I might get into their car and escape?

Constable Brown quickly returned, looking slightly off colour, although it was difficult to tell in the illumination caused by the car headlights. Not saying a word, he shuffled into the car, presumably to call up reinforcements. Having done that he came up to us and told "Terry" (his mate) to go and put the blue and white crime scene tape across the front gates and wait there until the crime scene team arrived.

In the meantime he invited me to sit in the back of the car. "I think you'll feel better sitting down, madam," he intoned in his comforting country burr.

"Thank you. I'd give anything for a drink."

"I don't think we should go back into the house."

"It's alright. I understand."

Having seated me in the car, Brown went around the outside of the house. Thank goodness it was a dry night. He wouldn't disturb any evidence along the concrete path – if there was anything to find. He came back and checked up on me. "You alright, madam?"

"Fine."

"Look, I walked round that way and came to the end of the path. I can't see that anything's been disturbed. What's round the other side?"

"The driveway to the garages. And above that the flat where – where -."

"Housekeeper?" I nodded. "Okay, love, you stay there and I'll go and have a quick shufty."

He went around the corner out of sight and I sat wondering what he would find. The body of Dan? I shuddered at the thought.

When he returned he looked okay. "The garage doors are open. There's an old Rolls Royce Silver Wraith in there. The flat's dark so I don't know if anyone's in it. I called, but didn't get an answer."

"There should be a Volvo 340 in the garage. Why didn't you go up and look in the flat?"

"Evidence," he stated succinctly. Coward, I thought, but he then won me over when he added, "Like the Rolls."

I smiled at him. "My baby."

"Use her much?"

"Only when I'm in the country. I love driving her but if I have to go somewhere where there's a parking problem Dan Spencer drives her. He was supposed to meet me at the station with the Volvo. But he didn't turn up." Which reminded me. "Does that mean he's gone to the station while I was coming back here in the cab and we passed each other?"

"Dunno. Know the Volvo's registration?"

"Hang on." I rummaged in my handbag (once described by someone as a holdall – cheek!) and came out with my Filofax. "Here it is." I dictated the number.

He called in the number and description of the car to the control room so someone could check at Brockenhurst railway station and see if Dan was there or somewhere along the route.

Then a small convoy of vehicles arrived. Among them was a dark blue Ford Mondeo. It was the boss and his constable. Then came the police surgeon, a van of uniforms (who were detailed to secure the site – they wouldn't be able to do much more outside until daylight), a mortuary van and SOCOs. And a pair of divers to go into the pool to remove the body and check under water for evidence.

Whew! Would have been cheaper to put them all in a bus.

I watched their arrival from the back of the police car and assumed that the dark-haired gent to whom Constable Brown explained the situation was the boss man. Superintendent or Chief Inspector. Whatever.

He listened intently, occasionally nodding his head or putting a question to the tubby figure in the straining uniform. Eventually he turned and spoke to some of the other figures crowding behind him. He must have told them to hold their horses, except for a couple who went round the corner of the house, presumably to check the flat. Then he came over to the car.

"Mrs. Marjoribanks, I'm Chief Detective Inspector Kettle."

"Miss Marjoribanks," I reacted automatically, then stared at him.

"I beg your pardon, Miss Marjoribanks. Actually that answers my first question, which was if you knew where you husband was." He smiled at me.

"No, ta. I don't have one. But I know you, don't I?" I was almost sure it was old "Steaming" Kettle.

He began an automatic response, "No, I don't..." He paused, took my arm to help me out and walked me over to the light spilling from the open door. His eyes crinkled in a way I remember happens whenever he's thinking. He's thirty years older now, but then so am I.

"Walker Road Primary and Seniors?" I nodded. "Good God! You're…"

Chapter 2

I didn't give him time to finish. "Cleo Marjoribanks."

"Gawd! Wot you doin' ownin' a drum like this?" His carefully improved English lapsed back to our childhood in Plaistow, East London.

I had to laugh. "Wiv what's happened you'll soon find out," I retorted.

That brought him back to earth. "Right. Now, Cleo old girl, we've a bit of a problem. The house is going to have to be gone through so you won't be able to stay here tonight. Is there anyone you can stay with? A friend or relative?"

"Don't know anyone around here. I only moved here a few weeks ago. The locals barely nod to me."

"Hmmm."

"S'alright. I'll go and stay at a hotel in Lyndhurst. The only thing though, I need to get some clothes and things. Oh, and I'd love a cuppa. I'm dry as the Sahara."

"I'll have my constable, Jenny Dixon," he nodded in the direction of the young lady, "go into the house with you to help you pack then drive you to the hotel."

"She needn't do that! I can drive meself in the Roller."

That made his eyebrows almost disappear under his hair line.

"I'm sorry, Cleo." He shook his head. "Can you hang on a minute? Before you go upstairs I need them to fingerprint up there."

He went away and left me standing there. I used the wall as a prop again. A couple of overall- and cap-garbed people – couldn't tell whether they were men or women – went into the house and began working their way up the staircase. Help! That awful powder all over my nice new paintwork. As it happened Janet must have dusted the banister that morning because they didn't find any fingerprints on it. Then they disappeared, presumably looking for my bedroom.

"Why can't I take the Roller? They weren't supposed to use it. Not when I'm not here. All Dan does is take it out to wash it, make sure there's petrol in it and that it works proper."

"I'm sorry. Look, Cleo, I'll have someone call ahead and book a room for a night or two."

"Okay. And what about that cuppa?" I finished, giving him a cheeky grin. If my memory served me right, he also liked his cuppa.

"I'm sure we have an expert at making tea somewhere around."

"Ta."

"Jenny!" The young lady strode over and Steaming Kettle introduced us. "Can you go upstairs with Miss Marjoribanks to help her, then take her to whichever hotel we can get a room in?"

"Yes, sir. Come on, Miss Marjoribanks."

"Oh, gosh, this 'Miss Marjoribanks' business ain't half posh, innit? Why don't you call me Cleo."

"Okay, Cleo. I'm Jenny."

"That's better."

"Oh, Cleo, do you have any keys for the Rolls Royce and the flat over the garage?" Steaming asked. One of the two men who'd gone round the corner had returned. I guess they needed the key for the flat.

"And the house keys?"

"Might as well," Steaming smiled.

I walked towards him and beckoned him to me. "I don't want to shout this information all around the village.

10

In the kitchen you'll see there's an old fashioned pantry. Inside it on the wall are some cupboards. One of them is the key cupboard. Can't remember myself which one so you'll have to try them all. When I gave her the keys Janet – that's Janet Spencer what's in the pool – put them on key rings with labels."

"Thank you very much. Okay, Jenny?"

As we went into the house, me leading the way upstairs and not touching the dusty banister, I repeated my request, "You know, I really would love a cuppa."

"Wait a minute." Jenny leaned over the banister and called, "Anyone brewing up in the kitchen? We could do with some tea up here."

Steaming turned and looked at her, quirked an eyebrow and nodded briefly. I noticed that his dark hair is now attractively flecked with grey.

"Come on, Cleo, let's go and get you sorted out," Jenny suggested.

"I'll have to get the cleaning company in again," I mourned and she patted my back.

In the bedroom, while I was getting a suitcase from the back of the cupboard, one big enough for everything I would need, Jenny looked around at the room with its white furniture, fitted cupboards and silver and white striped wallpaper. I reckon it all contrasts fantastically well with the cornflower blue carpet and pastel blue curtains. And she began a little gentle probing. "Nice room." I smiled at her. "How long have you been living here? It's a lovely house – what I could see of it," she added ruefully.

"Not long. You should have seen it when I bought it. The woman who'd lived here until she died was too old to do anything and she kept cats. I don't think anything had been done to the place for years. I had to have it fumigated

11

and all re-done. The pool room is where the old conservatory was."

"I haven't seen the rest of the house," she reminded me as she sat down in one of the pair of pale blue armchairs and crossed one trousered leg over the other.

"No, of course, I forgot."

Jenny shrugged, "Must be nice to have your own pool."

"Except it'll have to be cleaned out now," I pointed out. "I'm not sure whether I'll even be able to go into that room again."

"Give it time, Cleo. Perhaps you could have a pool party," she suggested, her brown eyes twinkling.

Wonder what she'd look like if her hair was longer? The chestnut hair was short enough to give her a boyish look. Easy care hair, I guess.

It was my turn to shrug. "Don't know. Perhaps I'll have the room redesigned. Or something."

"Must be nice to be able to afford to do whatever you want when you want," she mused, obviously wondering where the money came from.

I did my mind-reading act, looked up from the caftan I was folding and said, succinctly, "Lottery. And that's strictly between you and me." I paused, "Oh, and I guess your boss and all."

She acknowledged that with a smile, "I can't really not tell him."

"I'm sure you can't, love. So, I won the lottery and did all the important things as far as my family's concerned. Did all right by them. Actually the only people who know about the win are those distant relatives and a handful of close friends. They're the ones I know I can trust to remain discreet."

"Where were you living before you won?"

"Out in Essex. I'm your original Essex girl."

"I'd have said more London."

"Yeah, well, grew up in East London, but East London or Essex. Same difference. Paid my dues, flogged my guts out doing a boring job in London."

"What was that?"

"Secretary in public relations."

"Must have been interesting."

"Alright." I actually hadn't been that enamoured with it. "But glad to finish with it."

"I'm lucky. I've a job that interests me."

"There you are, then, if you get qualifications you can do these things. My only qualification were shorthand and typing." I sighed, then smiled. "Still I didn't have a bad time of it, but I'm glad to be doing what I'm doing now."

"I take it you've been away? You said something about coming from the station?" Jenny probed gently.

"Been up in town for a few days doing some shows and concerts. And shopping. Came back tonight. To this." I took a deep breath, shut the case and yanked the zip round. "That's the case done. Oh. I haven't done the sponge bag. Come on. Bathroom."

She followed me into it and let out a gasp. It's tile throughout – even the ceiling. You can lie down in comfort in the bath. And it has a whirlpool - just the job after ten or more hours on shift.

I saw her eyes take in the bath and read her mind again. "There's one of them in the main guest suite – you can always have a soak there."

She had the grace to blush. "No, I, er…."

I chuckled. "I mean it, girl. When I was working I would have given my eye teeth to be able to soak in one of them after a hard day at work, then battling on the underground. Anyway, I take it you like the bathroom? You don't think the turquoise suite too much?"

"It's cool – in both senses of the word."

"I think so. Don't know why but the designer tried to persuade me to have avocado, but I thought that went out of fashion years ago."

"Me too."

I turned to the business in hand and began stowing toiletries and make-up into what some would have called a small suitcase. No way is it a sponge bag. Knowing full well why she was sticking to me like glue I asked, "I guess you want to know where I was tonight, don't you?"

"It would help."

"You're in luck, love, because I went to a concert given by the London Symphony Orchestra at the Barbican. I know my tickets and program don't prove nothing, but I'm a member of their fan club and was backstage afterwards. I know some of the chaps so they can alibi me." I gave her a huge grin. "Okay?" I wasn't about to mention Raoul Gomez. I'd had an early dinner with him before the concert. Tell you more about him in a bit.

"Should be easy enough to check."

"So my alibi's okay and there's nothing I could have done here. As I said, I know the tickets don't prove anything. I'm not stupid you know."

"Cleo, I never said or even thought you were," she told me as we trooped back into the bedroom.

At that moment there was a tap on the door and a child in a constable's uniform entered bearing a tray with two cups and saucers, milk jug and sugar bowl. "We didn't put in the milk or sugar."

14

"Thanks, love," I gave him my best smile. "Here you are, Jenny, help yourself." The constable wheeled about and left the room.

Jenny was looking puzzled. "Don't worry, love, all he had to do was open the fridge for the milk and the sugar bowl was on a shelf." I told her. "He didn't have to think, you know."

We exchanged that smile all women exchange at the uselessness of men, and sat down side by side on the bed to sip the refreshing brew. It wasn't too bad. That kid's got a great future as the cop shop brewer-upper.

In the car on the way to Lyndhurst I brought up the subject of my old job. "Be honest, Jenny, you're dying to know if I just threw in the towel at work."

She squinted sideways at me and grinned. "Of course. I thought that was what everybody did when they came into that sort of money."

"Because I didn't want anyone knowing I'd come into money I worked out my month's notice." I fiddled with the seat belt – why do they always try either to strangle me or make me an Amazon?

She thought for a few moments, then said, "I can understand that. Yes, it makes sense. I think we all dream about winning the lottery or coming into a lot of money and chucking in the towel, but I doubt if many do it exactly that way."

"The people who amaze me are the ones who win the lottery then say they will carry on working! What on earth for? Apart from anything else, it isn't very fair to the unemployed, is it?"

"True, but as I've discovered doing this job, there's nothing so strange as people."

15

On arrival at the hotel Jenny carried in the suitcase and must have been marveling at its weight. It hadn't looked as if I'd packed enough clothes for a month, but I do believe in playing it safe.

As we parted, I asked, "Has Dan Spencer been located? I feel I ought to be the one to break the news to him."

She shook her head. "I haven't heard anything yet, apart from the fact that he wasn't in the flat. Don't worry, the news will be broken carefully." I nodded and she left. Whoever is looking for Dan Spencer is taking their time about it, I thought as I went up to my room.

So, who is Raoul? Not my bit of stuff – just a great friend. Yeah, when I first knew him I fancied him something rotten, but I got over that. Now, of course, I realize I'm not everyone's cuppa tea. Oops, sorry, I was going to tell you about Raoul. He's a violinist with the orchestra. No, he isn't Spanish, but his parents are. He was born in London but looks Spanish. You know, all dark hair (except for a fascinating white streak) and smoldering dark eyes.

The first time I clapped eyes on him was at a concert at the Royal Festival Hall. He's why I joined the fan club – to meet him. We hit if off straightaway – as best mates. As they say, if you can't win 'em, be big sister! Little did I know that even he was going to be involved in my current problem.

Chapter 3

Well, as you can imagine, news of the murder was all around the village the next morning. And rumours flocked thicker than starlings at dusk.

I found out about it later in the day. During the morning I was safely tucked away in Lyndhurst and didn't know what was going on.

Following a late breakfast I went for a stroll around the small town, looking in the shops, up one side of the main street and back down the other. I have to admit that I was a bit naughty. When I came to Queen's House (the headquarters of the Forestry Commission it said outside), I found a door open and peeked inside. Turns out I was looking in at the Verderers Court which is (as I also discovered later) a courtroom. Well, it does look like it even if the pink walls are a bit strange. There were rows of benches on the tiled floor, a neat chandelier hanging from the white raftered ceiling and some pretty stained glass windows. Then I was out of there quick, before anyone caught me!

Next I took a stroll through the graveyard of the next door church of St. Michaels and All Angels (hedging their bets?). To my great surprise I found the grave of one of my favourite fictional characters. Her real name was Alice Liddell, and when she was a child she was the inspiration for Lewis Carroll and his "Alice" books. I'd always wondered where she had ended up after leaving Oxford.

By this time I was ready for coffee and a bite to eat and headed to a nearby cafe. And it was there that Paula Linley found me. Clever lady.

Why? Because we had never met. Apparently she'd been to the hotel and asked what I was wearing - a purple caftan (the nearest I had to mourning and I did think I ought to nod in that direction).

When she arrived I was away in a little world of my own, wondering who had done in Janet Spencer and where Dan and my Volvo were.

This woman in a navy linen skirt and pale green shirt-waister pulled out the chair opposite me, sat down and gave a regal nod at the waitress who made a quicker arrival than when I had tried to order coffee.

"Two coffees, please, Freda."

"Yes, m'm." I reckon she would have curtsied if she'd thought it appropriate.

I looked at this posh lady and asked, "You the Queen or something?"

"No. Just 'the lady of the Manor'," she told me using fingers for quotation marks.

"Oh yeah. Mrs. Linley." I'd heard of her. "I'm Cleo Marjoribanks." I stuck out my ring bedecked hand - well she was wearing a posh ring and what I think were real pearls - I had to keep my end up. We solemnly shook hands.

"Glad to meet you, Cleo. By the way, my name's Paula."

"Ta. Oh, ta." This second word of thanks was to the waitress who deftly replaced the cold coffee. "How about some toasted teacakes?" I looked at Paula enquiringly.

"Why not."

"Okay, love, for two please and put it all on my bill."

"You don't...."

I stopped her with an imperious hand. "Mrs. Linley, you're the first person in the village who has approached me. And I can afford it, anyway. Probably better off than you." I gave a cheeky grin.

She smiled, "The rumour factory got it half right, I expect."

The teacakes arrived and we tucked in, merely talking about such mundane things as the weather and the Forest. And me wondering why she had sought me out.

Mind you, when she talked about the Forest I could tell she loved it, her wide-set brown eyes literally glowed. I did think she could do something with her ordinary brown hair, though – like get a more fashionable cut.

When we'd finished, she brought up the subject of the murder.

"The police came to see me this morning about Mrs. Spencer. I'm sorry something so dreadful happened."

"Yeah. It was a bit of a shock. I'd had a few nice days in Town. You know, shopping, shows, and a concert, then came back to this."

"It must have been a terrible shock, but we can't discuss it here." We could almost hear the nearby ears stretching. "Until the police have finished with your house, why don't you come and stay with us?' she invited.

Weird, I thought. "It's kind of you, but I couldn't impose."

"No imposition. It will be more comfortable for you and easier for the police."

As I was curious to find out why she was anxious for my company, I relented and we returned to the hotel to collect my luggage and pay the bill.

While we were driving across the open moorland in her Toyota (I can never remember the model but it's rather staid), I suddenly felt my eyes fill. I couldn't help it. Shock, I reckon. Or maybe the kindness of this elegant lady. "There are some tissues in the glove box," she told me.

"Ta." I helped myself to the packet.

She drove into one of the car parks and stopped. "Delayed shock."

I nodded and blew my nose. "I doe. I can'd helb it."

"Have a good cry. I'm going for a walk. Perhaps I'll have a chat with those ponies." There was a group of the famous New Forest ponies not far away. "They sometimes let me get close. Maybe they sense that I am a New Forester."

Once I'd mopped up, I got out and went to watch her – she was telling the horses what had happened!

"Feeling better?" She asked when she saw me.

"And a fool."

She shrugged, "You're entitled in the circumstances. Come and meet the ponies."

"Don't think so, thanks." I was a bit scared of them.

"They won't hurt you. Just approach slowly and if one looks at you, look it straight in the eye."

I started to get nearer but one of the horses moved away so I stopped. "I think this is far enough."

She smiled at me, turned to her four legged friends and said goodbye, telling them to behave and be careful of strangers! Then I remembered that some had been badly injured by yobbos. Probably on drugs and thought it was a lark to be cruel to the friendly forest ponies. I know what I'd like to do to the wicked buggers! And it would hurt.

As we returned to the car I commented, "My gear isn't exactly the best for walking around here. Think I'll have to get some clothes like yours."

"Please don't, Cleo. You suit what you wear and I don't think you are a tweedy type."

"Maybe not. Perhaps I'll get some trousers and loose tops."

20

"That sounds better. Now, are you fit for the rest of the journey?"

"You make it sound like we live a long way away. I think secretly you are a funny lady."

She smiled. "Thank you. But don't tell my friends and family."

I guffawed (yes, I am a loud lady). "Oh, Paula, I like you."

"Thank you."

While we were driving along I cast my mind back to the previous evening. I'd phoned home from Waterloo Station and told Dan Spencer (my housekeeper's husband who does odd jobs and driving. Me with a housekeeper! I still have to pinch myself) to meet me at the station. There I was off the train and steaming 'cos Dan wasn't there. I think if I had known what had happened... Anyway, I gave up waiting and called a cab. No point in waiting for a bus – the last one had already gone. You know what connections are like with public transport.

And I let the cab go as soon as I got home. If he'd still been there, I think I would have left quick after I found the body of Janet Spencer.

As we turned in through the opened gates to Paula's home I had my first real look at the house. I'd only ever driven past it and you can't see much of it from the road with the high walls in the way.

"Wow!" I breathed. "It's smashing."

Paula smiled. "I think so."

It really is. It's Georgian, cream and very square like a child's drawing of a house. Admittedly, a child using a ruler – door in the centre and a pair of windows either side. Above are five sets of windows exactly over the others and the door. As we drove around the side to the garage I could see it was a lot bigger than it looks from the front.

Paula stopped the car outside the double garage. "This is where the stables used to be."

"You mean your stables?"

"The ones belonging to the house," she corrected me. "Gerard's father had them pulled down and the garage put up instead."

"Oh, right. You said your daughter's out riding. So where's the stable now?" It puzzled me because I'd assumed they had their own stables.

"Next door." She pointed to the side of the gardens away from the village. I remembered seeing a driveway with a small notice but hadn't realised what it was.

As we carted my luggage from the car to the back of the house I got some idea of the size of the garden. Herbaceous around the garage, formal – lawn and flower beds – on the other side of the house – out back a patio, lawn, roses and tennis court. Later I discovered that what I call the living room looks out over the formal garden and has French windows opening onto it.

"The old kitchen garden is where that wild garden is over there, next to the stables," Paula pointed out. "We decided to turn it into a garden to attract butterflies and wild life when we realised we couldn't afford the gardeners to keep up the veggies and fruit."

"So who looks after it now?"

"Lawn service. Same as the one you use. As you know, they also trim the trees and bushes. We do the rest."

"A lot of work."

"It's good for us. Helps us to relax."

I could agree with that as I potter about my own garden – small compared to this one, but large compared to my parents' home.

Indoors Paula showed me to a guest room and left me to unpack. "By the time you've finished I'll have some lunch ready. You do like salad, I hope?"

"That'll be okay by me. Is it just us two?"

"I'm hoping Margaret will be back from her ride. She went out early but didn't say when she would be back."

"She a teenager?" Paula nodded and smiled. "Typical," was my automatic response which I immediately realised wasn't on. I gave a rueful grin, "Sorry, Paula, I know she's your daughter, but some of my friends have problem teenagers."

Once on my own I sat on the bed – a double in a very ordinary room (no frills or chintz, thank goodness) and pondered some more about the invitation to stay here.

Paula's not the sort to invite strangers into her house. Did her husband know I was here? I could feel myself frowning and quickly rubbed my forehead. Don't want to encourage them lines, do we?

Oh well, I thought, standing up and opening the case to hang up a few things, let's see if I can find out what her problem is.

Margaret didn't make it for lunch, so just the two of us ate in the kitchen. Afterwards we sat out on the patio overlooking their well-kept garden drinking coffee and Paula filled me in on the morning's events as she knew them.

"I heard about the murder after breakfast. Gerard, that's my husband," she explained, "had left to go to a Verderer's Meeting in Lyndhurst" (I must have got out of

23

that Courtroom just in time!) "and I had just finished stacking the dishwasher when Mrs. Walsh arrived. She's the cleaner," she added.

"Morning, Mrs. Linley. Have you heard what's happened?" She imitated the New Forest burr and I laughed.

"That's good. Ever thought of taking it up as a profession?" I teased.

"You could call it my party piece, but I don't do it in front of the villagers as they might be offended. There's no point in growing up in the Forest and not being able to understand what people say to you," she said with a smile.

"I guess not. It's like when I worked I talked a bit more posh, but I bet you'd find that hard to believe?"

She gave me a considering look. "I'm not sure. I think you're a bit of a chameleon."

"Change me colours you mean?"

"Exactly. After all, look at the way you arrived here." No one could forget that! The gossips outside the village post office-cum general store had all done double-takes as I passed them in the stately 1949 Silver Wraith. The villagers by the cottage gates and a pair by the Church Lych Gate, stopped to gawp. I suspect some of them thought that it was Dame Edna Everidge, before they realised that what they had seen was a head of wild red hair and a pair of ostentatious red framed spectacles. Paula continued, "If that wasn't making a statement I don't know what is."

She raised her delicate eyebrows and pointed out. "You could have driven to your house from the other direction and missed the village altogether."

I threw up my hands, caught my necklace and, of course, it snapped showering beads everywhere. "Drat!" We scrabbled around picking up what we could find.

"Don't worry about the rest, Paula, I've got plenty more strings of beads." I took the cup off its saucer and tipped a handful of beads onto it. "I was going to say, I give in. Anyway, Paula, let's get back to this morning."

"Right. I assumed from Mrs. Walsh's comment that either the local drunk or some hooligans had caused a disturbance. Then she told me that your housekeeper had drowned in the swimming pool. I assumed she had slipped on the wet surface. But Mrs. Walsh soon put me right. Her pale blue eyes widened and she said, almost reverentially, 'they say she was murdered.'

"That was a shock so I suggested we both sit down and she tell me what she knew. At least that got her to take off her coat, so I knew she was stopping, although I wondered how much work she would actually do as I had originally planned to go into Lyndhurst to do some shopping. I suspected that after my departure our telephone wire would become red hot.

"She told me that the 'perlice' were still at your house. And that they were questioning everyone in the village. I asked about you..." She paused and gave me a doubtful look.

"What did she call me?" Still she hesitated so I guessed it had to have been an unflattering description, but I was curious to know what the locals called me. "Come on, Paula, I won't be offended."

"The Cockney Queen."

I roared with laughter. It was a milder nickname than I'd expected.

Seeing that I wasn't offended Paula went on, "I had thought an incomer as flamboyant as you would have landed a more..."

25

"Derogatory name?" I finished for her and she blushed. "Listen, Paula, I went to school in the East End. We were little bleeders and called each other horrible names. I've heard the lot. I'll tell you a secret. Have you met the Detective Inspector yet?" She nodded. "Well, we were at school together and his nickname was Steaming Kettle."

That relaxed her as we laughed.

"I take it that no one else in the police knows you two grew up together?"

"I've no idea. Can we get back to this morning?" I reminded her of the point of this conversation.

"Well, so far as your nickname is concerned, it shows you how well I don't always understand the villagers. You're obviously beginning to become a respected figure. I've seen you about the village, brightening everyone's life in gaudy caftan and straw hat, and am glad we've now met."

"So am I," I smiled at her, but that didn't stop my suspicions.

"I asked Mrs. Walsh if you were back yet. She said you were back from your holiday but didn't know if you were at the house. She did know that your Volvo wasn't there and thought you had found Mrs. Spencer.

"I suspected the police hadn't let you stay in the house and wondered if someone had put you up for the night, but she said you weren't in the village. That's when the police arrived so I told her to get started and I would see them.

"I was right. It was Inspector Kettle." She smiled and added, "I thought that only detectives on television and in films were good looking."

"Yeah. He's improved since school. I reckon there'll be a few fluttering hearts in the village."

"Not just teenage ones either. I'll bet he has a way with old ladies.

Anyway, to get back to reality. He had a constable with him, Jenny Dixon, and far too pretty for what must be gruesome job. There will probably be some male hearts throbbing."

"To say the least!" I chortled and Paula surprised me by grinning. And there I was thinking I might have gone too far. "Makes me feel so old when I see these young coppers," I added.

"Mmm," she agreed and we sat looking at the beautifully laid out garden.

I don't know what she was thinking about, but I was still trying to work out why I had been invited here. Did Paula have some deep, dark secret? There was something niggling at the back of my mind. Had she been having an affair with Dan? You know, sort of Lady Chatterley? I couldn't picture it 'cos Paula looks so cool and calm. Not quite Grace Kelly but along those lines.

Anyway, back to business and maybe she'd let something slip.

Chapter 4

The front door bell then rang and Paula said. "I'll go, you stay here," but I followed her indoors.

When she opened the door I heard Steaming's voice. "Good afternoon, Mrs. Linley. This is Sergeant Wiles. Did you manage to persuade Miss Marjoribanks to come back with you?" As if he didn't already know!

"Indeed I did. Why don't you come in and wait in the sitting room and I'll get her. She's in the garden."

"The kitchen," I carolled.

"Why don't we all go into the kitchen," Steaming suggested – trust him. Bet he wants a cuppa.

When they came in I was at the sink washing up. "You don't have to do that, Cleo!" Paula exclaimed. "Just put them in the dishwasher."

"Sorry, Paula, didn't think these few bits were worth it."

"Never mind. Come and sit down. The Chief Inspector wants a word with you. Oh, and this is Sergeant Wiles."

I dried my hands on a tea cloth and thrust out a hand to shake the young lad's. He looked startled but shook it. Good manners, but then he looks a bit straightlaced. Skinny with floppy blonde hair which would probably look better if he had a more modern haircut. And he's got those light brown eyes which writers always describe as sherry but I think they look like…. Oh, well, never mind.

"Now, everyone, sit down and I'll make tea or coffee. Whatever you prefer." Paula gave her orders.

We sat and while she was making tea for them I tried to tell them what I know (more like don't know) about my defunct housekeeper.

"We still haven't traced Mr. Spencer. Do you have any idea where he might be?"

"I suppose you mean you haven't found my car either?"

Steaming shook his head. "Sorry."

"I've no idea where he could've gone. I don't know nothing about them. Not known 'em long enough." Then remembered something that used to irritate him. Wonder if it still does? I began tapping my nails on the table.

"When did you employ them?" He frowned as he asked. Yeah, it did!

"Took them on a couple of weeks before I moved in. The agency found them." I stopped tapping.

"Which agency is that?" Blondie asked and scribbled down the details as I dictated them. "Thanks."

"Were they the only people you interviewed?"

"Look, Inspector," cor, listen to me being all formal with Steaming, but Blondie made me feel I ought to, "let me explain. I don't know nothing about housekeepers and such. I just went to the agency and told them what I wanted. They found some people and I went and met them to see which ones I liked, y'know?"

Steaming nodded, although I thought I detected a gleam of amusement in his eye. "Cleo, we do know something about you," he admitted.

I guffawed. "Should a guessed you'd bin digging about me, shouldn't I? Okay, so you know." I could sense Paula's curiosity so turned to look at her. "I'll fill you in one of these days." Back to the job in hand. "Right. So I met about four couples and thought I'd get on best with the Spencers. That's how come they work for me. But you've got to understand, I've not been at this house much. Too busy doing other things. So I didn't really get time to know them properly."

Blondie looked at me. "Didn't you have any conversations with Mrs. Spencer?"

"Mostly we talked about work. I didn't know what she was supposed to do." I grimaced. "And so we sort of discussed the outlines of what I wanted her to do and what she thought she ought to do. Came to an arrangement with it."

"Yes, Miss Marjoribanks...."

"Cleo."

"Sorry," he smiled (not bad), "Cleo. You couldn't only have discussed work. Didn't you discuss likes and dislikes? Didn't she mention friends or family?"

"No." I frowned the way I do when I'm thinking deeply, then looked from one to other of the detectives and added, "You know, now you've asked that question I think it's strange, but she didn't. I know I told her that my Mum and Dad died in a car crash some years ago," Steaming made a sort of noise but shook his head when I looked at him. Guess he hadn't heard about the accident, "and that I don't have any brothers or sisters. But she never said nothing about her family. Or her husband's. I don't know whether their parents are alive or whether they've got children, or what. Nothing. Weird, innit?"

Paula said afterwards that she thought it was strange because she can never get Mrs. Walsh to stop yacking on about her family and everything they do.

"Well, Cleo," Steaming stirred. "We've been through their flat but there isn't so much as an address book or bank books. Did you pay them by cheque or by cash?"

"By cheque. There's got to be a cheque book or paying-in book or a card somewhere."

30

"There's nothing in the flat and your Volvo hasn't turned up, so all I can think is that Spencer has taken off somewhere with them."

"Well, he's never said anything. Quite frankly I thought he was a miserable bugger. All we ever discussed was the garden and the cars. What needed doing. He did them because he got paid to do them, but he didn't do them with very good grace. In fact, come to think about, they might not have lasted long working for me, anyway. I can't be doing with all that. Life's life, get on and live it." I sighed, then gave him a smarmy smile. "Chief Inspector, when can I go back to my house?"

"SOCO's have more or less finished with it but I don't think you should go back and stay there just yet. Not unless you have someone to stay with you."

"Difficult. Well, would you mind if I go up to London? I've got a flat up there."

Paula jumped in quickly. "You don't have to rush off, Cleo. You can stay here. You're going to have to get another housekeeper anyway. If you like, I'll help you."

I smiled at her and heaved a sigh of relief. "Would you really?"

"Of course."

"Sure I'm not putting you out?"

"No. I wouldn't suggest it otherwise. Besides, I enjoy your company."

The police stood up and Steaming said. "Thank you very much, Mrs. Linley. Cleo, I'm afraid I'll have to ask you to identify Mrs. Spencer."

I could feel myself turn pale. "Do I have to?"

He nodded. "I'm afraid so, old thing." Blondie gave him a startled look when he called me that. Probably thought he was being too familiar with a witness! "No relatives and no husband."

I swallowed what felt like a plum stone. "Okay. When?"

"This evening probably."

I nodded, not looking forward to that. Then Blondie asked, "Could you give us a description of Dan Spencer?"

I closed my eyes and had a think. "About six feet. Broad shoulders, narrow hips. Fair hair brushed straight back. Side parting. On right. Brilliant blue eyes and a smile to charm with."

"Any distinguishing marks?" Steaming asked.

"Hands. Rough. Couple of scars on fingers but can't remember which ones."

"Can't have everything, I suppose." I opened my eyes to find him grinning at me. "Thanks, Cleo. I think that if you want to go to your house to get anything, it'll be fine. Provided, of course, that we have finished work there."

"And can I have my Roller?"

"Yes, you can have your Rolls Royce."

"Much as I love driving the Roller, I'd rather have the Volvo to go into Southampton to the agency."

"Don't worry, Cleo, we can go in my car," Paula said, "but I do look forward to riding in your Rolls Royce some time. By the way, have you ever been to the National Motor Museum?"

"Yeah, I love it. Shall we go along when this lot have finished with us?"

"I'd like to but I have other things to do. Maybe we can go another day."

She saw the police off the premises and returned to the kitchen where I was sitting doodling on a notepad. Actually, it was her shopping list pad and doodling helps me think. The last thing I wanted to do was identify Janet and, of course, I was worried about Dan. Where was he? Had he killed his wife? And, where the heck is my car?

Chapter 5

"Cleo, rather than sit around here doing nothing would you like to come along to the WI meeting this afternoon?" Paula asked as she came back through the door. "I have to get changed now and go down there as I'm the chairperson."

I looked at her and wrinkled me nose. "Nah. I don't think that's quite my kind of thing, Paula."

Suspecting what I thought about the WI, she sat down opposite me, put her elbows on the table, leaned across and asked, "What do you think the Women's Institute does?"

"Well, you know, its ladies wearing gardens on their heads, learning how to make things from scraps of cloth and dried flowers, and baking cakes."

She sat back and laughed. "Oh, Cleo, wonderful, wonderful. We've moved on a bit since then. Can you imagine me in a flowered hat? In any case, have you forgotten what happened to Mr. Blair at our conference in the year 2000?"

I looked at her with my head on one side, quirked an eyebrow, "No, can't see you in flowers and, yeah, I had forgotten the WI virtually hand-bagged the Prime Minister."

"Do come along with me, Cleo. We have a travel talk this afternoon."

"Yeah?"

"Yes. About the Mayan culture in Mexico."

"Sounds like it could be interesting."

"Come and get changed."

"What d'you think I ought to put on? I haven't got anything other than my caftans."

"That'll do. You'll liven the place up.

Townie that I am, it was only when we were strolling towards the village that I learned that when there isn't a pavement you have to walk facing the oncoming traffic.

"Not in the same direction?"

"No," Paula smiled. "If you're on the same side as the oncoming traffic you can step out of the way of an oncoming vehicle."

"Into the ditch?" I was only half serious and she knew it.

There are pavements on both sides of the road once you get into the village proper. As the main street isn't straight but has a sharp bend (almost like a corner) about halfway along it makes sense. The shops are in the centre and small houses, some terraced, flank them.

I think I'd better tell you about the village now so you'll know what I'm talking about later on.

Trewith Green is a bit off the beaten track, between two busier roads. I think the War Memorial is a bit of a laugh. No, not the memorial itself, but its location as it is on the edge of the pavement where the road bends – not on the inside part like you'd expect, but on the bit that sticks out. And it's got a little iron fence with spikes all the way around it. When I asked Paula about it she told me, "The fence was put up after several cars had hit the memorial." So now any cars aiming for it end up with dented wings and maybe a punctured tire! Also in an attempt to protect the memorial are speed bumps fore and aft so to speak. I don't reckon the dogs much like the spikes either! Of course it would make more sense to move the memorial but, apparently, when that was proposed, almost the whole village was up in arms against the idea.

35

Across the road from the memorial is the graveyard to our church, St. Mary's. There isn't a regular vicar any more but one who visits from another Parish. As attendance is down so much Paula told me that this happens a lot in the country.

We don't have much in the way of shops, just a General Store, a newsagent-cum-tobacconist-cum sweet shop, and a shop selling knitting wools, a few clothes, toys and gifts. And, of course, we have two pubs, the Queen Victoria (shades of 'Eastenders') and the Dog and Duck.

Probably the most important supplier in the village is the local garage, where the blacksmith used to be. He also does a roaring trade in bike repairs. Biking is a popular hobby in the New Forest, both with the residents and the visitors. Some of the residents who can't afford cars also have to rely on bikes to get about.

Most of the local residents have been here for donkey's years or, rather, their families have. There are a few people, like me, who retired from the big city to a more peaceful environment. Most people who still work either do so in the forest or in tourism. There are some young children, but not as many as there once were so the village school closed down and the kids are bussed to their schools. The school building is now used as the Village Hall.

As we strolled down the lane towards the Village Hall I asked Paula, "You told me that your husband is at a Verderers' Meeting. What's that? What do they do?"

"As a Verderer? He is actually a barrister but his work as a Verderer means that he is a judge of the New Forest." She then went on to explain about Agisters and Commoners, who are the police and land users of the forest.

Apparently, the ponies are owned by the commoners: people who own or rent a property or piece of land to which the privileges of rights of common are attached. Sounds confusing to me.

"The Verderers Court, which goes back to Norman times, is the oldest judicial court in Great Britain. There are ten Verderers who meet six times a year to administer the rights of common at the Verderers Hall in Lyndhurst."

"Where he is at the moment?"

"That's right. The five Agisters are appointed by the Verderers and deal with the management of the 5,000 ponies and the cattle that roam the New Forest."

"I've seen the ponies and some donkeys, but not the cattle."

"You will. But there are also twelve New Forest keepers employed by the Forestry Commission to look after the wildlife, conservation, and recreational facilities."

I thought about all this then asked, "It all goes back a real long way, doesn't it? What would I be? As owner of The Larches. A Commoner?"

"I don't know. You would have to look through the Title Deeds and papers of your house."

"Give me something to do. By the way, Paula, after the meeting I'm going to go and pick up the Roller. You don't mind if I park it in your driveway, do you? You've got plenty of space there."

"Knowing Gerard he'll probably insist on your putting it in our garage."

"No, I don't want to put you out."

"Gerard is as much in love with old cars as you are."

I chuckled. "Well we'll have something in common. Another thing. Do you want to come with me and have a look around the house?"

"Oh, I couldn't."

"Come on, Paula, you know you're dying to see it. You've got to be as curious as at least half of the village."

"Well." She couldn't help smiling because I was right. "Actually I would like to look at it but for another reason. To lay the ghosts."

"Oh yeah." Light dawned. "Lady of the Manor. I get it. You visited the old girl."

"Unfortunately, yes."

"Don't worry. Remember, I saw inside that place before I had it done over. I knew I'd got a bargain there and, yeah, I knew I'd have to spend some serious money on it."

"I'm sure you did." I could see her wondering where that money came from and a light began to glimmer in the back of my brain.

At this point a middle-aged lady bustled up, rather unsuitably attired in a drop waist summer dress in green and orange floral which made her sallow complexion and lumpy figure look even worse. What a contrast to Paula's pale blue silk dress.

"Good afternoon, Mrs. Linley. Good afternoon, Miss Marjoribanks." It was Mrs. Cheetham, the gossip guru as Paula later told me. We greeted her as she started walking along with us - on Paula's right - and leant forward to look at me (on the left) and said, "Sorry to hear about your housekeeper, Miss Marjoribanks." You notice I didn't invite Mrs. C to use my Christian name.

"Yeah well," I didn't say nothing else and there was no way I was going to give Mrs. C anything for her grapevine.

By now we were at the Village Hall and I was introduced to some other ladies. Wonder if any of them will have anything in common with me? It'll surprise them if they do!

As she was "chair" (I always thought that was a piece of furniture!), Paula left me with a couple of the ladies.

"Sorry to hear about your housekeeper," the first one said.

"Yes, terrible thing to happen. We've never had anything like that happen around here before."

And it's my fault I suppose? "Mean within living memory?" I asked pertinently. For those who don't know, the New Forest was created by William the Conqueror so that he could go hunting and his son, William Rufus, was killed here.

They looked at each other. "Er, well, er, yes," the first one agreed. Then a third lady joined them, was introduced and, as she was about to make a comment to me – presumably about Janet – the others said they had something to discuss about another meeting and all three left. I look around, couldn't see anyone I knew so went and sat down in the back row of chairs. What is amazing is that when you're sitting and others are standing, you become invisible, which is how I heard something ver-r-r-y inter-resting.

"Does anyone know where Dan is?" a voice asked quietly.

"No. The police are still asking about him."

"What are we going to do if he doesn't come back?"

"More to the point, if he's murdered his wife, do we want him back?"

"That's a good point. I hadn't thought of that."

Well, I thought, that's a turn up for the books. Dan's the obvious so she's been too busy thinking about her own plans. Or whatever. What has he been getting up to with

39

the village ladies?   Can't be affairs, unless he plays threesomes. I wanted to laugh out loud at this ridiculous thought but, fortunately, Paula called the ladies to order.

The lecture, complete with slides, was interesting, but I think only a few of us could have answered questions afterwards.   Some of the ladies were definitely not concentrating. Even Paula, who was sitting at the front with her back to the audience, sensed the inattention. She told me so afterwards.

Having politely applauded the lecturer we were then invited to help ourselves to refreshments. Not wanting to seem greedy, even though I was parched, I took my time approaching the tables with helpful ladies behind them. Hmm, I thought as I looked at the cakes and biscuits on offer. Most of them were shop bought and the home-made ones looked like they were made from packets. You know, brightly yellow and dry looking. I may not be a cook but my Mum baked fabulous cakes so I do know the difference. Looking at the empty plates I guessed they had held the real things. No wonder there'd been a rush!

I got a cup of tea then sat down again in my invisible mode.

It worked. I didn't dare turn around to look at the two ladies who thought they were having a secret discussion, but it got my ears flapping.

"Who do you think killed Dan's wife?"

"Did someone kill her? I thought she'd drowned."

"So why are the perlice asking all these questions?"

"Isn't that what they usually do when someone dies in funny whatsits?"

I think she means suspicious circumstances.

"Well, that's what this is, innit?"

"S'pose so. Haven't thought 'oo did it. D'you reckon Dan did?"

"Be daft if he did. He'd got it made 'adn't he? Wife doin' all the work, free board'n'lodging. All e' 'ad to do was take the cars to the car wash."

Eh? My baby in the car wash? He was supposed to hand wash her. Wait 'til I get my hands on him. Then I tuned back in.

"What about 'er boyfriend?"

"Did she have one?"

"Well someone seen 'er in Lymington with a bloke. Couple of times."

Janet with a lover? Oh boy!

"P'raps 'e killed 'er if she'd tried to break if orf."

"Could be, but what are we going to do about Dan? I tried his mobile phone but couldn't get an answer."

"Me either. I suppose we 'ave to wait until 'e gets in touch with us."

"Yeah, but the next big......" and they moved away.

What big thing? Orgy (oh yeah). Heist? I wish people wouldn't do that – walk away just when the conversation is getting interesting.

Chapter 6

After the meeting, as we were strolling along towards the house, which is out the other side of the village to Paula's, I asked about Steaming's morning visit to her house.

"The Chief Inspector wanted to know if Gerard was in, but, as you know, he's at a Verderers' Meeting.

"The constable looked puzzled, but I wasn't sure whether it was about the Verderers because she pointed to a photograph of Margaret, which is on the bookshelf, and asked who it was. I could see that it was on the tip of her tongue to ask if Margaret was a granddaughter. I explained that the pictures were of my sons James and Edward who are married and live in London and Scotland and that Margaret is my daughter." She smiled ruefully. "She was, of course, out on her horse somewhere in the forest. When she's home from school she seems to spend more time on the horse than at home. She is at that early teens stage when she knows best," she added. "Fortunately she is a good horsewoman and the Commoners and Agisters know her."

"Isn't it a bit dangerous though? You know, dangerous men and all that?" I asked.

"Cleo, I'm exhausted from trying to talk sense into her. Neither threats nor pleas make any difference. I just have to hope for the best and that she will soon learn some discretion."

"A typical teenager."

"Exactly. And she does have a mobile phone."

"What's she going to do with that when someone attacks her, throw it at him?" She shrugged and sighed and I was sorry I'd said it. Me and my big mouth. "Sorry, Paula."

"You're right, of course."

I tried to console her, but she was obviously worried about her rebel. "What did the 'perlice' say?"

"When Mrs. Walsh came in with the coffee the Inspector told her to stay, saying they had something to tell us. Mrs. Walsh said, 'If its about Mrs. Spencer, we know'."

I chuckled. "The village telegraph is alive and well."

"Exactly. I introduced them and she looked them up and down and said, 'Yus. I've seen yer in the village'."

"There's no answer to that."

"The Inspector simply nodded and managed to control the smile I could see hovering about his lips and suggested the constable go with Mrs. Walsh." Paula nodded. "I suspect he is very astute because he commented on her knowing a lot about the village."

"Oh, Steaming always was a sly one."

"Any woman would tell him her darkest secrets when he smiles." Yeah, I remembered it well. The molasses dark eyes twinkled and even teachers believed him. "I poured out the coffee and we sat down. Obviously he wanted to know if I knew Mrs. Spencer."

"And did you?"

"Only to greet in passing if we met in the village."

"What about her husband?"

She shook her head. "I don't think I would know him if I saw him," then turned to look at a garden and it made me wonder if she was lying. "Cleo, you're beginning to sound like the Inspector."

"God forbid!" Me a copper? And you like Steaming! That shut me up.

Paula smiled. "He also asked if I knew you. I told him no, but knew who you were and told him about your arrival driving through the village in the Roller."

43

We laughed. "What did he have to say to that?"

"That you were a character."

"Bloody cheek. And I bet he pointed out that I could have come in from the other side of the village." She merely nodded.

She went on to tell me that her alibi had been the same as a number of other ladies in the village. At the theatre in Southampton. An organised outing that Steaming already knew about from other interviews. He'd also wanted to know if Gerard Linley and Margaret had been with them. As it was a hen party, obviously Mr. L wasn't with them and Margaret chose not to go.

"I'll bet that was because she wouldn't be seen dead going to a farce and certainly not with the village deadheads." I exclaimed. I should have kept my big mouth shut again. She turned red and fiddled with her pearls. "Sorry, Paula..."

She flapped a hand. "You're right, of course. It caused the mother-and-daughter of a row." We had now reached my pride and joy and were strolling up the drive. "Oh! This is much better," she waved a hand at the garden. "You haven't made many changes to it though."

"No. The house is 1920s and I felt the garden ought to stay more or less as it was. I really only had it tidied up and re-planted. That's all."

The house has spanking new paintwork and sparkling windows and looks fabulous, even if I say so myself.

"It's.... Oh, Cleo, I can't tell you how it pleases me to see the house like this. It was breaking my heart."

"It nearly broke mine when I first looked at it," I retorted. "Come on. Oh, look, they've just finished," I added as the front door opened and the Scene of Crime team with their bits and pieces came out to load up their van.

"Are you Miss Marjoribanks?" a bespectacled young man approached and asked.

"Yes."

"Here's the keys for you." He handed them over. He'd obviously been primed about me.

"Thanks. You all finished now?"

"Yes. You can go back in."

"Thanks."

We saw them off and went in. Apart from fingerprint powder it wasn't too bad. Paula stood there in the hall looking all around. "Cleo, this is wonderful. My memory was of a room with that awful glossy brown embossed paper on the wainscoting, and rather dingy and dirty cream walls.

"This is absolutely superb," she enthused as she looked around at the light hall. No dado rail, just magnolia walls and apple green carpet. Years of paint had been removed from what can now be seen are some rather nice light oak doors.

"What do you think of the doors? They were a surprise, I can tell you, when we got all that paint off. I was going to have them painted magnolia, but when they called me I came down here like a shot to have a look. Beautiful. But I've had new brass doorknobs and fingerplates put on because I think these look nicer than the bakelite things that were on there."

There are some nice paintings on the walls, mostly of Mediterranean scenes. When I saw her looking at them I told her, "I got them in Kos when I was on a Greek Islands cruise. I saw them and knew I'd have a use for them to brighten up a corner."

"They fit beautifully in here." As she was looking around I watched her eyes pass across the staircase and up at the landing to see something she'd never seen before: An absolutely gorgeous stained glass window depicting a mermaid on a rock, combing her hair. "Where did you get that from?"

I chuckled. "It didn't come from anywhere. That was another one of the finds. It had been boarded over. When I was looking around outside I saw this dirty window with boards behind it and had to work out where it was."

"You're joking."

"No. Nice bit of Art Nouveau, innit?"

"Have you had it valued?"

"Not yet, but I think I'm going to have to because of insurance. And you never know, it might be one of them famous artists designed it."

"I can't believe you haven't had it done yet. I don't think I would have had the patience to wait so long."

"When you've been as busy as me, Paula, you will. Now let's have look around the rest of this place and see how dirty they've left it."

If the hall was a revelation to her, the rest of the house stunned her. I think if she didn't already have her own lovely home she would have coveted mine. She said as much on the way out to the garage to get the Roller.

That stopped me in my tracks. I looked at her to make sure she was serious. "You really mean that, Paula?" She nodded and I was happy as a man who'd been given a new electric toy.

"Yes, I do. I think you've done a wonderful job."

"Ooh," I heaved a sigh of relief. "I'm so glad you said that. I had so many arguments because everybody said I ought to get a designer to do it. And I didn't want a magazine house. Know what I mean?"

"I know exactly what you mean. I think you've done a wonderful job. It's you. Your taste."

"You know that?"

"Of course. Some of it is very unusual, some of it is very luxurious, but none of it is over the top. Do you know what I'm looking forward to now?"

"What?" I asked, still rooted to the spot.

"A ride in your Rolls-Royce, please?"

"Sorry."

So we arrived back at Paula's in style just as Margaret came strolling up the path. I didn't know whether Paula was pleased to see her or not. In one way I think she was, as I heard her murmur "well, there you are, you see, you go and spend the whole day out and you don't get a chance to ride in a wonderful car".

"Come on, ducks, let's go in and you can introduce us."

"If she hasn't shut herself in her room."

"Doubt it. Teenagers usually can't resist a bit of curiosity, even if they try not to show it."

But there's no knowing with teenagers, is there? All she did was flounce upstairs to her room – we heard the door slam.

I didn't have time to think about it. There was a message on the machine – from Steaming, would I call him?

"Wotcher. It's me. What do want?"

"Are you busy?"

"Just got in. Why?"

"If I send Jenny out to pick you up could you face doing the ID now?"

"Yuck. I was hoping you'd find someone else."

"I'll be there with you." Big deal.

"Oh, alright. And, by the way, wouldn't it be easier if you used my mobile?"

"Don't have the number." I gave it to him but I'm damn sure I'd already given it to him.

With the speed at which Jenny arrived I'm sure she had already been on her way, but I didn't bother to comment. Guess that's the cop way. Assume you're not too far away from base, will drop everything and do as you're told!

Well, it was every bit as bad as I thought it would be. The pong in the mortuary – or whatever they call it – is godawful. Enough to make you throw up though, fortunately, I didn't. How they can work in it is beyond me!

Besides I'd never seen a dead body before, which surprised Steaming - he thought I'd ID'd Mum and Dad.

"How wrong can you be, chum?" I told him after he'd finished apologising and I'd returned to the land of the living. Yeah. I passed out. She didn't look too bad but had a nasty gash on the temple. Apparently that's what killed her. "An uncle saw Mum and Dad for me."

"I really am sorry, Cleo. I just thought you were tougher."

"Well, I'm not," I snapped.

"After some of the things you did at school you could've fooled me." I threatened him with the handbag and he stood up. "Want to get out of here?"

Good idea. He took hold of my arms to help me up off the floor and we went to an office where this bloke, the pathologist, gave me a tot of brandy.

Anyway, I confirmed it was Janet, then Steaming drove me back to Paula's where I had a shower and washed my hair to try and get rid of the smells.

On the way back to Paula's I asked, "What's your sergeant's name?"

"Wiles. Why?"

"I know that," was my irritable response. "What's his Christian name?"

"Oh. Jeremy. I only ever call him Wiles."

"Jeremy? Poor bugger. Can you imagine the kids at school calling him Jerry?" For the uninitiated 'jerry' is a slang word for a chamber pot. Along with 'po' and 'gazunder' (goes under the bed!). "Which was probably one among several names," I added.

Steaming grinned. "Yeah. We had a Jerry in my class," he recalled.

I rolled my eyes. "Jeremy's an alright name if you're an actor or posh. At least at a public school like Eton or Harrow they would probably use the full name."

"You think?"

"Don't you?"

"No. Kids are kids are kids."

He was probably right. I really feel sorry for children whose parents don't think long and hard before naming their offspring. Mine? I'll keep you guessing on that one.

I was in time for dinner (which Paula had delayed slightly) but I didn't really have much of an appetite. Understandable I reckon. Anyway, Margaret did do us the favour of joining us for dinner that evening (even teenagers don't like starving unless they're trying to get skinny), although she barely opened her mouth and afterwards went back to her incarceration. Sociable type, obviously. I noticed Gerard raise his eyebrows at his wife, who shrugged and I tactfully pretended not to notice. Must be a bit embarrassing for them.

As Paula didn't have any appointments the next morning she suggested we go into Southampton.

"To the registry office?" I asked.

"It would be a good idea to set things in motion as quickly as possible. You do want a new housekeeper I take it?"

"Of course." I grinned. "And don't forget I have to go to the police station to have my fingerprints taken. For elimination purposes." I used the finger signal to put quotes around those last two words. "What about Margaret? Does she want to come with us?"

Paula shook her head. "No idea. She had breakfast with Gerard and left. Presumably out on the horse again."

"Doesn't she ever get saddle-sore?" It's amazing that anyone can spend so much time horse-riding.

"If she does she's never said. Anyway I don't think she's riding all day long. Probably goes and communes with nature." She forestalled my next comment. "And don't forget, she does have a cell phone."

"Fat lot of good that'll do if someone attacks her." And my thoughts ran on, What is she supposed to do with it? Point it at him and hope the rays stop him in his track?

"Sorry, Cleo, you have to know teenagers to know that there isn't anything you can say or do to get some sense into their heads. They know all the answers."

I thought for a bit. "True," I conceded, "and I don't have kids. I know I thought I knew more than my parents when I was that age. I suppose you....", I paused and smiled. "No, I guess you weren't like that."

"Like what?"

"Rebellious. I can imagine you being a little Goody-Two-Shoes."

She smiled at that description. "Of course. I was too scared to disobey The Law".

"Can Maggie do karate or anything like that?"

"I doubt it but I suspect she would put up a pretty good fight. She's quite strong. You have to be to control a big horse like Star."

"And I guess she could get the horse to protect her," I mused.

"I'm sure. Anyway, enough of Maggie. Let's get going to Southampton."

We did what we had to do in Southampton and came back here. Of course, with everything going right in the morning Sod's Law came into operation in the afternoon and things started going awry.

Chapter 7

As Paula had some telephone calls to make and letters to write, she chased me out into the garden telling me to relax. Which was fine until Margaret arrived on the scene demanding that I give her some money - a thousand pounds to be exact.

"You what?"

"A thousand pounds. You can afford it."

"Even if I could I wouldn't even lend it to you. Or anyone, come to that."

"It's not fair." That tone of voice and phrase were familiar. "Why should you have all that money? You're not fit to have so much. You're not even properly educated and can't speak properly. Where did you get the money from anyway? Steal it? Or are you a gangster's moll?" Gangster's Moll? Where on earth did she get that one from? It's even before my time! When I didn't respond but just sat looking up at the demon from hell, she went on, "I know. You sell your body. No, that's not right. No man would want your body," she sneered. "You're a madam, aren't you?"

Talk about itchy palms. If she'd been my brat she'd have a ringing in her ears.

I gave a quiet laugh and used my posh voice. "You really don't like the thought that I can legitimately have a lot of money, do you? I'm not going to tell you where I got it from because it isn't any of your business. You know, Maggie, your problem is that you're a spoiled brat."

She stamped her foot in rage (I'd never seen anyone do that before. I thought it was author's imagination). "I'm not! I'm not!"

"No? Anyway, what do you want a thousand pounds for?"

Mumble, mumble while she scuffed a foot on the lawn.

"How about speaking up? I can't hear what you want it for."

"A computer."

"You've got one."

"I want a better one."

"In that case do what I did at your age."

"I'm not selling my body," was the outraged response.

"Who said anything about that? Do what any honest citizen does. Get a job. There are plenty of jobs you could do during the school holidays."

"Daddy doesn't like the idea of my working before I leave school."

"But he wouldn't mind your taking money from a stranger? I think that's called stealing, isn't it?"

"Not if you give it to me."

"But your father wouldn't mind?" I repeated.

"Oh... Oh..." Unable to think of a suitable reply she turned and fled across the garden, I assume to go to the stables and her horse.

Feeling in need of a drink I got up and went in to the kitchen. And found Paula sitting at the table looking as if all the stuffing had gone out of her.

"I guess you heard that." She nodded. "I'm sorry, Paula. I'll pack my things and move back home."

"What have Gerard and I raised between us? I've never heard Margaret behaving like that before."

"No." I couldn't say any more. I pulled out a chair and sat down

"Cleo, I'm sorry, I don't know what to say. I'm mortified."

"What for? Just because your daughter has been behaving like a typical teenager? I'm the one in the wrong here."

"No, you're not. It's true what you said to her. She is a spoiled brat and I just don't know what to do."

"Don't you think that's because of what the doctor's always tell us women – 'it's your age'?"

She gave me a watery smile and nodded.

"I think the biggest problem with Maggie at the moment is that she's in love."

That brought her head up. "What?" Paula gasped.

"Didn't you realise that? Why do you think she's away all day? Obviously meeting someone. I certainly don't believe that codswallop about wanting a new compuyter, do you? She probably wants the money so they can go away for a holiday. Or something. Maybe he wants to buy a car or a motorbike."

"A thousand pounds won't buy it."

"No, but it'll make a deposit."

"I don't know, Cleo, I think you're exaggerating."

"I don't think so. I can remember being in love at that age. It was the first time. And, no, it wasn't with Steaming. You wouldn't have fallen in love at that age, would you?"

She shook her head. "No, I was still at boarding school."

"And didn't get the chance to meet boys," I finished.

We discussed the problems of bringing up teenage daughters for a bit, then, to change the subject, I asked her, "Do you have any idea why Janet was killed? Any rumours."

"Not really. I think I once heard something about gambling. His, not hers," she added hurriedly. "Not having met them I'm afraid..."

"Gambling!" That's the first I'd heard of it. "If I'd known I wouldn't have hired   them. Sorry to sound so harsh about gamblers, but I've worked hard all my life and having a gambler about the house could have caused problems." I stopped and thought. "Come to think of it, perhaps it has."

"Maybe, but don't think too much about it now. She may have been killed for a very different reason."

Maybe, but the glimmer at the back of my mind was beginning to grow into a glow. Between what I had overheard and the reason for Paula befriending me, the dots were beginning to join up.

I stood up, "I'm going to go and pack my things. I mean it about going home.   It would be far too embarrassing for all of us, and you and Gerard need to have a long talk with your daughter this evening."

"But you can't stay alone at your house. The police don't yet know who the murderer is. Perhaps he'll come back for you. Perhaps he thought it was you he killed."

I gave a shout of laughter. "Come on, Paula, how could anyone mistake Mrs. Spencer for me?"

She agreed reluctantly. "Even so..."

"Forget it. If it makes you feel any better I'll call Steaming and tell him. They can put on an extra patrol or whatever they do in the circumstances."

The first thing I actually did when I reached home was call the people who had installed the pool to have them clean it out. They promised to do it the next morning. Then I called Steaming and left a message to say I was back home.

Later on, while I was looking in the freezer trying to decide what to have for dinner the front door bell pealed.

Snatching up a caftan and throwing it on over my shorts and bra I started for the hall. The bell rang again. "Hang on! I'm coming!"

At the door was a smiling and apologetic Constable Dixon. "Sorry, Cleo, thought you might be having a siesta."

"Fat chance. You better come in. Got more questions?"

"Nope. Come to take up your offer of the spa bath. Soon as I heard you were back here....."

I snorted. "Tell that to the Marines. Your boss sent you. Either to keep an eye on me or to question me. Or maybe both."

"I told him it wouldn't work," she retorted with a grin. "But I'd still like a go in the bath."

I waved her upstairs. "You know where it is and presumably how it works?" She nodded. "Go ahead, but remember the twenty minutes max. Then come down and help me raid the freezer for dinner. I take it you're staying the night?" I raised an eyebrow and nodded in the direction of the overnight bag she was holding.

"Of course," was the demure reply.

Later we sat either side of the kitchen table digging into pizza washed down with red wine. "So, Jenny, what questions are you supposed to ask?" I wasn't going to waste time.

"Dunno." She thought for a bit, a frown of concentration bringing her delicate eyebrows closer together. "Here's one. Where do you keep your jewellery?"

"Good stuff or everyday junk?"

"Good stuff."

"Safety deposit in London. No chance of wearing it down here."

"I assume by everyday junk you mean gilt and plastic?"

"Yeah. Usually matches the caftans." I chuckled. "I guess the reason for that question was in case I'd caught Mrs. Spencer stealing it?"

She nodded.

"She'd have been very welcome to the junk but I doubt if she would have taken it, do you?"

"Unless she was a kleptomaniac."

"Doubt it."

"Well, was she blackmailing you about something?"

I sat back and looked at her. "I'd be a fool to admit that, wouldn't I? Apart from my lottery win, my life's an open book. No secrets. No hidden lovers, no ex-husbands, no children. I've never stolen in any shape or form and I've not murdered anyone." I took a deep breath. "Neither am I a 'gangster's moll' or a 'madam', as was suggested earlier today." I roared with laughter at that recollection and she smiled politely.

When I explained what had happened at the Linleys she didn't know whether to be shocked or amused and settled for the latter.

"I've been called all sorts in my life, including various versions of a "madam", but it's the first time I've been called a Gangster's Moll. I wonder where a teenager got that expression from?"

"It is a bit old fashioned, isn't it?"

"Even for me!"

After the pizza was gone I suggested taking our coffee out into the garden where it was pleasantly cool.

I sat on the swing seat and Jenny kept her feet on the ground in a comfortable wicker-work chair. "So, Cleo, what else have you done since your win?"

I swung for a bit. "Went off for a holiday to Monte Carlo. First class all the way; it was fantastic! When I come back I bought a flat in London. By the River Thames in one of them converted warehouses. It's got those high ceilings, a balcony from which I can see the river, Tower Bridge, and the Tower of London. Sometimes I think about my grandfather who was a Lighterman on that river. I can even vaguely remember when ships were anchored outside the building!

"Anyway, back to modern times. As you can imagine, the flat is all very, very modern. The latest in furniture and all that jazz.

"And I've got a cleaning lady. Tracy. She's in her mid-twenties and has a young daughter but no husband. He lost his job and just hung around waiting for the world to offer him another one. She got fed up with his whinge-ing and threw him out. Must've taken guts. She works for several other people in the flats and has been vetted by the Management Committee. So she's honest."

"You didn't have to interview her?"

I shrugged. "In a way, and not in the way I should have with the Spencers," I admitted. "Thank goodness Paula Linley's going to help me with replacing them."

Jenny smiled. "What do you do with yourself in London if you aren't working?"

"At the moment, not a lot. I go to the theatre – musicals and comedies are my favourites. And I sometimes

58

go to concerts where the music is music, if you know what I mean."

She puzzled over that. "I don't think so. Do you mean modern pop sort of music or classical?"

"Light classical." She nodded. "I want to spend some time here trying to get to know a few people and find out something about the area with the occasional weekend back in London. Then I really need to get down to planning my life a bit better."

"In what way? Charity work?"

"No. Education. I like to travel and I know that it's easier if I can understand the other languages. And I want to have some more music lessons. I've got a grand piano here, have you seen it?" She nodded. "I've got a good upright in the flat. I started learning to play when I was a kid but once I was out to work my Mum told me I had to pay for the lessons myself. I couldn't afford them so that was that."

"Sounds like you've got it all planned."

Later we watched a bit of telly and drank a few glasses of wine before heading for our respective bedrooms. You'd think that after the day I had had and the wine, that I would have fallen asleep straightaway, wouldn't you?

Wrong!!!!!

Between the overheard conversations and Paula's strange behaviour I knew there was definitely something going on. Come on, why would the Lady of the Manor suddenly take it into her head to befriend a virtual stranger, let alone invite her into her house? There had to be an ulterior motive. Now she tells me Dan was a gambler, but that she didn't even know what he looked like. That is definitely a lie.

59

What could it all have to do with her? How had she known he was a gambler? And, the biggest question of all is, does she think I was in cahoots with him and whatever he was involved in that included other people in the village?

And I know you're thinking that I'm a right one to talk about gambling when I've won the lottery. Yup, I can see you library readers ready with your editing pen. I don't call the occasional flutter on the lottery or a horse race gambling. Gambling's a disease that makes you waste your money.

Chapter 8

I may not be much of a housewife but even I can tell when supplies are running low. Tea and coffee were both almost finished up so I did a recce and made a list. Time to go to the village shop. Even though this would have been a job you'd expect Janet to have done, because I'd wanted to try to get to know the locals I'd done the village shops whenever I was at home.

And, being lazy, I'd taken the small Volvo. Apart from it being a bit pretentious to take the Roller, there really wasn't anywhere to park it. Between the road not being very wide and the big bend you can only park a small car anywhere near the shops and as the pubs were both built before the invention of the motor car they don't have car parks.

As I still don't have the Volvo my only choice was shanks's pony. Time for comfy shoes, straw hat – with a bright gauze scarf tied around the crown, the ends floating behind – or drooping down my back if it isn't windy – and sunglasses. Right, shopping bag with a couple of small ones folded up inside and I was ready for my half-a-mile walk. Why three bags? Well, you know how it is when you go shopping for a couple of things and end up with a couple of dozen.

Talk about give me the fright of my life! There I was strolling along, enjoying the dapple shade thrown by the trees and who should pop out of the lane a few yards along the road but Mrs. Cheetham. That lady who introduced herself to me when Paula and I were on the way to the WI lecture. So what was she doing on this side of the village?

"Good morning, Miss Marjoribanks."

"Good morning." I didn't want to encourage her.

61

"Going shopping?" she asked as she fell into step beside me. I resisted the temptation to make a sarcastic reply. She probably wouldn't understand, anyway.

"Yes."

"Must be difficult doing without your housekeeper."

What does she want?

When I didn't reply she went on. "Of course, I didn't know her but she seemed like a nice lady. Must have been awful for you. Finding her, I mean." Fortunately she didn't seem to expect a reply. "I think I would have passed out or something if it had been me. Did you?" I shook my head. "I think you must be very brave living by yourself in that house. Scary now too, I expect. I know how lonely I feel now that Bertie's gone."

While she rattled on I thought, Bertie? Husband or dog? Run away? Died? Oops she's stopped, obviously expecting a reply. "Living alone doesn't bother me at all. I've done it for more years than I care to remember. Actually, I quite like it. You'll get used to it."

Her face showed her disappointment. What had she been angling for? An invite to stay or did she want to be my new housekeeper?

"Have the perlice asked you a lot of questions?" she asked, trying for a recovery.

"Of course."

"They didn't ask me many. Just if I'd seen any strangers in the village. Silly question if you ask me with the ramblers and cyclists around." She was right. Although we're off the beaten track for motorists, we do get a lot of people who are hiking or biking through the forest. "Pity they didn't ask me more because I could tell them lots."

Really? I thought.

"Like that Dan Spencer. Always in and out of the ladies' houses. I can guess what he was up to."

The mind boggles!

"And her. She was always driving off in her car somewhere."

Her car? And where? And always?

Before I could ask for enlightenment, "Anyway must go," she said and she went. Turned about a scuttled down the side road we had just passed. The Crescent, which answered why she had appeared at the other side of the village the other day.

Wondering at her speedy departure I continued on towards the General Store and saw two ladies standing outside having a good gossip. Had the sight of them been the reason Mrs. Cheetham had made such a hurried departure?

"Good morning, Miss Marjoribanks."

"Good morning, Miss Marjoribanks."

"Good morning," I smiled at them. "Lovely day," and pushed open the door. Things are looking up. They said my name and smiled!

When I first came to Trewith Green I'd pictured the General Store as being one of the old-fashioned ones with a long counter and someone behind it to serve you and, in one corner, the post office. Not so. To compete with the big boys in town this was now a small supermarket complete with a check-out counter.

Apparently the post office used to be here as well. That was until Royal Mail, in its infinite wisdom, decided the only way it could save money was to close down the village shop branches. Thus many village shops closed to the further inconvenience of the villagers.

All heart these big business aren't they?

63

As I had already discovered, some of the old folks don't have cars. This is because they either never learned to drive or can no longer afford to run them. That being the case, how on earth does the Royal Mail expect them to collect their weekly pensions? Okay, have it paid into the bank. Where are the banks when they need cash?

And our village bus service is a joke, to say the least. One bus in either direction in the early morning for the workers, and one bus (each way) in the evening to bring them home.

Of course I ended up with three full bags of shopping. There are some things I cannot resist, such as McVities dark chocolate digestives. I salivate at the thought of them.

Having paid the usual King's Ransom and had a chat about the lovely summer weather with the lady on the check-out I struggled out of the shop, paused to check for traffic before crossing the road and – lo and behold! – Paula in her Toyota.

She stopped, opened her window and called, "Need a lift?" Silly question

"Yes, ta." I crossed over, put the bags on the back seat and got in beside her. "Went in for the usual half-a-dozen things."

"So I see," she responded dryly as we headed off. "I'm just off to Lyndhurst," she explained.

"No time for a cuppa?"

"Not this time, I'm afraid. Got a dental appointment."

"Oh yuck."

She chuckled. "Check up."

"Hope he doesn't find anything."

"Me too."

"Listen, just a quickie. Why would Mrs. Cheetham be lurking near my place?" And I went on to relate the one-sided conversation.

"She's a strange lady. Word of warning, Cleo, she is the biggest gossip, which is why people avoid her."

"What she doesn't know she'll make up?"

"Exactly."

"I'm still trying to work out whether she was obliquely asking for an invite to stay and keep me company. Or trying to find out if I want another housekeeper."

"Could be either. Maybe the invitation with a view to becoming the housekeeper."

"Well she's out of luck. I don't like her. By the way, who is or was Bertie?"

"Her husband. He died last year."

"Of boredom?"

"Could have been. No one knows exactly because she told people different things."

"Doesn't she have any family?"

"Oh yes. As soon as they were old enough the three of them fled the nest."

"I'll bet none of them wants her now."

"Doubtful," Paula agreed as she pulled up at my kitchen door. "By the way, Cleo, who did you think Bertie was?"

"Didn't know whether it was her husband or a dog. And, from the way she said he'd gone, I couldn't work out whether he was dead or had walked out."

We laughed, then I struggled out, retrieved my shopping and waved her off.

As I put away the shopping I was still wondering about Mrs. Cheetham. So she was the village's biggest gossip and she had told me she knows some things she could have told the police. Or was she lying? Surely if she had some info she could call the police and tell them? Wouldn't she? Shouldn't she? Perhaps I should mention it to Steaming.

Chapter 9

I was popular with the police the next morning. Jenny left, the pool people arrived to clean the pool and I was in the study leafing through a pile of home style magazines and making notes when Steaming and Blondie (mustn't think of him as Jerry otherwise I might laugh!) arrived.

"Where do you want to sit?" I asked as they stepped into the hall. "The sitting room for comfort, my study which is untidy, or the kitchen? We could have coffee."

"The kitchen, please." Steaming's always quick on the uptake.

While I prepared the coffee pot we passed time on generalities such as the weather and the work being done to the pool. I plumped down on a chair. "Right, Chief Inspector, start the questions while we wait for the coffee."

His first question surprised me. "Did you hire someone to kill Mrs. Spencer?"

I was gob-smacked and looked at him in stunned silence. The coffee pot plopped and gurgled. "Do what! Are you crazy? I didn't even really know the woman."

"I know you said you employed them through an agency, but once they worked here you must have had conversations with them."

"And as I told you, it was only to do with work."

"Indulge me and tell me again," he invited. If we'd still been kids at school I'd have clobbered him one.

Instead I took a deep breath, forgetting I was twiddling with beads. Of course they snapped and went all over the place. "Leave 'em," I told Blondie who was down on his knees. Talk about Jumping Jack Flash. He sat down again and we played pushing the beads into the centre of the table before I explained - yet again - about my visits to the registry office then continued, "Although I arrived on Thursday, the Spencers weren't coming until the next day, which was the first of the month.

"And, before you ask, after the decorators and everyone had moved out I paid the agency to get a cleaning firm in.

"The Spencers arrived, by cab, bright and early. I gave them a key to the flat and Janet helped her husband carry their luggage up to it, then came to the house. The first thing she asked me was if I'd had breakfast.

"I had and pointed out that the dirties were in the dishwasher. I offered her coffee, which she was reluctant to accept until I told her that we had things to discuss and it would be easier with coffee.

"She gave me a nervous smile and insisted on pouring out. I showed her the cupboard where the china is and left her to it. It was interesting to sit at the table and watch someone else get organized. I don't like housework or cooking so she didn't have to worry that I would interfere!" I paused and grinned at my audience who nodded their understanding.

"Anyway, I knew from her application form that she was fifty-five and that they had worked in the past for old ladies." I stopped while I poured out the coffee and handed it around. Then I sat down and continued, "As she seemed to be quiet and had a comfortable figure I think the old ladies had been at ease with her.

"We sat here while I repeated what I'd told her at our interview, adding that once she knew exactly how often she would need a cleaning lady she should let me know. I also suggested that she find the cleaning lady when the time came.

"She agreed, then asked what I wanted her husband to do. She didn't think that there would be very much for him. I had to agree but pointed out that we would be able to find odds and ends which the builders and decorators hadn't quite got right. And, of course, he cleans the cars."

I thought back. "You know, when she smiled she looked almost beautiful. Her pale blue eyes lit up and a dimple appeared in one of the chipmunk cheeks." I sighed, "Pity about the disappearing chin, but we can't choose our looks."

When I looked at Steaming I could see he was trying not to laugh. I used to try doing that to him in class, especially when we had a teacher we didn't like. Back to the subject.

"I gave her another key to the flat and when I did that she took a plastic bag of key-rings and tags out of her handbag. Before I knew it she had all the spare keys on the right rings. I also gave her a set of house keys and a key to the Volvo telling her to feel free to use it when I'm not around. Apart from keeping it running smoothly, I didn't want the Roller used.

"We then returned to the subject of Dan and what he could do. She said he could always mow the lawns if there was a motor mower. I told her I have a lawn service so he needn't bother, but could keep an eye on them to make sure they did the job properly. Apparently he isn't any good with plants. I also told her I wouldn't object if he wanted to hire himself out part time. For some reason she didn't approve. I still haven't worked out why not."

I sat back and regarded them. "That's about it, I think. Any more coffee?"

While I poured some more Sergeant Wiles, who had been scribbling notes, exchanged a look with Steaming.

69

With the mugs back in front of them he took up the questioning. "Did you know that Dan Spencer gambles?"

I shook my head. "Not until Mrs. Linley mentioned it as a rumour. I guess that's why Janet didn't want him out of her sight. But, no, I didn't know that at the time."

"He didn't ask you for extra money at any time?"

"Nope."

"Could he have fiddled any bills? For petrol, that kind of thing."

"No way. I may not be 'well educated' but I am savvy enough to check my bills before paying them."

They smiled at that and Blondie went on, "When we searched the flat again we did find a savings account book."

"Where?"

"Bottom of the flour bin." Steaming grimaced and shifted uncomfortably on the chair.

"You mean no one thought to look under it when searching the flat?" I was astounded at the stupidity.

"Not there. It was in a plastic bag inside under the flour."

"I bet a woman found it," I commented dryly and they exchanged a look.

"Told you she'd say something like that, didn't I?" Steaming said to his minion who nodded. I merely raised my eyes to look at the ceiling and refrained from comment.

"Don't you want to know about the account?" Steaming asked me.

Of course I did, but I wasn't about to give him that satisfaction. "None of my business."

"Tell her, Wiles, before her nose gets as long as Pinocchio's." I'll get him one day!

"It's in Mrs. Spencer's name and from the total we can only assume that she knew about his gambling and insisted on banking their earnings." He then told me the total and it knocked me silly. Nearly a quarter of a million pounds! How could a couple like that earn and save so much? Especially if he gambles. Silly me. Perhaps he was lucky – several times.

"And inheritances," Steaming added dryly. Ah. "I expect they were saving for early retirement. Thing is, Cleo, some quite large sums have been withdrawn."

"On top of that total?" I was aghast.

"No. From it."

"So where is it?"

"No idea. Maybe she had another account, but we haven't found any other books."

"If she did have another account why bother to put it in that one to start with?

He shrugged and changed the subject slightly. "Did you know Mrs. Spencer had a brother?"

"No. As I've told you, we weren't exactly bosom buddies. Come to think of it I suppose I should have insisted on knowing the next of kin, shouldn't I?" I grimaced at this failure on my part.

"Even if you forgot to do so she should have supplied it," he tried to comfort me.

"Thanks for that. So where is this brother?"

"Not at home. No one at his place of business knows where he is, neither do his neighbours. He took a few days holiday and that is as much as they know."

"Can't you trace him by his car?"

"No car. At least," he amended quickly, "that we know about."

"He could…. Sorry, I shouldn't be telling the police how to do their job. I'm sure you've already checked all channels."

"Of course. We don't think he caught a bus and his nearest railway station is Victoria."

"No chance!" I crowed as he named one of the large London termini.

"Exactly."

At that moment a chiming issued from Steaming's jacket. He patted his pockets and brought out the mobile phone.

Blondie and me found it difficult to understand the content of the call from the, "Yes. Fine. Where? Okay. Wait for us."

Phone call over Steaming stood up – as did Blondie, "You'll be glad to know, Cleo, that your Volvo has turned up."

"Not?"

"No. Empty," he reassured me. "An Agister found it in a copse. We've got to go and meet him now and he'll take us to it." He then added, apologetically, "We'll have to take it in for forensic."

"That's okay. I've got the Roller. Anyway, I think I'll want to sell the Volvo." I pulled a yucky face.

Once they'd gone, which they did in quick order (Steaming didn't even finish his coffee!) I phoned Paula to ask how an Agister could find the car when the police couldn't.

"The Forest is enormous and the Agisters and Forestry Commission Keepers know it better than the police," she told me. "They patrol it every day and the car was obviously in an 'off limits' area.

"I see. I wonder where Dan Spencer is?" I mused and we chatted about this for a while and I told her about my interview.

It wasn't until after we'd disconnected that I remembered I hadn't told Steaming about the overheard conversations or what Mrs. Cheetham had told me. Now I wondered whether Janet's 'lover' might not have been her brother. Would he have killed his sister?

Chapter 10

Thank goodness I had already had breakfast the next morning before Jenny Dixon called to tell me they'd found Dan.

I asked if he had admitted killing his wife. There was a deathly hush. "He's dead?" I hazarded. "Suicide?" The easy answer and a relief all round for the village.

"His body was washed up on a beach."

"How do you know it's Dan Spencer?"

"Soggy papers in his pocket but you'll probably be asked to ID him."

"Not again!" I wailed.

"Just a minute, Cleo, the Chief wants a word with you."

"Okay."

"Cleo?"

"That's me."

"Hang on a minute. I'm going to my office." Uh-oh, secrets. He didn't keep me in suspense for long. "You there?"

"Nah. Gone for a fly in me jet. Course I'm here."

"You always were lippy."

"Look who's talking?" I was aghast (I think that's the word I want). He was always in more trouble than me with our teachers. I heard him give a deep sigh.

"Can we get to the matter in hand?"

"That's what I'm here for."

"Assuming this is Dan Spencer, he was shot. Don't tell anyone." Bossy-boots.

"Think I'm stupid? I do read mystery novels, you know."

"Okay, okay."

"So, do you think he shot himself?"

"Don't know. But the Volvo wasn't anywhere near the river."

"Wasn't it?"

"No."

"Which means what?"

"He had a long walk."

"Ho-hum. Find the brother-in-law?"

"For one. For two, find enemies."

"And the Best of British! Gambling for one. Women?"

"To be found out."

"By the way, ducks, I've been meaning to tell you about a couple of conversations I overheard at the WI meeting I went to."

"Leaving it a bit late, aren't you?"

"Do you want to know about them or not?" I asked dryly.

"Of course I do. Sorry I'm bit narky, but…."

"Excuses, excuses." Anyway, I passed them on for what it was worth, adding, "The old ladies who the Spencers used to work for?"

"They're already dead."

"Their relatives, stupid." Oops I overdid that. He put the phone down a bit sharpish and before I had a chance to mention Mrs. Cheetham and her guesswork. Anyway, I didn't have time for more chat. Paula and I were going to Southampton.

I called her and gave her some of the news about Dan – the bare bones as it were – and confirmed the time she was going to pick me up. I reckon I'll have difficulty persuading another couple to take over so quickly from the

75

Spencers, but I need her to teach me in case she can't always come with me.

The agency had found four possible couples for us to interview and set aside a room for the purpose. Apart from my one or two questions I left most of the talking to Paula, but did take lots of notes. Afterwards Paula asked whether I had taken the minutes or been forming opinions! Both actually.

Then with a feeling of a job well done we went for lunch and I decided it was time to start clearing the trees from the wood.

"Paula, the other day when Steaming was interviewing me in your kitchen I said I would let you in on a secret."

She looked puzzled. "Sorry, Cleo, I can't remember."

"When he said they knew all about me?"

Her brow cleared. "Oh yes. You don't have to tell me you know."

Curiosity isn't just reserved for cats, I thought. "I want to tell you. I'm sure there are all sorts of rumours in the village and, let's face it, even your daughter thinks I'm either a gangster's moll or a madam!"

Paula looked embarrassed and fiddled with the salt cellar. "I-I-I-..." I put a hand over hers and reassured her. "Don't worry, I don't care. I think it's hilarious actually." I grinned and she smiled.

"So, Paula, let me tell you about my win on the lottery."

"Do what?"

"Lottery," I repeated succinctly. "My money's honest. Honest," I added with a smile.

She looked so relieved. "I am so glad."

"Thought it was ill-gotten gains, did you?"

"We-ell."

76

"Look, love, I'm not stupid. There had to be a reason why you sought me out and I've been adding up the numbers. Dan was a gambler. Ergo, was he also a bookie's runner?"

She gasped and put a hand to her mouth.

Bingo! If you'll forgive the pun. In case you don't know, a bookie's runner is a bit historical and goes back to when gambling on the horses was illegal in England, except at the races. Now we've got Betting Shops (or Turf Accountants for the nobs). As even I wouldn't go into one what are the chances Paula and some of the village ladies would?

"How did you guess?" Paula whispered.

"It doesn't take a Stephen Hawking. Take my advice and tell Steaming. And tell the other ladies to confess. I'm told it's good for the soul," I finished dryly.

"The stupid thing is that I'm not a gambler. No, really. You know, life can get pretty boring sometimes and it was just to add a bit of spice to it. I've always liked horses and one of my hobbies is keeping records of race horses; their form and lineage."

"Like the Queen does, you mean?"

"Exactly, but I'm not as expert as her."

"So what good is the knowledge if you can't put it into practise?"

She smiled. "It helps when Gerard and I go to the races at Goodwood."

"Heard of that place. Posh house, motor racing and Ladies Day at the horse racing."

"That's right," she confirmed.

"But then you wanted more than that?" I asked, referring to what was obviously her betting habit.

"Yes."

"Makes it more interesting when you're watching racing on the telly," I commented and she nodded. "Rather like me doing the lottery. How did you get to know about Dan?"

"Village ladies," was her succinct reply. She'd heard about him from them and made contact that way.

"Fine, but that still doesn't answer why you picked me up, so to speak. Care to confess?"

"This is so embarrassing, Cleo, especially now that I know you."

"Try. I've told you before, nothing embarrasses me."

She took a deep breath. "Well, Dan was also trying some blackmail…"

"The bastard," I interrupted, "I suppose he wanted you to place larger bets and give him a bigger slice of the pie?" She nodded. "So, back to the blackmail."

"Not only the gambling, but also about Margaret. He said he knew something about her," she put in parenthetically, then continued, "but it seems he was also trying it with some of the others. I have no idea what secrets they might have; perhaps it was simply their gambling."

"And you thought I might be part and parcel of it," I finished.

She nodded and looked ashamed. "I'm sorry."

"Don't be. I would have been. What about Janet?"

"She came to see me. Seems she found out about it all."

"And?"

"Blackmail. She'd get him to stop if I paid her."

"What a right pair I hired! Let's go to the pub on the corner and get a stiff drink," I suggested as we had now finished lunch, "I could use one."

78

That's what we did, me with a Scotch and Paula, of course, with a medium sherry, and I told her what I'd been doing with all that lovely lolly.

"Did I tell you I've got a little pad in London which makes it alright for when I want to go up town for a few days? Maybe do a bit of shopping or go to the theatre. In fact, Paula, when you want to you can always use it. Or, rather, you and Gerard."

"That's very generous of you, Cleo, but don't let's get too far forward with ourselves."

"You're right. I'm sorry, I tend to push a bit. You just got to tell me off when I get pushy."

She laid a hand on my arm. "Cleo, you could never be described as being pushy. If you were pushy you would have pushed your way into this village weeks ago."

"Yeah, well."

"I think you are actually rather shy, aren't you?"

I looked away blinking rather hard. Sometimes kindness is hard to take. "Sorry, I didn't mean to be rude," she apologized.

"That's alright. You are right. I am a bit. Perhaps that's why I tend to show off a bit. Put on all these gaudy clothes."

"I shouldn't worry. You give them something to talk about and you brighten the place up."

After that we split up to go and do our shopping and when we met up I was laden with bags. "More clothes?" she asked.

"Wait and see."

And what a surprise she had. As soon as we got home I left her in the living room with a glass of my best sherry and pounded up the stairs. When I came back down she

79

was relaxed in a comfortable armchair and got the shock of her life when I walked in. There I was in a safari suit. Shorts modestly covering my rather thick thighs and knee length socks covering shapely legs – even though I say it myself

"You don't look as – er…."

"Fat?"

"Well…."

"I know," I grinned. "I've already lost some weight since retiring. You have to remember that I did a sedentary job. Now I get more exercise. And I don't eat as much junk food."

"So what will you wear when you're slim and lithe," she teased.

"I'll think about it if that time comes. My bones are too big anyway. So what do you think?" I gave a twirl.

"Excellent. You won't frighten the wild life in that. But how will you get from here to wherever without the villagers seeing you?"

"A gaudy loose top over it. They'll only see me behind the wheel as I drive by."

Paula laughed.

"Now about these Safaris." I sat down beside her. "Tell me about them."

"They're run by the Forestry Commission. There are several covering different aspects of the Forest. You have to book ahead and meet them at the Tourist Office in Lyndhurst."

"When are the tours?"

She raised her eyebrows. "You think I'm the Tourist Board?"

I laughed and apologized. "Hint taken. I'll call them."

"Pardon my curiosity, Cleo, but did you only buy one outfit?"

"Good Lord, no. The others will be delivered, but I wanted your opinion on it."

Later Paula told me that despite the news with which the day had begun, driving home she felt revitalized and happy. But then, of course, she couldn't see into the future and was unaware of what it had in store for her.

Chapter 11

"Good morning. I'm Mrs. Walsh. Mrs. Linley said you're looking for someone to do yer cleaning? I've got a window now so I thought I'd come round."

I waved a hand to indicate she should come in, at the same time averting my head to cough, covering up a laugh. I only hoped Mrs. Walsh didn't realise I was amused at the incongruous use of Yuppy language in New Forest burr from this rather plain, wiry woman with the deepset blue eyes that I reckon don't miss a thing.

"I'm sorry about that. Do come in."

"You got a corf?"

"No, just a frog in my throat. Let's go into the kitchen." I pointed down the hall and followed her. "Yeah, I do need someone to do the cleaning."

I was further put out after I'd poured out two mugs of coffee and sat down at the table to see that the rummaging in the large shopping bag had brought forth a filofax. Which she then earnestly consulted, a frown on her face.

"Look, lemme see what time I've got free. When d'you want me to come? Once a week? Twice a week? Three times a week?"

"When I'm here probably twice a week, but when I'm not here I should think only once a week. Just to keep the dust down." I shrugged.

"Twice a week then. Lemme see."

We settled on days and times, Mrs. Walsh deciding that she would probably need four hours to get through.

With days, hours and money discussed, mugs drained and put into the dishwasher Mrs. Walsh dragged an overall out of the bag and donned it. "Mrs. M." She obviously had a problem with the pronunciation of Marjoribanks. "Could

82

you show me where the cleaning stuff is then I can get on. I take it you want your bedroom and bathroom done." She looked around. "The kitchen." It was a bit messy. "What about the dining room and lounge?"

"Why don't I show you where everything is and the rooms that I'm using. Do those now and if you've got time start on the others. Then you can do them as and when."

As we went from room to room she made some complimentary comments, then surprised me, "By the way, Mrs. M. you really oughter keep them gates shut."

"During the day?" Tell you the truth I don't ever shut them, they're big, heavy wooden things that weigh a ton. They'd stop a ten ton truck if it tried to smash its way in. Great security, but liable to break your back.

"Course. Gates is to keep out people you don't want in yer house or garden."

"Apart from occasional cars, cyclists and ramblers there aren't many people come by here," I pointed out.

"All the more reason. 'N' I'm not talking about strangers, neither. There's that Mrs. Cheetham, for one."

"Why would she come in?"

"Tryin' ter make friends wiv yer, in't she?"

"I suppose so."

"Take it from me, yer don't need 'er as a friend," Mrs. Walsh said darkly. "And she'll take yer flowers."

"Eh?"

"She 'n't no gardener. Bertie used to do it and fer others in the village." Probably to get out from under. "Now she thinks she c'n 'elp 'erself. Caught 'er at Mrs. Linley's once and I give 'er an earful."

I bet you did, I thought. I could just picture it.

She then changed the subject abruptly telling me that she'd just finished at Paula's. "Don't know what's wrong

83

with the young one. Looks as if she's been having a good cry. Teenagers. I mean what can you do with them, eh? I got one of me own. I know what they're like. All problems. These girls all think they're in love."

I didn't comment but filed the information away presuming that Margaret had been well and truly told off by her parents over the scene of two days ago. I know how these things tend to rankle. I remember it well. "Right, Mrs. Walsh, I'll leave you to get on and I'll be in the study."

"Alright, Mrs. M."

Once I could hear her banging about in the kitchen, I took out the mobile phone. "Paula, it's Cleo. Thanks for sending Mrs. Walsh. She looks to be a treasure, although I think she might be trying a fast one."

"What's up?"

"She reckons she needs four hours to get round here. Can you imagine, looking after one person?"

"She is very thorough," Paula consoled, "but you'd better keep a check on her and time it. Make sure you're there the first few times she comes in. Once you have a housekeeper I shouldn't think you would need her for that length of time. You'll only want her for the heavier work, won't you?"

"S'right. Anyway, Paula, what's this she tells me about Margaret's been crying? Been having another go at her, have you?"

"No, I haven't said another word. Neither has Gerard. We decided we'd leave it for now. Naturally we spoke to her the other evening and tried to get through to her about her manners. Of course we got the usual 'you don't understand', but I have no idea what is wrong now."

"Young love going wrong probably."

She sighed. "I've no idea."

"She there now?"

"Of course not. Out on the horse again."

After we'd disconnected I began – again - to try to plan the new décor for the pool room.

Once Mrs. Walsh had finished and I'd paid her, I snacked, then sat and wondered what to do with the afternoon. "Come on, girl, you're not going to sit around and do nothing all afternoon. What did you buy a house in New Forest for? To sit and look at four walls? Get out of it. Come on, get shifting." I hoisted myself up from the kitchen table and plodded upstairs to change into one of the safari outfits and, as I'd told Paula, put a short bright top over it. In the garage I looked at the Roller. "Well, babe, you're not really the car I'd choose to take into the forest, but you'll have to do for now. At least you're easily recognisable so no one's going to pinch you."

I drove to one of the several car parks and discovered that the Roller isn't exactly the best vehicle for driving on rough ground. It may be a well-sprung car but it hasn't got four-wheel drive and it was a bumpy ride in the parking area. Must go and see the car dealer tomorrow about another vehicle. Perhaps a four-wheel drive instead of a small car.

Once parked – well away from the village, I might add – I discarded the tunic (don't want to scare the horses do we?) and changed into my sensible walking shoes. I made sure my baby was locked then began walking along a footpath towards what seemed to be a nearby copse.

"Whew!" I paused about halfway. "That's a lot further away than what I thought." I stood there, arms akimbo (I tend to do that) and looked around at the gorse-covered heathland with occasional small stands of trees. As my eyes became used to the scenery, I could see quite a few horses in the area quietly grazing, some with growing foals. I shivered with fear and thought, "Shall I go back to the car? No, come on, be brave," I chided myself. "They won't hurt you. Think of them as like dogs. If dogs think you're scared they'll play up but if you ignore them they leave you alone. Come on, it's only because you've never been close to a horse."

With that I continued my walk. As I was nearing the copse I could see a saddled horse cropping the grass and wondered where the rider was. "Oh gawd, don't tell me someone's fallen off and broken a leg or something," I muttered.

I looked hard at the horse, it moved and I got the back view. "'Ere, horse, turn round I want to get a look at your front." Keeping me distance I moved slowly round until I could see its face. "I thought so. You're Maggie's horse, aren't you?" I remembered seeing it in a photo Paula had shown me. "Now what the heck's your name?" The reins were hanging down, "Come on, Cleo, be brave. Be brave."

I inched towards the horse. It inched away. I got a little closer and he moved away again. "Oh for gawd's sake, come 'ere! I want to take hold of those reins before you break your bloody leg. Now, come 'ere!" Surprisingly the horse did "come 'ere". I got hold of the reins. "Now what do I do? I'm not getting up on top of you even if I knew how.

"Come on, where is she? You're Maggie's horse. Where's Maggie. Come on, show me where she is." I was actually thinking of the horse as being like a dog.

I began walking into the copse, the horse quite close behind and getting uncomfortably close. I could almost feel it nudging me and I broke out in a cold sweat. "Don't get too close, horse. Don't run away with me, either. Hang on a minute." I stopped and it stopped. We both listened.

I could faintly hear the sound of sobbing. The horse whickered (I think that's what that noise is called) and flicked his ears. "That's her, innit? Come on, horse, here we go. You lead her to me." I stood to one side of the footpath and let it go forward and take the lead.

Margaret was sitting on the ground nursing a foot, her helmet on the ground beside her and her fair hair like a waterfall over her face.

"So why didn't you use your mobile and phone your mother?"

She shoved her hair back as she looked up and whispered, "Battery's flat."

"How clever can you be! So you've fallen off your horse. Please don't tell me you've broken your ankle."

"I don't know. I don't know," she sobbed.

"You hold your horse and I'll look at your ankle." I handed over the reins and struggled to get down onto my knees. That's not an easy feat at my size, as you can imagine. Neither is it a pretty sight. While the horse nuzzled his mistress I got hold of her foot. "I don't know how we're going to get this boot off. Can you wiggle your toes?"

"Yeah."

"Well it's not broke then. Probably twisted or sprained. Come on, let's get you up. I'm quite sure your horse will help you though how I'm going to get up I have no idea." The sight of me crawling towards a tree and using it to stand up was enough to bring a smile of amusement to her face and to forget her own woes.

"Right, your turn." I managed to get her standing on her good foot. "Now how are we going to get you onto the horse?"

"Dunno."

"Shall we see if we can get you up there? Or do you want to walk him and hang on to me?"

I could see the indecisiveness in her face – features that would one day be like her mother's. It would be a strain getting up on the horse but then again, it would be a strain to have to accept help from the woman she had labelled "gangster's moll".

"Come on, love, I'm not going to hurt you. I think we ought to try and get you up on the horse. Let's see if we can find something for you to stand on so you can hop up on. Seen any fallen trees around?"

"There might be something over there." She nodded to her left.

"Okay. Come on." We hobbled over to a conveniently fallen tree trunk and managed to get her on to that – standing on one foot. "How're you going to get onto the horse?"

"I can put my good foot in the stirrup and throw my other leg over if you can hold me steady."

"Right. Hang on." After a bit of a struggle to find the best way for me to stand to support her while she hopped over onto the horse we eventually managed it. "Right, love, do you think you're alright to go home like this or do you want to come out the car park? We can put you into the car and tie up the horse. No one's going to pinch him are they?"

"Don't think so."

"Right. So we get the horse tied up, I'll take you home and bring your Mum out to collect the horse."

"Alright." A very abject Maggie agreed to the plan and we trooped slowly back to the Roller. Then there was the problem of getting her off the horse but it seemed to know what was expected of it and, together with the aid of me and the car, she was down and onto the back seat.

"I'm going to tie your horse up to that tree over there. Is that alright?"

"Do you know how to tie a knot to hold it?"

"It's alright, love, I was a Girl Guide. Done me knots."

Back at the car she was in tears, presumably shock. Not being of a maternal disposition I wasn't quite clear what to do. I got into the front passenger seat and turned around to rest my arms on the back of it. I usually keep the glass wall down. I think of it as only for the posh people so they can cut themselves off from the chauffeur.

"Hey, come on love, it can't be as bad as that. It's only a sprain."

She hiccuped, "You don't know that."

"That it's a sprain? Course I do."

"Not that." She scrubbed her hazel eyes with a sodden handkerchief.

I found a packet of tissues in the glove box and threw them to her, "Cop hold," and waited until she'd had a good blow and, hopefully, recovered from her bout of crying.

"So, Maggie..."

"Margaret," was the truculent interruption.

I sighed. "Okay, Margaret. What's really wrong?" As if I didn't know it was something else.

"None of your business," was the muttered response.

"I know. Just call me nosy. So what's wrong? Had a row with the boyfriend?"

She looked panic-stricken realising there was no escape from this interfering old bat. "No."

89

"So?" I waited patiently.

Eventually, "It's worse."

I stayed silent, thinking she was going to say she was preggers, then it came out in a rush and I got the shock. "He's dead." Then came more tears. I hoped it wasn't who I was thinking.

Was it Dan Spencer? If so, what was he doing with an under-age girl? I sincerely hoped it wasn't what I feared. Tread very carefully, Cleo, I warned myself.

Chapter 12

"I'm sorry. You're right, it is worse than I thought."

When the latest bout of tears subsided Margaret peeked at me over the top of the current soggy tissue. "You've guessed who it is, haven't you?"

"Dan?"

She nodded.

"Want to talk about it?" I asked softly. Negated by the shake of a head. "Okay. Your choice. For now."

"Wh-wh-what do you mean?"

"The police."

"Oh." It took a while for her to assimilate the thought. "Will I really have to? I mean, no one knows. Except you, of course." She sat up as straight as she could with her legs along the seat. "You wouldn't! You're mean."

"Hey, hold it, kid."

"I'm not a kid. I'm a woman."

"A young woman if you want to be pedantic."

She gulped, then offered a watery smile.

"What did I say that's so funny?"

"Pedantic. It isn't your language."

"What do you mean?"

"It's a-a-a- oh, I don't know, but it doesn't suit you. Neither do those clothes."

I shrugged. What adult listens to advice from teenagers about their clothes? "I know lots of words, young woman. And the clothes won't frighten the horses," I smiled at her before turning serious again. "Now stop trying to turn the conversation. D'you want to rehearse what you'll have to tell the police?"

She conceded defeated, "Okay." And told me how she'd met Dan Spencer a few times when out riding. He'd been quite honest about being married and what he did, but had got the impressionable teenager's sympathy with his dreams. He had plans, one day, of making the big time with a secret invention. Unfortunately, his wife didn't believe him (neither did I) so she kept their savings in an account which only she could draw from. That meant he never had enough ready cash to buy the parts for his invention.

Of course Margaret had managed to persuade him to let her give him some of her pocket money, which was predictably plentiful.

And, of course, he had told her that when she was of age he would divorce his wife and marry her.

I had great difficulty restraining myself from saying what I thought of predators such as Dan Spencer. Good job he's already dead, I thought; otherwise I might do it myself. Aloud I asked, "And the one thousand pounds you wanted from me?"

She hung her head. "Sorry."

"What did he want it for?"

"To get away before the police accused him of murdering his wife."

"And did he?"

"No," was the vehement response.

I didn't push it. "One other thing, Margaret." We exchanged an understanding look.

"He never even kissed me."

I hoped my relief wasn't apparent.

"Okay, Margaret. Thanks for telling me. Do you want to go home now or come back to my place? When you talk with the police one of your parents will have to be present."

"Do I have to do it right away?"

"The sooner the better."

"Cleo, can you tell my mother? Please? And I'm sorry I said those nasty things to you," she finished in a rush.

"Forget it. You were upset. So the plan is we go back to your place and let your Mum strap up your foot. I bring her back here to collect Dobbin…"

She giggled. "Dobbin's a donkey's name. That's Star for the white mark on his face."

I grinned, "Would have helped to know that when I was trying to get hold of him."

"He obeyed you when you got bossy."

"He did, didn't he?" If I sounded surprised, it was because I was. I also realised I was no longer so afraid of horses. "That's the first time I've ever touched a horse. Or got that close, come to think of it."

"Poor you."

"City girl – woman – that's me," I grinned. "Back to our plan of campaign. I'll tell your Mum when we get here then she can get over it while riding Star back home."

"Will you come back? Please," the blue eyes pleaded.

"Okay, but I don't think I'll be allowed to stay with you when you talk to the police."

"Oh."

"Don't worry. They're smashing. The Chief Inspector looks like a film star and the Constable is a pretty, er, young woman." I'd almost called Jenny Dixon a "girl".

During the drive I asked, casually, "If you heard me with Star why didn't you call out?" Silence from the back. "I get it. You didn't want me to find you."

A whispered, "Yes."

I heaved a sigh. "Some day, Margaret, you'll be older and wiser."

93

In the car riding back to collect Star I was a bit quiet trying to work out how I was going to break the news to Paula. She broke in on my musings, "I'm sorry if Margaret has been rude again, Cleo," she essayed.

"Oh, sorry, I'm a bit quiet, love. Nah. She wasn't rude. Fact she apologized."

"Well there's a change in the weather."

Yeah, I thought, and I know why and I'm not looking forward to telling you. "Right, Paula, here we are and it looks like Star's got company." Some of the wild ponies were cropping grass around Margaret's horse.

"Protecting him," Paula explained.

"Doing a better job than humans."

"Of course," she smiled, "and thanks for the lift." She was about to open the door but I put a hand on her arm.

"Not yet, Paula, I've got to tell you something."

The tone of my voice and expression on my face must have told her it was something she didn't really want to hear.

"Truth is I dunno how to tell you. It's bad, but not that bad, if you know what I mean?"

She shook her head, looking mystified. "Sorry, but I don't. Either news is good or bad."

"Yeah. Well." I took a deep breath. "Seems like Margaret knew Dan Spencer."

"I suppose she met him about the village sometime." When I didn't respond she frowned and looked closely at me. "Oh my God! You mean really knew?"

I nodded, "Afraid so, but," I hurried on, "not that well." I then told her what Margaret had told me.

Paula sat gripping her hands and trying to breath normally.

"Come on, love, scream or shout or swear. I don't care. We can even scream together if you like."

"I-I-I-I don't know what to say."

"I do. If someone hadn't already done for the bastard I'd do for him myself."

She gave me a watery smile and sniffed, and I handed over another packet of tissues. "Have a good cry and blow."

That was all she needed. I gave her a hug. Don't think she's had one in years. Once recovered she apologized. "No good saying I don't know what came over me!" she exclaimed.

"Yeah, well," I was a bit embarrassed. I'd succumbed to an instinct when p'raps I should have been more reserved.

Paula took hold of my hands. "Cleo, thank you for being there for me. And for Margaret. You did right."

I was relieved. "Good. I didn't know whether I was doing it proper or not. I only know that we've got to tell the police. Or, rather, Margaret has."

"Will you stay with us when she does?"

"If they let me."

"Thanks."

We sat in the car staring at the horses. "Paula, who do you think did it?"

"What? Killed Mrs. Spencer or Dan?"

"I think it's obvious that Dan killed her. Probably because he wanted money for gambling. No, who killed him?"

"No idea," she shook her head.

"Could have been something to do with gambling, but it's a bit of a coincidence. Course it could be the same person did for both of them."

95

"Who? They didn't have children, did they?"

I shrugged. "Who knows? She's got a brother if the police can find him. No one knows where he is which is why their names haven't been released to the press yet. He might be on holiday, on the razz, or on a blinder."

At Paula's puzzled look I explained that by razz I meant a "dirty weekend – so to speak" and a blinder meant he might be boozing somewhere.

"Maybe. No one in the village has seen any strangers."

I thought about that, wondering for a moment what she meant. Then I realised. "Yeah, but to get to my place he wouldn't need to go through the village, would he? Not if he's got a car. Anyway, why would he kill his sister?"

"Money", my friend said succinctly.

"True. But suppose she was already dead? He wouldn't have been able to get into the house. And the police didn't find any strange fingerprints. At least," I amended, "they haven't mentioned that."

"But you don't know for sure."

"No. No one broke in though. Actually, come to think of it, I don't know what she was doing in the house at that time of night."

"Going for a swim?" Although she meant that as a serious comment, when we exchanged a look we both giggled. Once started it was difficult to stop but eventually I gasped. "We shouldn't be laughing." Then started again. "Delayed shock. I'm going." Paula was the first to recover and opened the car door. As she stepped out she said, "See you back at my place."

As I was wiping tears from my cheeks, I just flapped a hand in her direction and sat panting and letting out the occasional giggle. Once recovered from what I reckon was nervous tension I started the car and returned along the country byways to the Linley house, wondering what the police would make of Margaret's news.

Chapter 13

Poor old Paula got a fright when she came back from stabling Star. Margaret and I were upstairs in her room playing on the computer and making so much noise we didn't hear her, not even when she came belting up the stairs to see what was going on.

"Oh." She was in the doorway; we turned and laughed at her. I could just about picture her thought. Maggie (sorry, girl, but you'll always be Maggie in my mind) treating the woman she'd labelled a whore, like a best friend.

"Hey, Paula, this is great. Have you ever played computer games? I hadn't. I'm going to have to buy some. They're fantastic."

She shook her head, looking dazed. "How did you get up here?"

"With difficulty!" we chorused and giggled, then Maggie explained, "With the banister on one side and Cleo propping me up on the other."

"Don't you think we should call the Inspector and get it over with?" Paula brought us down to earth.

"Yeah. You going change?"

"Yes, I must."

"Do that and I'll call Steaming."

"Who?" Maggie demanded.

"Sorry, kiddo. Chief Inspector Kettle," I told her primly.

She chuckled. "I like it. Did you make that up?"

"A very long time ago. We were at school together."

"Were you….?"

"NO. Just fighting friends," I put in quickly. "You be alright here on your own while I call him and your Mum changes?"

She nodded so Paula and I left her playing with her favourite toy.

"I wish Gerard wasn't in Court today. He should be here for the interview with the police." Paula sighed. "I'm not looking forward to telling him of his 'angel's' latest escapade."

"Can't help you there, old girl. Go and get changed and I'll go down and get on with the phoning." I wanted to use my mobile out of their hearing so that I could warn Steaming to take it easy on the kid. Of course, he wasn't in so I left a message asking him to call Paula and got a message that someone was going to take me to ID Dan's body sometime later.

To be quite honest, I didn't think he'd want me around when he interviewed Maggie.

When Paula came down I told her, "You don't need me. You really need Gerard. Apart from anything else, I need to get showered and changed. They want me to do the ID later."

"Of course you must go and get ready. I'll explain it to Margaret."

"Tell her I'm sorry I can't be with her."

"Of course." Paula gave an understanding smile.

"When Steaming phones tell him and perhaps he'll leave it until Gerard can be here."

"Maybe he'll think it's too urgent to wait. That's why I would like you to stay."

"Don't think he would let me stay anyway. You can tell me all about it later." I jotted Steaming's number down on the pad by her phone. "I've left a message for him to call you, but that's the number – just in case. Actually I think Maggie'd like to get it over with quick and not with her Dad present."

She sighed. "I think you're probably right. Thanks for everything, Cleo."

"That's alright. Give me a bell and let me know how it goes."

"Of course."

As I was going out to the Roller I paused and had a brainstorm. "Oops, nearly forgot the gaudy. Can't have the villagers thinking I'm normal, can we?" I charged out to the car, grabbed my top and went back indoors to put it on. As I left I gave Paula a hug and dashed off.

This time I was taken to the morgue in a cop car with a couple of uniforms in front. Was I glad we didn't have to drive through the village. Rumour would have gone around that I'd been arrested!

Blondie, a.k.a. Detective Sergeant Wiles met me. And a WPC – probably in case I fainted again.

I didn't and the body was Dan. Couldn't see any bullet holes so he wasn't shot in the head – thank gawd!

Guess what Steaming and Jenny had been doing while I was at grisly corner? S'right. Interviewing Maggie.

Paula diplomatically left a message at home instead of calling me on the mobile. When I called she told me all about it.

"So they didn't take long in coming then?" I asked.

"No. Just as I was hoping they wouldn't come until this evening when Gerard would be here, the Chief Inspector and his Constable arrived."

"So what happened?"

"We went up to Margaret's room. She and I sat on her bed, Jenny Dixon used Margaret's desk and the Inspector sat on the edge of the armchair. I don't think he was too comfortable with the idea of sitting that low."

"No, well, he wouldn't be, would he? Can't seem to be in charge. How was Maggie?"

"Funnily enough she let me put my arm around her. That's the closest we've been for a long time."

"Maybe this has given her a fright." Of her life, I hoped. Perhaps she'd appreciate her parents in future.

"He told Margaret that he has a daughter the same age as her...."

"What!" Well blow me down with a pea-shooter. Steaming married and with kids! Who'd have thought it? As a kid he was always a rebel. Like me. I never thought he'd get married. Just shows you, don't it?

"Shall I carry on?" Paula asked dryly.

"Oh, yes, of course. Sorry about that but the thought of Steaming married and with kids just gob-smacks me."

"So I gather." I could hear her smiling.

"Right, love, carry on."

And she did. Apparently he offered Maggie the choice of telling him or telling Jenny the news. Maggie chose Jenny. Well, she would. Jenny's younger, pretty, and a woman and much more likely to understand, isn't she? But Paula did say that although Steaming went out of the room, he didn't shut the door so he was obviously listening.

Maggie took a bit of persuading. I think she wanted her mother to tell the story, but she did get around to telling Jenny what had happened, albeit slowly and with lots of prompting from the constable.

"Did she come out with anything she hadn't told me?"

101

"Did she tell you they used to meet in that glade where the car was found?"

"No."

"Apparently Dan used to drive his car there and meet her. And I asked her about the money she asked you for."

"His wife was dead, he couldn't sign the checks and didn't have any money to make a getaway."

"Right. I must say, I was and am very angry with that man."

"Yeah. He got what he deserved. Sorry if that sounds vicious but men like that make me very, very angry."

"I agree with you." She huffed. "And here I am thinking I am a reasonable, caring and understanding woman."

"Come off your high horse, Paula. We women have got to stick together when it comes to con men and rapists and the like." We chatted along those lines for a bit then I brought her back to the matter in hand. "So what happened after Maggie told Jenny everything?"

"She ended up in tears. It was just like having my baby back."

"Who knows, maybe this'll bring you closer."

"We'll see."

"What happened next?"

"We left Margaret and went downstairs." They found Steaming in the hall – still quick and light on his feet that one – studying a picture on the wall. I could just see him with his hands behind his back, Prince Philip style. He always did fancy himself as Royalty.

When Paula asked him he admitted that he had been listening outside the door. In the kitchen she poured out some stewed coffee for them (I like it!) and made tea for Maggie.

I'm not sure whether Steaming was being delicately diplomatic or is just a wally. He described Dan Spencer as a "not very nice man". Not very nice! He was bloody diabolical, and that's me putting it mildly.

"Sounds like he's going soft in his old age," I commented.

"Probably put it that way for my delicate ears."

I laughed. "Yeah, you're probably right. So what happened with your interview?"

"I wasn't very clever. I told him that I hadn't known what was going on and that if I had known I would have tried to put a stop to it."

"And he wanted to know how."

"How did you guess?"

"Obvious, innit, when you think about it?"

"Of course."

"So how did you get out of that?"

"Told him I had no idea. It's just one of those things a parent thinks at the time. Fortunately he agreed with me. Then asked if Gerard knew."

"Which of course he doesn't yet."

"Exactly. I told the Inspector that. And told him I didn't know when to expect Gerard." Apparently after he's finished in court he has to go back to his office to leave his robe and wig there – I'd love to see him tarted up in that gear.

"I suppose he wants to see Gerard?"

"Yes. I think he went straight to the office when they left here."

"Not a time-waster our Steaming."

"And I think he'll want to see you about all this."

"You told him I'd got the info out of Maggie?"

"Well he did ask how I knew about it. By the way, he wasn't totally surprised. Why would that be?"

"No idea, love."

"Anyway I told him about Margaret falling off her horse and you finding them. I also told them about Dan and the gambling," she added.

"And the village ladies?"

"Yes, but I couldn't tell him who they are."

Couldn't or wouldn't?

Why wasn't I surprised when, not long after Paula rang off, Steaming called? Invited himself over for dinner and all.

"You've got a nerve, Steaming. Anyway, I can't cook." Gotcha!

"I can."

"Eh?"

"I can cook. What have you got in the fridge?"

"Haven't looked. Anyway, there's stuff in the freezer."

"You really can't cook?"

"I said so, didn't I?"

"How did you exist before?"

"Frozen meals in the microwave and take-aways. Sarnies for lunch." Explains my size, doesn't it?

He wasn't going to take no for an answer so I let him come. Wonder what his wife would have thought if she knew where he was going to spend the evening? Oh well, that's his problem, not mine.

With my sieve-like memory there was one job I hadn't yet done. My Mum always reckoned I deliberately forgot to do things. I didn't. Honest. Problem is I get easily distracted and forget about the nitty-gritty jobs.

104

I decided that I couldn't procrastinate any longer and headed off to the flat over the garage. Complete with cleaning gear in case there wasn't any over there. Even though I'd avoided the place I knew there'd be that awful powder stuff the cops used for fingerprints, all over everything.

When I opened the door I had to step back. It ponged. Stale cigarettes and booze. Just like a pub the morning after.

Be brave, woman, I chided myself and went in to get all the windows open. First stop was the kitchen to clear out the fridge. Two dustbin bags of the stuff. Teach me to either do it myself sooner or get someone in to do it!

Curtains down for the laundry and dry cleaners. Bed linen and blankets ditto.

Exhausted I sat in an armchair in the living room and looked around. Hmm. Every bit as bad as I had imagined. With dust – ordinary type – all over everything and the state of the bathroom I wondered whether Janet had ever cleaned the place up. Didn't look like it. So what did she do with her time?

No way was I going to clean it. So much for good intentions! I'd ask Mrs. Walsh if she wanted the job.

In the meantime I realised the seat was uncomfortable. I stood up, picked up the chair cushion, shook it, ran my hand over it and felt something inside. Fortunately, it had one of those zip-on covers so it didn't take long to open it and pull out – a notebook.

How on earth had Steaming's lot missed it? Obviously they'd only picked up the cushion to look underneath and maybe feel down the insides of the chair. And replaced the cushion upside-down.

I opened it and found lists in writing I didn't know. Ergo, Dan's notebook. I sat down to take a better gander at it. At first I thought it was his gambling record, then gradually, it began to make sense. It was his 'runners' book. The initials being those of the ladies for whom he had placed bets, their winnings (if any) and his 'commission'. Wowee! Wait until Steaming sees this, I thought gleefully.

It'll make his day. Now he won't have to have his group question all the ladies, only the ones who match up to the initials.

I wish I knew them better. Wouldn't it be nice if one of them has an exceptionally violent husband who found out about her gambling?

Chapter 14

When Steaming came round to prepare dinner he got his back on me by getting me to wash the veggies while he prepared some steak he'd brought with him. It wasn't until he'd cooked and served it all – at the kitchen table which was quite cosy – that we got down to brass tacks.

"I hear it was you got the story out of Margaret Linley?"

"Yeah. Well she was in shock so I reckon as I'm almost a stranger it was easier than telling her parents."

"No kid tells their parents those things, do they, Cleo?" He raised an eyebrow.

"What things? We never got up to anything when we was kids."

"Oh come on, girl, rumour was rife around you."

"You what?" I was aghast. Yeah I'd had boyfriends when we were in our teens but never more than kissing and a bit of petting. My Mum would've flayed me if I'd done anything else.

"Well, you did rather…" He didn't finish because I stood up and threatened to smash my plate over his head. "Okay, Okay. You didn't. But we always thought you did."

"Gossip behind the bike shed?"

He had the grace to blush. "Well, yes. But didn't you girls do the same?"

"Yeah, but we had the sense not to believe it. At least, most of us did. Men!" Are they really still that naïve? I shook my head in disgust. "How about getting back to the discussion? What did you mean when you told Paula you weren't surprised that Maggie told me?"

"Been on the phone already, have we?"

107

"Enough of your sarcasm, Steaming, or I'll tell Blondie and Jenny what your nickname is."

"They probably call me that anyway – out of my hearing." He sounded resigned and I guess he's right. "Remember when we were kids and if anyone had a problem they came to you?"

"Oh that. Yeah. The original Claire Rayner. I probably got them in even more trouble."

We exchanged a few reminiscences until we'd finished our meal when I poured coffee and we went into the lounge to relax.

"Did you go and see Gerard Linley?" I asked as we settled down in facing armchairs by the window, coffee on a table between us.

"Yup."

"And?"

"Confidential."

"Oh come on, mate, I'm me, remember. I found Janet, I've got info for you. If you can't trust me who can you trust?"

"If I tell you, you mustn't say a single word to anybody."

"Course not."

"Not even to Mrs. Linley."

"Listen, Kettle, the only person I know here is Paula and I'm not stoopid enough to go blabbing to her and giving her more grief. So who would I tell? I'm the stranger in town, remember? Anyway, Gerard will tell her."

"Okay, okay, don't get your drawers in a twist. Oh, and by the way, thanks for adding to my problems." I raised an eyebrow. "The bookies runner."

108

"That's going to add a few names to the list, innit?" I grinned.

He nodded, then told me about the interview with Gerard while I kept my secret. Well, I thought if I gave him the book now I wouldn't get to hear about this interview.

"We were waiting for him as he came out of court and he found a room where we could sit and discuss things. Remember, Linley had no idea what it was about at the time, but guessed it had something to do with the murders.

"He actually assumed we were going to ask his advice, but being a civil and not a criminal lawyer couldn't imagine what advice he could give us.

"We sat around the table and I told him what had happened between his daughter and Dan Spencer.

"Of course, being a barrister, he's schooled in keeping a poker face. He showed no signs of emotion or anything and simply told me that was bad news." I snorted at that understatement. I could just picture Gerard with his prematurely white crinkly hair and protuberant blue eyes (they probably look like ice when necessary), saying that. "That obviously he wouldn't want his family to be mixed up in anything unsavoury. And, of course, he wanted to know how he could help us?"

"With your inquiries?" Steaming grinned and nodded.

"I'm sure you told him," I commented dryly.

"The most obvious question was whether he already knew. He looked straight at me and shook his head. No, he didn't know, then told me that teenagers can be very, very secretive. I agreed with him and pointed out that fathers have even less contact due to being out at work all the time."

109

"As you've got kids you'd know, of course." I aimed a hard look at him but he merely nodded and carried on with the story.

"He reckons he's luckier than me because he is sure to see his daughter at the weekends. Told me, as if I didn't already know, that Maggie goes to boarding school during the week.

"He didn't like it when I told him I'd heard rumours about her being rather hot-headed and that's why she's at boarding school. He didn't bother to comment but looked as if he'd just sucked a lemon. Anyway, I then asked if he thought she had made up this story about her and Spencer."

"Well, mate, don't keep me in suspense. Sitting there like the cat that caught a couple of birds."

"Give us a chance to drink me coffee, woman!"

"Speak nicely and I'll pour some more."

"Yes, please," he gave me his best smile so I poured. "Okay." He sat back to continue the saga. "He doesn't think she would. That if she says that's what happened then it did."

"Did you ask if she might have exaggerated or left out anything?"

"Of course."

"And?"

"He qualified his answer. He didn't like to think she had omitted anything. If he thought that then certainly he would have to insist that she see a doctor. But he felt that although she can be a little rash," (oh, yeah?) "he thought that like most teenagers, she has her head screwed on right and they wouldn't have allowed her to go riding in the forest on her own had they not been reasonably sure that they could trust her." He ran out of breath at that point!

110

What a hoot! I laughed. "How typical of parents. Of course we can trust our children, they're always very good," I mimicked some I'd heard – you know, such as on telly after a kid's committed a crime. "Did you point out that she's just proved that they can't trust her?"

"Of course and he reckons that its his business to investigate that."

"That's true. What about Dan's body? Did he have anything to say about that?"

"He knew it was found this morning and I told him Dan had been shot. Which brought me to the dumb question of whether he owns a gun or guns."

"Why dumb?" Sounded a perfectly sensible question to me.

"Cleo, there are very few people living in the forest who don't own some sort of weapon."

"Oh."

"When I told him we need to check his weapon or weapons to eliminate them, he reckoned it was a very polite way of saying that we suspect him."

"Even though I like Gerard, I suppose in the circs you have to suspect him," I mused.

"Everyone until they are eliminated," was Steaming's tart rejoinder.

I put up my hands in self-defence. "Okay, okay. So have you got his guns?"

"Yeah. He invited us back to his place where we picked them up and took them to the lab."

"You don't honestly believe he shot Dan, do you?"

"As I said just now, old thing, everyone is suspect. If his guns are eliminated then that puts him a few rungs down the ladder."

"When will you know that?"

"How do I know? It depends when the lab and ballistics can deal with them."

I know what you're thinking. Hand guns are illegal in this country so all Gerard would have are rifles. What do I know about firearms? Zilch. And, let's face it, Steaming is a senior copper. He isn't going to tell me everything.

After he had told me all that I casually handed over the notebook and told him where I had found it. He was not a happy bunny. I wouldn't want to be in his office in the morning. After a quick glance through it he put it in his pocket.

Then, ever so casually he asked, "By the way, Cleo, why didn't you tell me about Raoul Gomez?" As he was studying his fingernails I almost offered to give him a nail file – and not just for his nails!

"None of your business that's why."

"Everything is my business at the moment."

"Everything that's happened here is. Not my private life in London." I stood up, picked up the coffee pot and flounced out of the room. Now what?

Of course being the gent he is Steaming brought out our empties. "Sorry, Cleo, but I do need a better answer."

I'd been at the sink rinsing out the coffee pot. I sighed and turned around, leaned against the sink and crossed my arms. And felt the drops of water on the edge of the sink soak into my dress. Whoopee.

"I didn't mention Raoul because I know he didn't kill Janet – he was playing that night. Anyway, as he's never been down here he's never met the Spencers."

"So?"

"So it wasn't important. How did you find out?"

"Gossip in the orchestra. You going to tell me?"

112

So I did. Not the bit about fancying Raoul. That really is private. And if Steaming is jealous... What am I thinking about? Why would he be jealous? Silly me.

When I finished Steaming smiled. "Thanks, love. Sorry I had to bully you into that, but you know how wrong gossip can be."

Was it my imagination or did he look relieved? If so, why? Could he really be jealous? That's given me something to think about.

And if you're wondering, no, he didn't stay the night. In fact, he left not long after that and I got a chaste kiss. No, not a chased one.

Chapter 15

Needless to say I didn't get much sleep last night. Oh yeah, I guess I must have dropped off eventually but with so much happening my mind was in a complete tizz. And I really didn't like to think that that nice man, Gerard, could have killed Dan Spencer. The thought is absolutely abhorrent. Wow, that's a posh word for me, innit? Anyway, as I say, I must have dropped off sometime, but there I was awake at five o'clock this morning and did what I'd vowed I'd never again do in my life – other than when catching a plane, of course. I got up. At five o'clock!!!

And put on a full pot of coffee. I had a suspicion I was going to need it.

While I was breaking my own rules I decided to be a very brave girl now that the pool was cleaned and re-filled - lay a ghost. No, not naked bathing – can't stand the sight of my own body and, in the circs. a good thing too.

And, yes, I did go around the house first to check that it was empty and that all the doors and windows were shut and locked!

Then I went into the pool room and stood there dithering. Should I climb down the steps or flop in like a whale. Oh, come on, come on, come on. Eventually I sat down at the shallow end and dangled my feet. It was quite refreshing – not freezing cold but I don't have the water too hot. Might as well just jump in the bath if you're going to have it that warm! I do like the pool to be refreshing.

I slipped down into the water, ducked up and down a few times getting my brain into gear, and eventually dog paddled my way around safely keeping one foot on the bottom.

So there I was having me dog paddle with Beethoven's Fifth filling the space. That's one of the things I like about living in a place with no close neighbours. I can put the music on as loud as I like. It was just a pity that I looked up at the windows. I did open up me mouth to scream but sank instead with a mouthful of water. Shouldn't 'ave taken me foot off the bottom. At least I didn't have far to go down. I bobbed up again and managed to get to the side, coughing and spluttering, and hauled myself out.

It was a man looking in at me. Good job I'd put a swimsuit on, innit? I got me robe and put it on quickly because I'm still not a pretty sight in a swimsuit. If he thought I was going to open the door or window, he'd got another think coming. I grabbed the phone and he started waving at me and I thought, What's up with him? I turned down the music and went and opened a small window high up (by turning a handle on the wall) and yelled at him, "You'd better have a good excuse otherwise I'm calling the police."

"I'm Janet Spencer's brother."

"Oh yeah. I don't even know her brother's name."

"Honest."

"I'm not letting you in. If you want to see me you can come back in the morning and bring your driving licence or something with you to prove who you are. I'm not opening up now."

"Oh, please," he begged.

"No." And I shut the window, walked out of the pool room and turned off the lights.

I went back upstairs. There was no way I was going to allow myself to be pestered by him but, of course, he kept ringing the front door bell and banging on the door. In the end I opened the bedroom window and called down to him to shut up, otherwise I would definitely call the police.

"I've told you to come back later. I'm not stupid. Even if you're really who you say you are, how do I know that you didn't kill your sister?"

"Oh, come on, missus, why would I do that?"

"It's been done before. There doesn't have to be an excuse. Family members kill each other all the time. Now, GET. SCAT. I do have the phone in my hand and I only need to push one button and the police will come screaming up and you'll be in jail. Actually, that's not a bad idea because they want to speak to you anyway."

"No, listen, missus, I gotta speak to you first."

"No, I think I'm going to call the police. I've had enough of you."

"Please."

Am I fool or am I a fool? "Alright, I'll do a deal with you. I won't call the police but you go away and come back at ten o'clock."

"But where am I going to sleep?"

"I have no idea and I couldn't care less. I assume you came in a car so wherever your car's parked, go and sleep in it."

He seemed to accept what I was saying and went away. Of course I didn't sleep. I was worrying about what he was doing, what he was up to. Was he going to set fire to the place? Would he try to break in? Oh dear. I left all the lights on as a deterrent. Then I remembered the coffee. I went downstairs, poured some out and, kind hearted soul that I am, poured some into a flask and put it on the back step, quickly locking the door again. What would these people do without me?

116

Whether Steaming was in bed asleep, alongside his wife, or whether he was at his office desk, I really didn't care. I called him on his mobile.

"Good morning, Steaming."

"Good God, Cleo." He had definitely been asleep. "What on earth do you want at this ungodly hour?"

"Ungodly? It's six-thirty. Why aren't you up and at work?"

"Come on, woman. By the time I finished at the office and got back here it was well past midnight."

"I've got news for you, sweetheart, I haven't been asleep at all," I exaggerated.

"You haven't? What's happened?"

My goodness, that was quick, I thought. "I've had a visitor."

"I know you've had a… Oh, okay. What?"

"Well there was me at five o'clock this morning having a swim, minding me own business and this man appeared at the window."

"Are you alright?"

"Of course I am. I'm not stupid enough to open the door to a stranger at that time. I'm even leery about doing it during the day."

"So who was it? Why didn't you call the police?"

"I threatened to. He says he's Janet Spencer's brother."

"I'll be right there."

"No you won't. You'll wait."

"What do you mean I'll wait? I need to speak to him."

"I know you do but I made a promise. I told him I wouldn't call the police until after he's spoken to me 'cos he said he wants to speak to me first."

"You can't let him in…!"

117

"Listen, sweetie, I don't even know his name or what he looks like. Can you help me out?"

"Oh. Right. His name's Jack Smith."

"That's original."

"Honest."

"Alright, his name's Jack Smith. Any idea what he looks like?"

"Not much idea."

"Do you reckon he looks like his sister?"

"Couldn't tell you. He's got a beard, that I do know." The man at the window had a beard.

"Mind you if he's got the same chin as his sister that would be why he's got a beard."

"True."

"But you've got nothing about how tall he is or anything?"

"The description we got from the neighbours is that he's about five-ten. Actually it varied from five-eight to six foot so let's say five-ten. Broad shouldered. Brownish hair, I believe. Sorry, Cleo, but I don't have the papers here. Somebody said they thought it was grey-ish, but anyway, it's either brown or grey or a mixture. Oh and he's got blue eyes. That was something most agreed on that he's got nice blue eyes," he parodied one of the ladies who had been questioned.

"Does he drive?"

"Originally we were told he doesn't have a car but we discovered that he does own a clapped out Ford Escort. One of the older models."

"That gives me some idea if he comes back and doesn't look like that. Or isn't driving that car. Mind you he might have a rental car."

"That's true, but what will you do if he doesn't look like that?"

Chapter 16

Steaming was so concerned about my safety that he'd obviously forgotten that I'd already seen Jack Smith! After some arguing I agreed to let him have access to the house but, as I pointed out, he couldn't come before Jack Smith because Jack might be watching the house and would see him arrive. We arranged it that Steaming would leave his car outside on the road and walk up to the house on the lawn so no vehicle or footsteps could be heard, and I would leave one of the doors to the pool room open enough for him to slip through. I would also leave other doors ajar so he could make his way through the house without being heard. I was to take Jack into the kitchen and we would sit either side of the table. That way if I was in any danger Steaming could save me. My hero!

Actually he did do that a few times when we was kids. I'd get into trouble with the boys. They always got the wrong impression of me. Steaming was quite right when he said that about giving the wrong impression. The trouble was that I developed early, so I was quite an attraction to the boys and I wasn't always this plump size either.

Well, my parents (or any of our parents) didn't have much money, so we went without pocket money. Obviously there was no buying of sweets and fast food. We just ate what was put in front of us, and if we didn't like it we left it and went without. Ergo none of us were exactly overweight.

But, of course, when you've got boobs arriving earlier than your friends' and people like Diana Dors and Marilyn Monroe as the icons of the previous era whom we could still remember, what do you expect?

Anyway, to get back to today. Promptly at ten the doorbell rang and I had a look through the peephole. Yes, he fit the description, so with the chain on I opened the door and said, "Got some I.D.?"

He silently thrust a tatty driving license and Visa card at me. They had the name Jack Smith and the address on the driving license was the one from London that Steaming had mentioned so I returned them, then shut the door, released the chain, and invited him in. "We'll go to the kitchen."

He handed me the empty thermos. "Thanks, missus."

"At least you didn't die of thirst or cold. Not that you could at this time of the year."

"No."

"Sit down. Here's some fresh coffee." I gave him a mug and went to the cooker to do a fry-up – he looked like a man who could eat a fry-up, but how anyone can eat greasy food first thing in the morning beats me. (Yeah, I know I can't cook, but anyone can throw food in a frying pan). And, of course, I had to stall for time to ensure Steaming was in place.

He tucked in and I had some toast with my coffee. When he'd finished I put everything into the dishwasher and sat down again. "Right. What did you want to see me about?"

"What I want to know is about Janet."

"What about her?"

"I just got a postcard to say she was working here. And that's all. I don't know how long she'd been here. Why she wanted me to know. Nothing."

"I can't tell you anything. She was just my housekeeper."

121

"Yeah, but how did she come to be your housekeeper. In the past they've always worked for old ladies. When I saw you in the pool I thought 'uh-huh, something's different. This is not an old un.'"

"Ta very much." I told him how Dan and Janet came to be working for me.

"How did she die? I mean all I heard was that, you know, this policeman came to my door and asked me if I was her brother and told me that she'd died but didn't tell me how or anything. So I don't know if she had a heart attack or what the cause was."

Unless he really didn't know anything it was good acting because I certainly had my suspicions as to why he had come around now she was dead. Especially now, since I know how much money she'd managed to stash away over the years. Was he after the money? My, my, could be. Murder's been done for a lot less.

"I don't know. If the police told you that why didn't they question you at the time?" Bearing in mind that he hadn't been at home when the police went there… He probably didn't know that I know that. Wonder how many more lies he'll tell me?

"It was just this young copper came, told me and then went. You know. I didn't know what to think so I just packed a case and left."

"I thought you'd gone on holiday?"

"That's what I told the neighbours."

"What about work?"

"I am on holiday. It's my holiday time. I wasn't actually going to go away. Then I decided I'd come down here. Then I thought no I couldn't, so I went away to think about it."

What a lovely explanation. So clear. "What do you want from me?"

"How did she die?"

"Drowned. In my pool. What I was doing this morning was laying the ghost."

"Oh my God. I don't think I could have done that."

"No, well she was your sister. I hardly knew her. But I found her."

"Oh. That must've been awful. Why didn't her husband find her?"

"For a start she wasn't supposed to be in the house at that time of night."

"Why not? She lived here."

"No she didn't. She worked here. They had their own flat over the garage which is that other building."

"Oh! I thought she'd lived in here."

What did that expression on his face mean? Why didn't he know about the flat? Uh-oh. Does that mean that if he'd known she'd lived in the flat, he'd have broken in there last night?

"What else can I do for you?"

"Can I go and get her things out of the flat?"

"I don't think so. I'm not sure that the police have finished with it," I stalled. "You'll have to go and see them and find out."

"But I need to get her things."

"I'll tell you what I'll do. When the police say so I'll get her things, pack them and you can have them."

"But can't I just go in and see where she lived?"

"I don't think so at the moment. You might be able to go in there with a police escort."

He deflated rapidly. "Oh. Alright. I suppose I'd better go then. Where's the police? In Southampton?"

"I think they're a bit closer than you might think."

"You got a station here in the village?"

"No, but I'm sure when you leave here you'll find them. Or they'll find you. One or the other."

"What d'you mean? Have you put 'em wise?" He stood up, the chair shoved violently backwards, and he leant over the table quite threateningly. At the same time Steaming came steaming through the kitchen door.

"Alright, lad. Enough of that."

"Who are you?"

Steaming flicked his ID. "The police. Who are you?"

"Jack Smith."

"Are you?"

Jack Smith subsided into the chair and held up his hands in submission. "Sorry."

Steaming still stood there, looked at me, looked at him, "I heard most of what he said. Interesting really."

Hang on, he's up to something. When I heard a car pull up outside I guessed that he had Blondie with him.

"So, Chief Inspector," hark at me all formal!, "what's this all about?"

"Well, Miss Marjoribanks, let me introduce you to Brian Spencer."

"Do what?" Cor, stone me. "You mean to tell me that this isn't Jack Smith?"

"Nope."

"But he showed me his driving licence and credit card.

"Oh yeah. Thing is, what he doesn't know is that Jack Smith was picked up last night and he has a driving licence on him which is quite new. He'd lost his and he also had some credit cards on him, but one is missing."

"I see. So this man here," I pointed across the table –
and with my nails it looked pretty vicious, "is Dan
Spencer's brother."

"Right."

"But that's the man you described to me on the
'phone."

"Yes, last night I received a description of this
gentlemen. He's been in trouble before."

"I might have guessed that, mightn't I? D'you want to
take him away? Get rid of him. Then you can come back
and tell me all about it later."

When they left (yes, it was Blondie driving the car), there
was what we think was a rental car parked in a field
gateway just along the road. Steaming said a low loader
would be coming to pick it up. I guess they want to give it
a going over, just in case. Hope they don't find any bodies
in it.

Chapter 17

This is getting confusing. I've got Janet drowned in the pool and Dan shot dead. So who did what to whom? Then we've got her brother. His brother, who's now come out of the woodwork. And she's saved up a lot of money and possibly moved some of it elsewhere. Offshore? Maybe. So who killed her?

I got a pad and pen, drew a line down the centre, put Janet's name on one side and Dan's on the other. Now, suspects. Jack Smith and Brian Spencer went under both of them. Gerard went under Dan. Who else could there be? The village ladies or their husbands?

I sat and sipped more coffee and thought about it, tapping my pen on the table. The caffeine must have kicked in. What about the old ladies they worked for? I must ask Steaming about that and made a note to remind myself. I wouldn't mind betting that some of those old girls had eventually made their Wills out to Janet and Dan. I wonder if any of the families had threatened to sue and had settled out of court? Now that's a thought.

I wish I had computer access like the police. Or even a contact in criminal law. That wouldn't half help.

I then came back to the family. Did Brian kill Janet and promise to share the money with his brother but then killed Dan so that he'd get it all himself? Or did Janet's brother, finding out that Janet had been murdered, assume Dan had killed her and went after him?

Of course I ended up going around in circles and finally gave up.

My musings were interrupted by the telephone. It was Paula.

"Hello, love, how're you doing?"

126

"Feeling a bit relieved."

"Good. They've decided Gerard couldn't have done it, have they?"

"Not exactly. He's more or less off the hook."

"He either is or he isn't. What do you mean?"

"The guns that he gave them couldn't have killed Dan Spencer because they're rifles and he was killed with a handgun. But, of course, for all the police know, Gerard might have had a gun they don't know about."

"Oh gawd. Steaming can't be that stupid, surely."

"It isn't so simple, Cleo. The main thing is establishing when Dan Spencer was killed and they aren't expecting those results until later today."

"What do you mean?"

"If he was killed on Thursday morning then Gerard couldn't have done it because he was on duty at the New Forest Show."

"I was going to go to that!" I wailed. "With all this business going on it went completely out of my mind. Damn."

"Never mind you can go next year."

"Sure. We're very manana, aren't we? That's the trouble. You promise yourself you're going to do something then keep putting it off. So getting back to the subject. If Gerard was at the Show he couldn't have killed Dan?"

"Exactly. But if he was killed at night there'd only be my word for it."

"It gets more and more complicated. You don't know what's been happening here this morning."

"You haven't had a break-in?" She sounded really worried.

"No. Nothing quite as bad as that," and I told her what she had missed.

"Poor old you. You should set the burglar alarm before you go to bed."

"The trouble is that I'm frightened I'm going to set the damned thing off myself. Get up during the night to go downstairs and get a drink and walk straight through the rays."

"You make sure you're well locked up."

"Don't worry, ducky, I do. But I'm still mad at Steaming for having me on like that. Me thinking it was her brother!"

"You never asked for their next of kin, did you?"

"No. Never thought of it."

"What about the agency? They must have had a note of the next-of-kin."

"Couldn't have done, could they? Which means the Spencers didn't tell them. But I tell you, Paula, they certainly cleaned up after them with the amount of money in that account."

"How much was it?"

I told her.

"Wow! So how many old ladies did they look after in their career?"

"Don't know."

"How many do you reckon they helped on their way?"

"No idea, but it wouldn't surprise me if they did. I tell you one thing. I'm glad I haven't got to sack them. Does that sound cruel in the circumstances?"

"No. I think I can understand where you're coming from. How do you know how much longer they were going to let you live?"

Oops.

"Come to think of it, I don't have any close living relatives."

"But you do have distant ones and friends. That makes a big difference."

"Thank you, Paula. Yes, I do have friends. Now that I know Steaming's in charge of this area of Serious Crime I would like to hope that if anything had happened to me they wouldn't have got away with it."

"Don't think in those terms, Cleo."

"I know. Think positive. Think positive."

"Cleo, we haven't discussed those couples we short-listed, have we?"

"Don't worry about that, love. I've already phoned the agency and told them no. I didn't really feel that comfortable with either couple. I'll just have to make do with Mrs. Walsh for the time being and hope that something turns up."

"The best way is to get someone on personal recommendation."

"Paula, you don't have to go away and leave your house empty."

"That's true but if you have a good burglar alarm you can always leave keys with me and we'll keep an eye on the place."

"Would you really?"

"Of course. Why don't we fix up that you have Mrs. Walsh in as you have her now and she can come in less often when you're away. Then if ever you need a chauffeur we can find one. I'm quite sure there's a capable driver or two in the village who would love to drive your Rolls Royce."

"I guess."

129

"Don't worry about it for now. So, Cleo, what are you going to do for the rest of the day?"

"I don't know. I'm getting bored with changing my mind for designs for the pool room."

Paula chuckled. "I bet you don't ever change it."

"I wouldn't bet on that."

"Why don't you see if you can get on one of those New Forest Safaris? Maybe they have a space to spare. I'm sure there is one scheduled for today."

"That's not a bad idea. Perhaps I'll phone them up and see. Thanks, Paula." We chatted a bit more then I wished her luck with the results of the autopsy on Dan Spencer and we rang off.

I got myself booked on the safari and went off to change into one of my safari suits. At least I'd be keeping out of trouble. Or so I thought.

Chapter 18

Those were famous last words weren't it? Nothing can go wrong on the safari, could it?

On the way from the Tour Office our guide – Keeper Tony – explained how the Forestry Commission works, "There are twelve Forestry Commission divisions each in charge of a keeper who controls the numbers and health of the flora and fauna. The north forest, where we're going is made up mostly of oaks, beech and planted conifers. The conifers were planted by the Forestry Commission after the last war and aren't indigenous." Later we were told that, as they mature and are felled they aren't being replaced. Those areas will be allowed to go back to what they were originally – heathland.

As we drove through the forest it was smashing. No traffic, just a few walkers. We went so slowly we could see some of the deer. I was in seventh heaven. I've never seen wild animals so close and so unafraid before. I certainly don't count going to the London Zoo as getting close to the wild animals, although it was great when we were kids. Tony told us that there are about 1,700 deer in the forest. That's a mixture of Roe, Seeker (imported from the Far East) and Fallow – and the antlers, which grow each year, can weigh a ton!

I didn't believe that but when we were up on the moorland we left the van and he heaved out this box of antlers and passed one set around – I nearly dropped it!

What I found hilarious was to learn that bucks don't feed for a month during the Rut – it's a wonder they've got the strength to do anything! I know making love makes me hungry.

Well, the van went off and left us – we were going to have a walk. Was I glad I had me walking shoes on! During the stroll Tony pointed out lots of things but I won't bore you with them.

One bit of info though is that the New Forest has the largest area of lowland heath in England. Lowland? We were pretty high up and could see for miles!

I don't know whether anyone else looked up at the sky, but one thing I did see were the big black clouds rolling in our direction. So there I am in with no umbrella or raincoat, nothing to protect myself from the rain which soon started. I made a dash (well, as dashing as someone my size can) for some nearby trees. Of course some of the clever-clogs in the group had anoraks which they donned. I never gave it a thought that it might rain which is stupid as you can never rely on the English weather. Actually it then began pelting down so heavily the others came over to the shelter of the trees as well!

The tree I was under was a rather gnarled old thing. No idea what type it was – haven't yet learned the differences. Certainly not a pine tree. More a deciduous one – you know what loses its leaves in autumn. Anyway, there I was leaning against it getting me breath back. Something was sticking in my back so I moved and turned to look. It was a bit of a knob of wood sticking out with a hole in it. Of course curious Annie doesn't stop to think about things like snakes or anything like that – I put my hand in the hole.

And got the shock of me life – it was metal, whatever it was. Don't ask me why I did it but I got a tissue out of my bag, put my hand back in the hole and lifted up this metal thing – and dropped it quick. It was a gun.

Needless to say I was no longer listening to Tony but I was in a right old state. What is a gun doing in a hole in a tree in the New Forest? Would it be too much of a coincidence that this could be the gun that shot Dan Spencer? After all, the Volvo had been found in the forest. Yeah, I know that had been nearer to where I live, but if I'd shot someone I wouldn't exactly get rid of the gun in that location. Would you? Personally I'd probably have thrown it in the sea, but then I'm not a murderer.

Come to think of it, I didn't know where Dan had been shot. Maybe he'd been shot here and the car simply dumped somewhere else. No, think straight, girl. The car couldn't have been up here so he couldn't have been shot here, but if this was the gun then whoever did it had to know the forest pretty well.

I did get myself together. When questions started, I inched my way over to Tony until I was standing beside him, tapped him on the arm and nodded him away from the group.

"Just a minute, ladies and gentlemen," he said apologetically as he moved in my direction. "I'm sorry but there aren't any..."

"Oh, it's alright. I don't want a loo. Listen. That tree over there that I was standing under. There's a gun in a hole in the tree."

"What?"

"There's a gun in there."

"You mean like a rifle or something?"

"No. It's more like a pistol. That kind of thing."

"I'd better go and get it."

"No, no, no!" I grabbed him as he made to go charging over there. "I'm Cleo Marjoribanks. You know, the lady whose housekeeper was drowned and housekeeper's husband was found shot dead?"

"Oh." It took a minute for it to sink in. "And you think this might be the gun?"

"Well, it's a possibility, isn't it? I don't know a lot about crime, but I do know enough about it from books to know that we shouldn't touch the gun but should contact the police."

"I'll call nine-nine-nine." He made to unhook his mobile phone from his belt.

"Don't worry. I know exactly who to call." I got out my mobile and called Steaming at his office. Of course neither he nor Blondie were in but Jenny Dixon was there. "Jenny, its Cleo Marjoribanks."

"Yes, Cleo, what can I do for you?"

"I'm on this safari with the Forestry Commission up in the northern part of the New Forest."

"Very nice too."

"I'm not phoning just to tell you that. The thing is that I was standing by a tree and I've found a gun in a hole in it."

"Oh." She seemed to be lost for words. I could almost hear the gears clicking creakingly in her brain.

"So what do you want me to do about it? Do you want me to take it out or will you send someone to pick it up?" I prompted her.

"I guess I'd better tell the boss first."

"Tell one or other of them. I can stay here – I don't mind hanging around. I'm soaked to the skin anyway so it won't make any difference. But they're going to have to meet someone from the Forestry Commission to bring them out here because it's private roads and all that jazz."

134

"Okay. Is there anybody with you from the Forestry Commission?"

"Yeah. Tony."

"Can I have a word with him?"

I handed over my phone. "It's Detective-Constable Dixon." They conversed for a bit. It was agreed that he would contact his boss to arrange for someone to meet the police to guide them to where we were, while he continued with the safari and I waited by the tree.

In the meantime the bedraggled group were muttering among themselves and some were sending me murderous looks for holding up the tour. Then Tony led them off and I rather suspect that the safari took a slightly different route back from the one planned. And that it got cut a bit short.

I just stood there where it was all quiet, not a soul in sight, never thinking that maybe the owner of the gun might come along to retrieve it! I have no idea why I didn't think of that. So I waited and waited, and enjoyed the peace and animals – certainly plenty of rabbits. I just hoped there weren't any creepy crawlies or those slithery things around. Thank goodness there weren't any horses or cows in sight.

Eventually Tony returned with the van, followed by Jenny driving Steaming. I showed them where the gun was, then was more or less summarily dismissed. Steaming asked Tony to take me back to where I'd left my car and guide the SOCO team out to the tree.

"I hope you don't think my car is parked anywhere near here?" I asked him. "It's down at the Tourist Office in Lyndhurst." He looked a bit disconcerted. "Either you'll have to let Tony take me all the way back there and have your people wait until he returns or...."

135

He put up a hand. "I'll get one of my people to take you down there. Sorry, Cleo, I didn't realise you'd come up in the van on the tour."

An apology! Wowee! I'll treasure that. He then took me to one side. "A piece of info for your delicate lugs, old thing. Your mate Gerard is off the hook. The time of death hasn't exactly been established but it's been sufficient to let us know that he was on duty at the New Forest Show."

"Told you so," I poked my tongue out at him.

"Never grow up, do you?" he grinned, patted me on the shoulder and went back to Jenny. I did wonder exactly what Jenny had told him about my being in the North Forest. Hadn't she told him I was on a Safari? Or had he assumed   it   met   somewhere   near   here?

Anyway, off we went, Tony and me to the outskirts of the forest. When I asked him where the rest of the party was he told me another van had been sent to collect them. Oh. When we arrived I saw a police car was parked complete with driver. While we had been driving towards it, Steaming had given the driver his instructions. Tony would prevent anyone entering that part of the woods and then guide the SOCO team in. After dropping me the policeman would return and stand guard!

Hope he didn't have to do it by himself for too long.

Driving home in the Roller I remembered that I had to get another vehicle organized and that made me feel a bit more cheerful – a kind of celebration. I'm definitely going to get a four-wheel drive. More sensible than the Volvo.

You'll never guess what was sitting on the driveway awaiting my arrival? You've got it – the Volvo. At least that got me shifting to call the dealer in Lymington as soon as I got indoors. Yes, they have some four-wheel drives and are quite happy to do an exchange. The problem is that I have to drive that damned car there in the morning when I go to test some of these four wheel drives. I'm looking forward to the testing but not to driving the Volvo.

Maybe with another night's sleep I'll be able to get myself over that.

What would have been very nice is if Steaming had told me that they had finished questioning the two brothers, Janet's and Dan's, and that they were sort of beyond suspicion at that point. Why? Because I got another nasty shock that evening. Fortunately this time he came to the front door. I looked through the peephole. Stranger. No idea who it is.

"Who is it?"

"Jack Smith."

"I've heard that one before." Except that it had turned out not to be Jack Smith but Dan's brother, Brian. I suppose that was as good a proof as any. In any case, he had the same look as his sister – chipmunk cheeks and disappearing chin. The eyes were different – beady and close together. I cautiously opened the door – with the chain on and he made to push his way in. "Oh no, sunshine, do that and I shut this door and call the police."

"No. No, don't do that. Please, Miss Mar-jori-banks."

"Marchbanks."

"Miss Marjoribanks, I actually don't want to come in, but what I do want to do is look around the flat where Janet lived."

"Why?"

"Dunno I just want to. You know."

"I don't really."

"Oh please," he whined.

I wasn't quite sure what to do about this. There was nothing there other than their clothes because the police had been through it with a fine tooth comb and I'd found what I assume was the last bit of 'evidence', so I knew there weren't any documents and such like there. "I can tell you one thing, Mr. Smith, you're not going to find any money or credit cards or bank statements or building society books because the police have them all."

There was a momentary sly look in his eye as if he knew something the police didn't, which gave me pause for thought. "Tell you what. I'll come over there with you because I really don't think you should be there alone. I'm sure the police would prefer somebody to be with you and, also, I want to make sure you don't take anything out of there without police permission."

"But Janet's things are mine now."

"We don't know that do we? She might not have left them to you."

"Well who else would she have left them to?"

"Dan. Who died after her so they would belong to Brian." He shut up. "Look, I'm not going to go into this with you any more. Either go away or come up there with me."

He gave in. "Okay. I'll let you come with me."

Eh?!!! Who owns that flat? Anyway I closed the door and went to get the keys.

I took the precaution of putting on a caftan with my mobile in one pocket and, with my house keys in the other, was a small canister of pepper. We went to the flat and he took a desultory look around. I didn't sit down as I thought I ought to keep on my toes. Of course he didn't find anything. When he'd finished I escorted him back down. "That's it. I told you there's nothing there."

138

"I know. It's just that I wanted to see where she spent her last few weeks. Thanks a lot, Miss Marjoribanks."

"Okay." He sauntered off down the garden path which left me wondering where he'd left his car. Parked outside? And what did he really want from the flat? A bank book in his and Janet's names? If the latter it meant he didn't have it and the police still had to find it.

Chapter 19

Before I attempted to drive the first four-wheel drive vehicle of my life I insisted the salesman take us somewhere quiet and safe – where I couldn't do any damage. Other than to the car, of course!

If I'd felt immediately at home behind the wheel of my stately Roller (and very much in charge), when I took my place behind the steering wheel of the Land Rover I felt as if I owned the road. Rather like sitting up in front of a bus. I can understand how people can get used to them and think they own the road.

It didn't take me long to get used to the weight, size and power of it. I tried a couple of others before making a decision – the Land Rover, of course. Definitely for the "country" me.

One of the advantages of having it means that I'll be able to park up in the forest and sit in it with the binoculars to watch the horses. Yeah, I know I've got used to Maggie's horse, but these New Forest ponies are a bit wild. Don't know as I'd trust them.

When we were back in the showroom dealing with the paperwork, the salesman went off to speak to his boss – or someone. (I think it was probably to do with persuading me to buy an extended warranty or have a burglar alarm fitted – anything to part you from yet more of the readies.) Anyway, back to what I started to tell you. There I was sitting with a mug of coffee when one of the other salesmen came over for a chat.

I'd noticed him sitting, not quite chewing his fingernails, but looking slightly nervous each time he glanced at me.

"Excuse me, but you're the lady whose housekeeper…"

"Was drowned in the swimming pool. Yes, I am."

"That's what I thought. And the car was…"

"I'm trading it in. That's why I'm getting this Land Rover. Actually I think it'll be better than the Volvo for me, don't you?"

"Yes."

I was puzzled. It didn't seem like he'd come over for a chat about cars. "Did you want something?" Well, there's nothing like asking, is there?

"I'm a bit puzzled." Really?

"Why? What? About my car?"

"No. You know this is a small town." Nothing like stating the obvious. "The house next door to where I live is a B&B. You know, one of these guest house B&Bs?"

"Yeah." I encouraged him.

"Well, there's a bloke been staying there for a few days." What's odd about that? That's what the B&Bs are for! "We expect strangers in town in the summer."

"Ye-es." I'm wondering where this is leading.

"But they usually only stay for a few days then they leave. But this man's been several times. Not just now, but I've seen him other times. I don't know why, but I think there's something strange about him."

This from the most unlikely looking car salesman I had ever seen – weedy, thinning sandy hair and water-green eyes. And nervous, to boot.

"What do you mean there's something strange about him? What does he look like? Does he have two heads or something?"

He gave me a nervous smile then described Jack Smith and his car – an old Ford Escort.

141

"You haven't mentioned this to anyone else?"

"No, I didn't think it was my business."

"I think it might be a good idea if you were to call the police officer in charge of this case."

"Why? Is he the murderer?" He paled and his fingers went back to his mouth. He was definitely chewing his nails now.

I flapped a hand. "No, no, no. Don't get me wrong. I may be wrong in what I'm thinking about this person, but it would be better for you to telephone this gentleman." I wrote down Steaming's name and direct line number on a scrap of paper. "Tell him who you are and what you've seen. And leave it to them."

"I dunno. I don't know that I could do that."

"Why not?"

"Well if this bloke's the murderer and he found out I'd told the perlice..."

I sighed. What would you do with them? No wonder the police have a hard job when witnesses won't come forward. "Tell you what, would it help if I do it?"

"That's what I was hoping. That's why I told you."

As if I hadn't already guessed. "Alright. What's the address of the B&B?"

I jotted it down and he thanked me, adding, "You won't let on to the police that I...?"

I wonder how he thought the police were going to accept what I tell them? Of course they're going to want to know where I got the info from. Oh well, I'd try and stall Steaming on that one, but he's no fool.

As I drove out through the garage gates I saw a woman flapping her hand at me. Oh no! Mrs. Cheetham. I pulled over and stopped. She opened the passenger door (thank goodness for electric locks – I'd never have been able to stretch that far across). "Going home, Mrs. Cheetham?"

"Yers," she puffed. Well, she had had to run a few yards to catch up with me. No, I didn't do it deliberately. I swear!

"Hop in." I leaned over to grab her shopping bag as she dumped it on the seat so she'd have two hands free to haul herself in.

I'd had to stop for her as it is village policy for the more fortunate to help the less fortunate. (Mind you, in these circumstances I was wondering who was what.) With an almost defunct bus service those of us with transport give others lifts to and from the towns.

"How did you get down here?" I asked. Surely whoever had brought her would be waiting to take her back?

"Mrs. Davis. 'Er at number twenty-four." Means absolutely nothing to me. "She's gorn to Bournemouth to see 'er Mum."

"How were you going to get back? Wait for the bus?"

"If necessary."

No answer to that is there? I suspect she'd seen me driving the Land Rover otherwise how did she know where to find me? Bet she'll be boasting to her neighbours that I chose to honour her with a drive in my brand new vehicle.

I think there is nothing worse than having to listen to someone rabbiting on about people you don't know. And, quite frankly, have no interest in, but Mrs. C seems to love dishing the dirt.

Out came her opinions on how certain young ladies bring up their children – or don't in her opinion. Then there was the gossip about who were friends or falling out with each other.

"Course the ones I really blame for their youngsters going wrong are the floozies 'oo go to Southampton for a bit of 'ow's your father."

I was tempted to ask her if she was referring to sex – or rather, sexual encounters – but soft hearted as I am I couldn't bring myself to embarrass her.

"How do you know?"

"They tell me."

"That they are going to Southampton to meet a man?" I couldn't believe they'd be so brazen.

"No, but I know."

Oh yeah. "How do you know they're going to Southampton?"

"That's what they tells me."

Ah. One way to get out of giving her a lift into one of the smaller towns and having her hanging onto the coat-tails when there.

"Do you ever go to Southampton?"

"N-o-o-. Not m'own. Used to go with Bertie sometimes. Big and noisy and dirty. Don't like it." She shook herself like a wet hen.

After I'd dropped her off at her house (a terraced Victorian not a lot unlike the place I grew up in) and was on my way home I had a niggling at the back of my mind that among all the drivel, she'd actually told me something significant.

Chapter 20

I had thought to go and show Paula my new acquisition but by now I had other things on my mind. Obviously one of them was the information about what sounds to be like Jack Smith's regular visits to Lymington. He wasn't going to be there for nothing. Not when his sister wasn't that far away.

To be quite honest I was feeling a bit fed up with everything that's going on.

Now I've got the Land Rover you'd think all I'd want to do is go out and use it. In one way I did but on the other hand I wanted to get away for a bit. I was pretty sure Steaming wouldn't agree to my going away for a holiday overseas, but at least I could go up to London for a few days. Maybe have a shopping spree, see a show or something. And, of course, p'raps I could see Raoul – if the orchestra's in town. Can't remember offhand. Anyway, I can console myself with that little trip.

I reckon when I've phoned up Steaming and given him the news about Jack Smith he won't mind my going away.

Needless to say when I did call he wasn't there, so I had to be satisfied with leaving a message to call me. Didn't think it worth calling him on his mobile. Mind you, in his position I'm not quite sure how much he should be trolling around the countryside rather than sitting at his desk doing some work. I would have thought being the boss man he should be at his desk telling others what to do. But then he always did have the get-up-and-go outlook on life.

As I couldn't talk to Steaming I called Paula instead to give her my news. About the car, of course.

"Hi, how's it going?"

"Hello, Cleo, how are you?"

"Been spending money."

"You sound excited. What did you buy?"

"A Land Rover."

"A what? A Land Rover?"

"Yeah. I couldn't bear that Volvo any more and as the police had finished with it they said I could get rid of it so I did. Traded it in for the Land Rover. Thought it'd be more sensible."

"Especially if you want to go into the forest. With the Land Rover you're going to be able to go further in than just sticking to the main roads."

"That's what I wanted to talk to you about. Or rather, Gerard, when I get back. To see exactly where I can go in it."

"What do you mean, when you get back?"

"I'm hoping, provided Steaming Kettle agrees to it, to go up to town for a few days. Just to get away from it, you know?"

"I do. It's been pretty hectic here between Margaret and then Gerard being suspected. But that's cleared up so what we have to do now is get Margaret back on track."

"What's she doing at the moment? Out on the horse?"

Paula laughed. "You've guessed right. Of course she's out on her horse. But I don't think she's going as far as she used to. She doesn't spend quite as much time out, and I've noticed that she makes sure her mobile phone is charged up every time she goes out. She doesn't know that I've seen her checking it before she leaves the house. I suspect that the day it isn't charged it'll be Mum, can I borrow yours?" Paula then changed the subject. "When are you planning to go to London?"

"I had thought tomorrow if he'll let me, but think I'll leave it to the day after. Give me time to get my brain properly into gear."

"How are you going? Taking the Rolls Royce or the Land Rover?"

"Oh no, I'm not taking a car. It's not worth it. I ain't got a parking space up there anyway. Go up by train."

"I'll take you to the station," she offered.

What a doll! "Nah, that's alright, Paula, I'll get a cab."

"I'll take you to the station," she repeated firmly. "I don't have anything else to do that morning."

"Great. Thanks. Tell you what, why don't you come up to town as well. You can stay overnight if you want."

"I can't do that. I've a meeting in the afternoon. If I can get some free time during the next few days and you're still up there I might come up for the day."

"Fantastic. Perhaps we could do a matinee or something."

We chatted for a bit longer. I was quite surprised that Paula suggested she come up. That'll be great. As I say, we were chatting on as women do – mostly village gossip, of course, when my phone beeped to let me know there was a call waiting. "Gotta go, Paula, another call coming in."

"Let me know what time train you're going to catch."

"Okay. With a bit of luck this is Steaming now."

We rang off and, sure enough, it was his lordship. I gave him the information I'd picked up. There was a deathly hush. "I can just hear what you're thinking. And I was thinking exactly the same thing," I told him.

"Cleo, I have no idea why they do it. We put out appeals but does anybody come forward? Only the ones who don't know anything but are full of their own self-importance. What's this guy's name?"

147

As you've guessed, I'd changed my mind about keeping him a secret. It was his story and as far as I'm concerned, he can tell it to the police. "Darryl," I told him, along with the name of the dealership.

"Thanks, Cleo, love. I'll get someone to go and take his statement."

"He didn't really want that. That's why he told me."

"Tough. I need the information on record from him. He's the one who's seen the bloke."

"I know, I know, keep yer 'air on. I'm just the messenger, remember?"

"Sorry, girl. Thanks a lot, love. At least that might give us something else to pull Jack Smith in on. And if we find it is him hopefully we can find out why he was around."

"Presumably to see his sister. Going to be interesting, ain't it? Why did he want to see his sister down there and not come up and visit her? I think it answers one piece of local gossip. She wasn't going to Lymington to meet a lover."

"She still could have, but I think you're right. Anyway why was she going down there to meet him when she's supposed to be looking after your house?"

"Oops. Your right, mate, d'you know I never thought of that. Bloody 'ell." That really did knock me for a loop. No, I didn't expect the Spencers to be at the house twenty-four hours a day and I know she had to go shopping, but if her brother was in Lymington she wasn't going to just go down there for half-an-hour or so was she? Considering I'm usually quicker on the up-take I reckon I do need some time away. "Look, Steaming, I'm a bit pissed orf, as they say round here. Be alright if I go up to town for a few days?"

"Staying at your place up there presumably?"

"Where else would I stay? That's what I've got it for." I pointed out sarcastically.

"I've got the number there haven't I?"

"And my mobile." Stupid lunk.

"How long you planning on staying there?"

"Dunno. Couple or four days. Maybe a week. Depends what happens. Shopping, museums, theatre. Something."

"As long as you don't go flying off somewhere foreign."

"I knew you'd say that. That's what I'd really like to do, but I'm prepared to make sacrifices."

"Yeah, yeah, yeah," he jeered.

I ignored that and continued. "I'll be a good girl. If I decide to move on somewhere else I'll let you know."

"Have a good time and don't get into too much trouble."

"As if I would." It was only going to be for a few fun days. How much trouble could I get into? Certainly none with Raoul, or could I? After all, one can always hope and the candle was still flickering.

It was good thing I'd decided against going to town for a couple of days. This morning I couldn't believe my eyes when I looked out of the kitchen window. I know Mrs. Walsh had warned me, but I hadn't really believed her.

There was Mrs. Cheetham, complete with gardening gloves, floppy cotton hat, secateurs and flower basket. Helping herself to my flowers!

I was out of there like a shot. "Mrs. Cheetham, what the hell do you think you are doing?" I yelled across to her.

149

She turned and looked at me. Then smiled. "Why I'm cutting us some flowers."

"I neither asked you to nor did I give you permission to help yourself." I'd reached her by this time.

"But everyone in the village lets me do it."

"No they don't. I've heard all about it."

Holding the secateurs in front of her like a weapon she simply smiled and said, quietly. "Pr'bably that troublemaker, Mrs. Walsh told yer. I could tell you some things about 'er and 'er family."

"I'm not interested, Mrs. Cheetham. What I am interested in is why you even imagine I would give you permission to steal my flowers."

"Oh t'ain't stealing. Course you lets me help myself. 'Specially as I knows all about you." She pointed the secateurs at me. Before she could do any damage with them I grabbed her wrist in both hands and gave it a Chinese burn. Made her drop them! I kicked them away from us.

"Yers," she said, rubbing her wrist. "They said yer vi'lent."

"Only with people who stupidly wave tools around in an irresponsible way. The 'they' I assume are the little people in your head?"

"You cow!" Wow, she used a 'dirty' word. "We all know yer money's ill gotten."

"The problem with people like you, Mrs. Cheetham, is that you can't bear not to know everything. What you don't know you make up. Now, get out of my garden and don't ever let me catch you again. If I find you stealing from me one more time I'll call the police."

"What, yer posh boyfriend from Southampton? He won't be interested."

Posh boyfriend? She should know! I started herding her around to the front of the house.

"Yer fink I don't know things, don't yer? Well, Miss Marjoribanks, or whatever yer name really is, I know lots of things. Like what Janet were really like. And she let me pick the flowers," she added.

Did she indeed?

"Yeah," she carried on, "me 'n' her 'ad an arrangement and I know lots about 'er and 'er 'usband."

I couldn't be bothered to reply or ask her what she knew. We'd now reached the road and I stood and pointed in the direction she should take. She went.

But left me with something to think about. Did she really know something about the Spencers? How good a 'friend' had she really been? I had thought Janet was reticent. In which case she wouldn't have made friends with Mrs. Cheetham. Not unless Mrs. C. had had something on them or that she had thought Mrs. C. knew something.

Chapter 21

Actually, that 'do' with Mrs. C did me good. Got some wheels turning over in my brain. Talk about ding-dong! Not Avon calling but bells chiming.

Remember Janet Spencer meeting a boyfriend in Lymington? I suddenly realised that what I suggested to Steaming about it being Jack, is wrong. Now that I've met her brother I know that he couldn't have been mistaken for a boyfriend. Not unless there's something radically wrong with people's eyes.

The pity of it is that I don't know who it was who said she saw them. Solution? Village shops. Good as the old Roman Forum any day. When murder's been done in a small village it isn't difficult to get people to talk about it.

I let the three or four in the shop waffle on for a bit before easing into the point of it. "Funny thing about Janet is that someone once said she had a gentleman friend. Can't see it myself."

A few murmurs of agreement then one lady said, "I did hear as how Mrs. Cheetham saw 'em once or twice."

"And we know she makes up stories," another retorted.

No, it hadn't been Mrs. Cheetham's voice I had heard. "Can't ask her," I commented dryly and they simply nodded their heads. "Anyone else who might know?"

"You might try one of the ladies that works down there."

Ah yes, but they are at work, not at home.

Seeing the look on my face, Mrs. Lawrence at the check-out suggested a name. "Annie Doherty. Works in the Nationwide."

I gave her a brilliant smile, "You're a star, Mrs. L." Paid for the shopping and hot-footed it home to get the

Land Rover. With a bit of luck I'd catch Annie during her lunch break.

Fortunately I do know Annie 'cos I do some of my banking at Nationwide.

Of course the car park was full so I ended up driving round and round in circles and getting more and more frustrated. Eventually I returned to the public car park and snagged a newly vacated space. With what car parks charge I wish I'd thought of it first and set up a business like the National Car Parks. I'd have been a multi-millionaire sooner!

I caught up with Annie and one of her workmates as they went into a sandwich shop. "Annie, you got a minute?"

"Of course, Miss Marjoribanks. Hang on." She turned to her friend with a request to get her a sarnie and a drink. "What can I do for you?" she asked me.

"Did you ever see Janet Spencer down here with a gentleman friend?"

"Of course. Two actually, but I think one was her brother. He sometimes came into the building society with her."

"The other one?"

"He would wait outside."

"Who was it, do you know?"

"I've seen him about, but I don't know him."

"What does he look like?"

She described him and I grinned. "That's brill, Annie. I owe you." I left her to rejoin her friend while I went back to the car for a think. Oh yes, I know who the gentleman friend is. Deciding I'd better not get on Steaming's wrong side, I called him. No answer but I did get hold of Jerry 'pot' Wiles.

"Sergeant, this is Cleo Marjoribanks. Is the boss there?"

"I'm sorry, Miss Marjoribanks," he still has a problem with informality you notice, "the Chief is at a Divisional Meeting."

"When do you expect him back?"

"Short answer? When he gets here. These things tend to go on a bit."

"I can imagine," was my dry rejoinder. "Do you remember that someone had said they'd seen Janet with a gentleman friend?"

"Vaguely."

"We assumed it was her brother."

"Right."

"I've now met her brother and it couldn't have been him."

"Why not?"

"Too much alike."

"Oh." Light dawned. "So we need to look for someone else."

"I think I know who it is," and I went on to tell him about my conversation with Annie.

When I had finished he thanked me and said he would pass the information on to the Chief. Otherwise known as Steaming.

"Thanks, Sergeant."

"Miss Marjoribanks, one thing."

"Yes?"

"You won't do anything silly or rash will you? He could be the killer," Wiles reminded me.

"No, I won't be stupid."

We rang off and I thought some more. I am in Lymington and he works in Lymington. If I meet him,

154

accidentally, in a public place, he can't do me any harm can he?

My guess was that he would either have a liquid lunch in a pub or be a fast foodie. And probably be as near to his work as possible. It wasn't too hard to find him – sitting on a pub terrace overlooking the river. As soon as he saw me approaching he gave me a wary look.

"Hello, just the person I wanted to see," I greeted him.

"I'm not talking to you. You told the police about me."

That's right, he's the car salesman who told me about Jack Smith. I pulled out a chair at his table and sat down. Fortunately he was sitting alone.

"This won't take long. Someone told me you knew Janet Spencer."

"Who?"

I pursed my lips. "Try again."

He sighed, took a gulp of his beer, looked at me and sighed again. "Yes. She was a friend."

"Bit old for you, wasn't she?" I grinned at him and he blushed!

Honestly he really is the most improbably car salesman I have ever come across. All I can think is that when he gets a potential client he must metamorphose into a charming personality.

"It's not what you think. She was a nice lady and took me out to lunch sometimes."

"I see. I suppose you met her when she brought the car in for a service."

"How do you know that?"

155

My turn to sigh. "Not that difficult. So she took you out for lunch sometimes. Did she ever take you to Trewith Green?"

"That's where you live."

"Right. So either she told you, you looked it up in the records or you've been there."

"I've been through it."

Yeah, well, you would to get to my place from Lymington.

"Did she take you to my house?"

"No. Her husband would have been there."

Makes sense. "So where did you go?"

"I told you. For lunch."

"And that's all?"

"That's all."

I stood up to go. No chance of getting any more from him.

"I suppose you're going to tell the Old Bill about it," he stated flatly.

"Unless you care to call them first and tell them?"

"Alright."

I left him, walked away and around the corner. Then I turned back to peek around that corner. He was standing down by the river using his mobile phone. As I'd split on him once he knew I would do it again.

Needless to say, I couldn't wait to find out whether he had called Southampton. I hurried back to the car where I could use my phone in privacy.

Steaming still wasn't in so I spoke to Jenny, "Don't say my name, love, and just answer yes or no," I instructed her.

"Okay."

"Did Darryl Barkin just call Wiles?"

"Yes."

156

"Good. I wasn't sure whether he would."

"Wiles isn't here at the moment. Let me guess that you had a chat with Darryl."

"Yes."

Jenny sighed, "Take care," she warned. "He might be okay in a crowd and seem inoffensive but you never can tell."

"Promise, Mum. Yeah, I'll be careful. Get Steaming to give me a call when he gets back. I've got an idea about Master Darryl."

"Thought you might have."

Oh boy, Steaming called this evening, spitting nails. Not so much short-tempered as land-mined.

"What on earth do you think you're doing talking to a possible suspect?" he yelled down the phone.

"Do you know something, you're wasting a 'phone call? I could hear you without it," I remarked.

"Stop being flippant. What do you think you're doing talking to Darryl Barkin? You should have let us do it."

"Hang on, Steaming, I called Wiles when I knew Darryl was friendly with Janet. Not my fault if I bumped into him when I went to the pub for a drink." Good job he couldn't see my crossed fingers.

"But you didn't have to bring up the subject of Janet," he pointed out. Quite reasonably I thought.

I capitulated. "Sorry, love, but it just sort of happened. He wasn't happy that I'd told you about Jack Smith."

"He wouldn't be, would he," was the tart rejoinder. "You got the alarm on?"

"Of course."

"Good. Just be very careful, that's all I ask."

"That's all?" I teased.

"You know what I mean. I don't want you to get hurt and I'm beginning to think you've a tendency to get into dangerous situations."

"I don't do it deliberately. Honest, guv. And I'm going up to London tomorrow, anyway."

"Good. Anyway, the message I got from Jenny said you've got an idea you want to discuss with me."

"Yup. I think Janet was using Darryl as a smoke-screen. He's much too young to have been anything else."

"I don't know. Look at Juliet Mills and Max Caulfield."

I chuckled. "Janet and Darryl aren't exactly a glamorous couple."

"Okay," he conceded, "so what's your point?"

"Janet went to Lymington to meet Jack, but a village is a small place and she knew Dan got about it. She also knew there was a very good chance that someone from the village might see her with Jack."

"Which they did."

"So she picked up Darryl and for the price of a few lunches, muddied the pond," I finished.

"Which makes you think what about Darryl?"

Damn, I was hoping he wouldn't ask that – just think it up for himself.

"Suppose Darryl realised that's what she was up to and got mad at her?"

"She invited him over one evening for a swim in the pool? While Dan was around? And he then killed Dan, I suppose?"

"Oh." So much for my good idea. "Forgot about Dan's presence for a mo."

"Just testing you. Think carefully, ducks. We don't know that Dan was at home, do we? He might have gone off somewhere for a night away."

"So Janet invited company. Maybe Dan had a lady friend and she thought she would teach him a lesson."

"Maybe, but all of it is speculation. I'm having Wiles do a check on Darryl tomorrow, after which we may know more. In the meantime, keep away from Lymington."

"Like I said, I'm orf to jolly old London tomorrow." If he is the murderer Darryl won't find me there, will he?

Chapter 22

"Hi, Trace, it's only me," I called as I went into my flat beside the River Thames, remembering that she would be there as it was her cleaning day. "Hi, toots, how are you?" This to the tiny figure that came dashing out of the living room wielding a duster in one hand and her favourite Telly Tubby, La-La, in the other. This was Tracy's four-year-old daughter.

"'Lo, Clee," she uttered. She never could get that O on the end of my name. Not important. At least I, her mother and she know whom she means. She's a pretty coffee-coloured tot with big brown eyes and Tracy's mousy coloured hair, but curly. I wouldn't say frizzy but very curly.

"You helping Mum?"

"Yeah. Come on. Come on."

Terse instructions. But I did follow her into the main living space. Tracy looked over and grinned. "Getting your orders are you, Cleo? Didn't know you was coming up today."

"It was almost a spur of the moment thing. I thought about coming up a couple of days ago, then a few things happened so I didn't know whether I'd be able to get away until last night. Didn't think it was worth giving you a call."

"They haven't arrested you then?" She laughed.

"Not so far."

"Want a cuppa? I've just put the kettle on."

"Good on yer, girl. Let's have some."

We went into the kitchen trailed by Jilly, now without her duster. I sat down on one of the stools at the breakfast bar and was offered La-La. I took her, gave her a kiss and

160

handed her back to Jilly because I knew that was expected of me. Tracy brought me up-to-date with the local gossip. It's amazing that even though we're in London and surrounded by businesses the area still retains something of its old neighbourhood atmosphere. Bit like being in a village in the centre of town. There are always a lot of comings and goings, especially in the converted warehouse where my flat is. Only a few of the 1980s Yuppies who survived are still here. Now it's a much more eclectic mix of people. Several like me are using these warehouse flats as pied-de-terres. Posh!

Suppose I'd better explain about them. It's an old converted warehouse and it's really nifty the way it's done. My flat's at the top which means that I've got a nice cathedral ceiling. There is a hallway which is rather strange 'cos most of them have front doors that open straight into the living space. Off the entrance hall there's a coat closet and a small toilet.

The living space is about two floors high with windows at the front overlooking the river. And a miniature balcony - not that we have much balcony type weather! Along the other outside wall I have a row of small windows along the top. What I've done because they're plain glass is hang stained glass motifs over them so when the sun shines through I get cathedral colours shining on the walls. There's a dining alcove and I've put a nice comfortable armchair by the front window as well as an arrangement of sofas and chairs. And, of course, the all-important upright piano. As Tracy often reminds me, the furnishings are minimal and ornaments almost non-existent which she likes as there isn't too much to dust.

Well, I don't use the flat much so there doesn't seem much point in having a lot of furniture and ornaments.

161

The kitchen isn't very large but as I'm no cook that don't matter.

You'd love the bedroom. Up a flight of stairs at the other end of the living space from the window - it's actually on a balcony. It's great if I don't feel like getting up – I can sit up in bed and look at the river. Of course there's built-in wardrobes and a vanity unit. The bathroom's off the bedroom and I have a whirlpool. I know Tracy sometimes uses it – I told her to.

That's it. Nothing terribly posh.

I must tell you, it was so funny this morning when Paula came to collect me. She really couldn't believe the sight that met her. Because we didn't have to drive through the village, I was already dressed for London: Royal Purple linen skirt (calf-length), a nice lavender and leaf green silk top that comes well down over the hips and covers a multitude of sins. You know the style I mean. No, it isn't a floral, but a swirly pattern. My pride and joy as far as the glasses are concerned are rimless ones. Because they are non-reflective they're almost invisible.

"My, you do look elegant."

"Thanks, Paula. As I'm going to the posh place I thought I ought to be dressed for it."

"I don't think anybody in the village would recognize you dressed like that."

"My hair would give me away."

"I suppose so," she agreed with a smile.

"I tell you, Paula, this is how I would have loved to have been able to afford to dress when I went to work. There are times when I'm up there that I'm almost tempted to pop into the office just to show them."

"And?"

"I always change my mind. Come on, let's face it; they weren't interested in me when I was working there, so they certainly aren't going to be interested in me now! Truth to tell they probably wouldn't even remember me."

Paula chuckled, "I find that very hard to believe."

"You better believe. They're all so into themselves and the 'yah, darlings' and cloning, they don't see other people."

"I have to take your word for that. I really don't know that type."

"You haven't missed much," I commented dryly, then changed the subject. "You know what's really nice now about traveling by train, is going First Class. I mean, it's not just that the seats are comfortable, but the carriage is clean. I really revel in that."

Once Tracy had finished her chores I paid what I owed and gave her a little bit more for looking after the place while I'm away.

After Tracy and Jilly left I checked my watch and found that I had time to call Raoul to see if he was working that evening. If not, perhaps he could take me out for dinner. That is assuming he didn't have a date. That's the problem with these good-looking men – too many dolly birds available! So far as I'm concerned I reckon that there's no point in knowing these wonderful men if they can't take you out. If he was working, then where and would it be a concert I would enjoy?

I did get hold of him. He was just about to leave.

"Sorry, Cleo, bit rushed. Just off to rehearsal."

"Where at?"

"Down at the church."

"The one in Borough? On the way to the Heffilump and Castle?" Sorry, as a kid I called elephants heffilumps and it's kind of stuck.

He chuckled. "That's it."

"How long will it take?"

"Dumb question. How would I know? Depends on the conductor."

"Sorry. Should have had a good thunk. Got a concert tonight?"

"No. Want dinner if we finish in time?"

"Thought you'd never ask!" Some men are hard work aren't they?

"Where are you phoning from?"

"London of course."

"I wondered. After all, you didn't say." No comment. "So I gather they let you off."

"Who?"

"The police. That whats-his-name, Kettle."

"How do you know him?"

"Tell you all about it later."

"I wouldn't have thought that my housekeeper and her husband getting knocked off made the headlines in the national press. There's been too much else going on."

"There have been one or two paragraphs."

"Alright. But I bet they didn't mention me, did they?" I hoped not!

"No, but it became a bit obvious for those of us who know you."

"How do you know Steaming Kettle?"

There was a bark of laughter from the other end of the line. "What did you call him?"

164

"Steaming Kettle. I'll tell you later. Anyway, I thought you were in a rush. Be alright if I come down to the church? I've got to eat now."

"So what's new?" he retorted. "Probably be best if you don't come into the actual hall. Wait outside in the lobby."

"Okay. See you later."

I was bloody mad that Steaming himself had been to see the orchestra. Or rather, Raoul. I couldn't imagine why. I should have thought it would have been sufficient for the City of London Police or the Metropolitan Police, or whoever to have done the necessary checking up on me. What was he up to?

Chapter 23

You know I still get a thrill knowing I don't have to use public transport to get me around London. Just call – or hail (depending where you are) – a cab! Fantastic. To hell with the expense. When the cab dropped me off outside the church I could hear the rehearsal still in full swing. Good. Haven't kept Raoul waiting. Have to confess that after lunch I'd sat in my favourite armchair overlooking the river – and fallen asleep. Couldn't believe it. The only time I take a siesta is when I'm on holiday. And that's because I'm often up later than usual at night.

I slept for about an hour and, knowing that rehearsals can go on a bit, took a chance on a dip in the whirlpool before tarting myself up.

I did as I'd been told and sat down outside the hall to listen. These conductors are fantastic. The orchestra played the same phrases several times and each time it sounded exactly the same to me but couldn't have done to him. At least I assumed it was a h24m and not a her. Still not too many female conductors yet. Talking of women and orchestras I'll never forget the time the wife of one of the older musicians asked my opinion of women in the orchestra. Of course I told her I thought it was great. They've never spoken to me since.

So there I was working on a small piece of embroidery... Oh, haven't I told you I do that? At the moment its cross stitch, my idea of embroidery by numbers. Actually I prefer fancier stuff but that isn't in fashion any more so I go with the flow.

Back to what I started to say. I was sitting there listening to the bits and pieces of music, including one whole movement of Beethoven, and some wives came in.

Of course a couple of them had to sit yacking and interfering with my listening but there's nothing you can do about that. I don't think they realised who I was because their conversation came around to the murders. Of course. The fact that their husbands had been questioned by the police was probably the most exciting thing that's happened to them for a long time. If you don't count the conductor who lost his place during a performance because he insisted on conducting without the music. Good job the orchestra's so good – they ignored him and played on.

"Apparently the woman who they think did it says she was at a concert at the time."

"Joe wondered about that. She's a member of the club. Can you imagine a member of the club being a murderer!"

I kept on sewing. Let them have their thrills. Anyway it would only embarrass them if I told them who I am.

"I'm not sure she is." Number one responded. "I think she's only a suspect."

"But it was her housekeeper, wasn't it?"

"I think so. Even so...."

"And the housekeeper's husband." Number two butted in. She was on a roll. "I wonder why she killed them?"

"Maybe she didn't. She's only a suspect," was the reiterated response.

At that moment we all became aware of the fact that the rehearsal was over. The doors to the rehearsal room opened and the conductor and his entourage exited, obviously in a hurry.

Then the musicians began to file out in dribs and drabs. The wives were quickly collected and hustled out, obviously they all had appointments to keep. The rest moved more leisurely and one or two stopped for a chat with me. They wanted to know what had been happening

167

down in the depths of the country. I gave them a run down as far as I knew things, "But I tell you fellers, and ladies, I don't know. I have no idea who did what to whom and when and why. We'll have to wait until the police have sorted it out."

"But aren't you scared of living down there on your own?"

"Why d'you think I'm up town now?" I retorted and they laughed.

Somebody looked a bit puzzled and I realised I hadn't seen him for some time. He obviously didn't know that, as the others did, I'd come into a bit of money. Someone will soon fill him in on that.

"Sorry to keep you waiting, Cleo. Got caught up in some technical stuff. I know I don't have to ask you if you're hungry," Raoul teased as we headed out to Borough High Street to find a cab.

Our first stop was his place to drop off his precious violin and let him get changed into something more suitable for dining out than jeans and tee-shirt. We then grabbed another cab to one of our favourite restaurants. Outside London (to the west, the other side from where I live, and where there's some pretty countryside) and it's by the River Thames. Somewhere quiet and peaceful – and romantic, for all the good that does me.

"So, Raoul, what's this about Steaming Kettle?" I asked once we were settled at the table with drinks and menus. I couldn't wait to find out what had happened.

Raoul chuckled. "Steaming Kettle. You do think up these names quickly."

"Not really. We went to school together."

He quirked an eyebrow. "You're kidding!" I shook my head. "Did you know he'd become a policeman?"

168

"No. Surprised the hell out of me when he turned up at the house. Imagine. I'd just found Janet in the pool, then he turned up? Anyway, what's it with you and him? I thought all they had to do was confirm my alibi?"

"Yes, well, you know what the grapevine's like. Somebody squealed."

"I never told him nothing about you. It wasn't important. Nothing to do with you."

"Nice of you to try and keep me out of it," he tipped his glass in my direction, "but as I say, somebody told them. The next thing I know he came to see me and wanted to know about our friendship. How long we'd known each other. All those kinds of details."

"Just being nosy was he? Sod."

"Calm down. Actually, I've got something to tell you. Let's order our meal first before the waiter gets his knickers in a twist."

"Okay." After much discussion we ordered and the waiter went away to deal with it. Then I leant forward over the table and said, "Right, you. Now, what's this mystery?"

"It turns out, but I didn't realise it, not when you told me what had happened. And you'd never mentioned their names and, quite frankly, it just didn't occur to me but..." He took another mouthful of wine. What was with him? He doesn't usually have problems saying what he wants. "You know my grandmother? The one that didn't speak English?"

"Ye-es." He was referring to his mother's mother. Those grandparents had come to England along with his parents, but they had never learned to speak English.

"After my grandfather died and she was on her own they got a housekeeper for her."

169

I closed my eyes. I could see what was coming. I opened my eyes to look at him. He nodded. "Good Lord. So what happened there? They didn't rook her of her money, did they?"

"I'm afraid they did. She also gave Janet some pieces of jewelry. We were going to take them to Court after Gran died but the lawyer pointed out that it would cost us more than we would get back so it wasn't worth it."

"I'm so sorry. I have heard since the murders that that was what they were like. I must say I didn't do a very good job of employment there."

"But you didn't know how to go about it. I hope you're going to be more careful in future." He smiled, his dimples appearing.

Why are these Latin men so good looking? Well, most of them. Trouble is they seem to keep their boyish good looks right up until they start to get past middle age then one day you look at them and find their faces have collapsed into a mass of wrinkles. But to get back to gorgeous Raoul and our conversation.

"At the moment I've just got a cleaning lady. I'm not going to have a housekeeper. Just a cleaner or two and a garden service."

"Do you have someone to advise you?"

"Yeah. Paula Linley. The Lady of the Manor." I described Paula to him while we tucked into our first course. After that we kept the conversation on lighter matters.

We went back to my place for coffee and then he departed. Just my luck, of course.

Toddle off with no 'how's-your-father' and leaving me with my thoughts about his grandmother and the Spencers. And the knowledge that I've got a friend with good reason

170

not to like them. Yes, he's Latin with a Latin temperament, but would he go to such lengths? I shook myself. Don't be stupid, Cleo, he was playing in the orchestra that night.

Yeah, but he could have organised it. Suppose the gunman drowned Janet, forced Dan into the car and made him drive him somewhere, then shot Dan, dumped him, then hid the car? No, that doesn't work. Dan wasn't killed the same night – he'd met with Maggie at some time after then.

Chapter 24

Was I glad Paula came up to town today! I think I'd have gone mad if I'd had another day like yesterday.

In the morning I'd been really restless. You know, pick up a book, read one page, put it down, make a cuppa, play the piano for a bit, stood looking out of the window. Thought a walk would do me good so tried a stroll up to London Bridge and back. Back to the flat. Then, bless her, Paula phoned to say she'd be coming to town for the day and could we do a matinee? Armed with my list of shows I went to the West End.

Yeah I know I could have telephoned but that doesn't pass the time and take your mind off murder, does it?

As luck would have it I got a couple of cancellations for "My Fair Lady" at the Theatre Royal in Drury Lane. If you know London you'll have a good idea what I did next – Covent Garden. Had a good browse around the shops and stalls (bought a sweater I couldn't resist), watched the street entertainers in the piazza then cut through to Charing Cross Road and Foyles Book Shop. Another good browse and bought a couple of novels. Yeah, mysteries. I do enjoy them and thought they might give me some ideas. Let's face it, Steaming doesn't seem to be doing much.

Apart from hassling my friends!

Anyway, today Paula and me met at Covent Garden where she bought a couple of things, then went into one of the restaurants for lunch.

Walking across the piazza we'd already caught up on news in general so once we were settled at a table sipping a very delectable (get me!) Sauvignon Blanc I opened the batting.

"I'm mad at Steaming."

"Why?" Paula prompted, raising one of her delicate eyebrows.

"He's only been up here in town pestering me friends!"

"Anyone in particular?" She smiled. Gosh she really is getting to know me.

I told her about Raoul – emphasizing we are only friends. "Honest." I tried to make it sound as earnest as possible. Then gave up. "Alright. I always fancied him something rotten, but as he didn't fancy me I settled for being good mates."

"I believe you but some may not."

"Meaning?" I gulped my wine. "Steaming? Jealous? Garn. Anyway he's married."

"Doesn't mean he can't feel jealous," she pointed out.

I thought about it. "Nah. Doesn't fit. We was school pals. Nothing else."

"Anyway, Cleo, what did he want with Raoul?" She brought me back into line at the same time as our food arrived. While we tucked in I told her about Raoul's connection to the Spencers.

"Would he or his family have arranged to kill the Spencers?"

"What would they have got out of it?"

"Revenge."

Oh. "No, I don't think so."

"But they are Latin."

"Not exactly 'family' though. But you've given me an idea. Suppose one of the families they worked for wanted revenge?"

"How would you find out?"

We thrashed it around a bit and got nowhere. Then it was time for the show which really cheered me up. We agreed it was better than the film and that Dennis

173

Waterman was a fantastic Mr. Doolittle. But then when you get a Londoner playing a cockney what can you expect?

After we'd had tea and I'd waved Paula off in her cab, I wandered down The Strand to Trafalgar Square, just enjoying the crowds – home-going workers rushing to the stations and tourists meandering along, some going into shops to look at souvenirs and some just enjoying London. There's no place like it in the world.

Eventually I grabbed a cab and came home to sit and play at changing the channels on the telly. Sometimes it's the only way it's even vaguely amusing. Don't know about you but I can't stand the sight of animals tearing each other apart or having it off. I do mean the four-legged variety. Come to think of it what they show on telly and in films these days of the two-legged variety isn't much different. And, of course, the wild life progs always seem to be on just when you're having tea or dinner. Great way to diet!

So far this summer's been pretty good but today it's a typical English summer – drizzling. Kind of day when I'd rather pack a case and get to the airport. No such luck in the circs of course.

I did the only other thing possible for a lady of leisure. Had a good soak in the Jacuzzi and hoped the massage of the bubbles and the scent of the candles would get my brain working. I was now convinced that the Spencers had been killed out of revenge.

Believe it or not, but it worked. I remembered a journalist I had had dealings with when I was in Public Relations. She was one of the few who would actually talk to a humble secretary – not just to leave messages, I mean. We'd even met for lunch a few times. Primrose is a black girl with beaded hair. I used to tease her about them because they always clanged against the 'phone. We probably hit it off because we're both from the East End; her parents settled in Leyton when they came over from Jamaica.

Primrose Day got teased unmercifully at school, not just because of her colour (I remember the black kids at my school and how mad I'd get at the awful brats who wouldn't leave them alone) but for her name. She was born on Primrose Day (April 19) so her parents thought it would be a good idea to name her for the day! (By the way, in case you don't know, the day got its name for Disraeli via Queen Victoria. It commemorates the day he died and as his favourite flowers were primroses….).

Back to Primrose. She used to hate her name but, having pulled herself up by her boot straps and become a journalist on a national daily, she now played on the name.

Why hadn't I thought of her before? Easy. I've left that life behind; been kind of busy sorting out my new life and… Well, you get the idea in my line of excuses.

"Hey, Queen of the Nile, where have you been?" she yelled down the 'phone. "I knew you'd left your old place. Where are you working now?"

"So long as you promise not to publish the story, I'll tell you over lunch."

"You're on." We settled time and place then she said, "I've just remembered something. There can't be two Cleo Marjoribanks – you're involved in murder."

"Like I said, kid, I'll tell all when I see you."

"Now I'm all agog."

"Bet you look funny. See you later." I rang off quickly before she could ask any more questions. Her journalist's antenna was at full mast.

Of course I got to the restaurant first – an Italian one we'd been to before. As we'd wanted to avoid work mates, the restaurants we chose were usually mid-way between our offices. Ironically around Fleet Street the once famous thoroughfare known as the home of the National Press whose offices are now scattered, mostly to Docklands. These were changes that came about in the 1980s with the introduction of new technology (computers, of course) which wouldn't fit into the old buildings. That was the excuse. Supposedly cheaper to get new buildings than renovate the old. Seems like the famous sixes to me.

But I digress.

When Primrose came through the door and stood looking around for me, I almost didn't recognise her. Her glance passed over me then returned as she did a double take and grinned.

"Wow!"

"Hey, lady!"

We exclaimed together then giggled as she pulled out a chair and sat down.

"You first," she invited, a wicked twinkle in her eye.

"Where are the braids and the pounds?" At 5' 2" just a couple of pounds over was murder to her hips.

"Great, innit?" She smiled. "It was time to get rid of the braids."

"Curly top," I teased her new short curls. "Actually I like it better."

"Doesn't deafen me. But what about you, lovely lady. You've lost some weight, hair's a different shade and that outfit didn't come from Marks & Spencer. I smell a mystery."

"Let's order first," I reminded her as a waitress appeared at the table.

Orders completed and drinks to hand, I went on, "Before I tell you my saga, Prim, what happened to you? You look more relaxed."

"Divorce."

"Eh?"

"Your fault."

I choked on my drink.

"Sorry, love, didn't mean it like that." She chuckled. "I was pissed off with his complaining I was never home when he was. As he spent most nights and weekends at football or in the pub with his mates I was right...."

"Pissed orf?" I supplied in a lah-di-dah voice which made her laugh.

"Yeah. Right. Anyway, as he resented my job and I could see how you managed without a man around, I realised I didn't need a prop. I mean, if he'd been supportive and consoled me when I needed it, things would have been a bit different."

"But he wanted to be macho?"

"Right on. He would have liked me to be 'the little woman' but he liked the money I brought home."

"More than his?" I hazarded.

"You got it. Life's great now I don't have to worry about him. I've even got a promotion."

"Congratulations. Doing what?"

"Crime reporter. One of them."

I sat back and grinned. Am I in luck or what?

"Before you tell me what you want...."

"Did I say that?"

"Why else would you call?"

"Now you're making me feel awful. I'm sorry I didn't keep in touch, but in the circs."

177

"Which are?" She raised her eyebrows, rummaged in her bag and pulled out some papers. Computer printouts. She turned them around so I could see what they were. Newspaper reports on the murder. "To live there and have a house that size you've got to have money. Ergo someone died and left you a bundle or…"

"No and yes. Don't finish that in public."

"Lucky old you. Tell me all about it some time, but let's get down to the nitty-gritty." She tapped the papers where they lay on the table beside her. "I smell a good story."

"Dunno. There's some things I can't tell you because the police haven't released them."

"I realise that, but promise me everything afterwards so I can do a profile of the crime. Maybe get a scoop."

The journalist's nose was definitely twitching.

"Of course. What we discuss now isn't for publication. Okay?" She nodded. "Thing is I've got an idea why the Spencers were murdered but don't know how to find out who by."

"And you think I can help," she stated. "Sounds like we might be able to scoop the Old Bill."

"I don't know about that, I just want to find out if my theory will work."

Chapter 25

"Sounds like an interesting problem. Shoot." She paused and giggled, "Sorry, wrong word."

"That's okay. Do it myself – all the time." I then outlined my idea.

"Hmm. Are you sure the police haven't already thought of that?"

"Doesn't sound like it from what I know of their investigation."

"Cleo," she leaned forward across the table, "they won't tell you what they're doing. They barely tell the press."

I patted her cheek. "Don't worry, love, I've got the inside track. Went to school with the Chief Inspector. Kettle's his name."

"Steaming's down there?" She sat back looking amazed.

"Know him?" I was surprised but coincidences do happen and she is now a crime reporter.

"Not exactly. Know of him. Used to be out at Snaresbrook but left. Got quite a reputation for solving cases. No one knows why he went or where to."

"P'raps he got fed up with violent crime and thought it'd be quieter down south. Though," I added thoughtfully, "why he would think Southampton would be less violent escapes me."

"Can we get back to what you want me to do?" Primrose smiled.

"Sorry, love. What I need to do is talk to people who the Spencers worked for. Or, rather, the relatives, assuming the old girls are all dead."

179

"Tough one if you don't know who they were. I assume you got them through an agency?"

"Yup, but they can't help. Police, you know."

"Of course. Do you have a computer?"

"Not in town. Got one at the house."

"Wow, two homes."

"That reminds me." I rummaged in my bag and brought out my folder of cards (posh, aren't I?) and gave her one of each – London and the New Forest.

She looked at them then at me and grinned. "Just around the corner from me. Only I'm renting."

"Why don't you pop round this evening then we can talk in comfort. You can have a go in the spa bath if you want."

"Again – wow! I'd love to. I'll have to give you a call later 'cos I don't know whether I'll be working."

"That's okay, I'm not planning on going out. If you ever fancy a weekend in the country you can always come down there. Assuming I'm home, of course."

"Oh yes, itchy feet, which you can indulge in now to your heart's content. Lucky old you. But I bet I'll stand out in the village."

"Yup." I grinned. "You'll only confirm their suspicions of me." She looked puzzled. "I'm the local eccentric." That fooled her.

"How can you be eccentric? You look normal."

"Not down there." I waggled my eyebrows which made her chuckle, "I don't wear normal clothes down there."

"I guess you wouldn't wear something like that outfit. What is it for the country? Twinsets and pearls or Bermuda shorts?"

Clever girl. "Definitely not twinsets."

180

She crowed with laughter, making several heads turn. "Oh, Cleo," she gasped, wiping tears from her cheeks, "I can't picture you in shorts."

"Wouldn't want to frighten the natives, would we? I only wear them when I'm rambling through the woods – and not a pretty sight," I admitted with a sigh, then revealed the secret. "Nah. I'm a gaudy caftans and beads lady."

Primrose grinned. "Yes, I can just picture it. Hat?" I nodded. "And Dame Edna glasses?" I nodded again. "I love it. Nothing would keep me away. Cleo, old girl, I love you."

That said, she noticed the time and had to dash back to the office. "Even if I can't get round tonight I'll give you a bell with what I manage to dig up ideas-wise."

And with that she was gone.

Back in the flat the light on the answerphone was doing its nut. Steaming – three times – would I call him urgently. Why didn't he use the mobile? No prizes. When I checked the battery was flat. Useful things mobile phones when you remember to keep them juiced up.

I called Steaming. "Thank Gawd," he greeted me. "Your mobile wasn't working and as I couldn't get hold of you at the flat I was worried."

"Sorry about that. My fault. I was lunching with a friend. What's up?" He was worried?

"It's Mrs. Cheetham."

"Oh no, what's she done now?"

"Nothing. She's dead."

"What! Heart attack or something?" Not a reason to call me I wouldn't have thought.

"No, she's been murdered."

"Not another one."

181

"'Fraid so and the news is worse. She was found in your garden."

"I told her the other day never to come into my garden again."

"She obviously didn't take much notice," he commented dryly. "Did she know you were going to be away?"

"No. The only people who knew were the Linleys and Mrs. Walsh and they wouldn't have told her."

"Perhaps she saw you drive through the village on your way to the station."

"First off, how would she know I was going to the station? Secondly, we didn't go through the village."

"We?"

"Paula took me to Brockenhurst and because I was dressed for London....."

"Rather than for the village," he finished with a chuckle.

"Exactly. Well, we went the long way round."

"Did you close the gates?"

"No. As I'm only planning on a few days and the burglar alarm is on it didn't seem worth it. Anyway, Paula said she'd check. Oh. Oh no, she didn't....?"

"No, no," he hurriedly reassured me. "I've spoken to her as I guessed she knew you were away. She just drove in, then walked around the house to check doors and windows."

"So how did she miss Mrs. C?"

"Mrs. C was behind the garage. She'd been dragged there. By the way, what would she have been doing in your garden? Did you ask her to go in and dead-head?"

182

"No way! Like I told you, I'd told her not to go into the garden. The other day I found her helping herself to my flowers. And told her off in no uncertain terms."

"So why would she go back when you're away?"

"More to the point, how did she know I was away?"

"Someone obviously told her."

"I get that, but who? Either that or someone phoned her pretending to be me."

"Luring her there which means someone overheard you when you were telling her off."

"And hoped I'd get blamed for her death. Oh yuck."

"But why?"

"She did say she had been friends with Janet and knew things about her and Dan. To be perfectly honest, I didn't really believe her."

"But someone may have. When are you coming back?"

"I was planning in the next day or so. If my place isn't a crime scene again?"

"The house wasn't involved this time. Unfortunately your crunchy driveway doesn't take prints."

Crunchy? Just because I've got pebbles. They look nicer than asphalt and concrete and don't go out of kilter like paving stones.

When Primrose came round in the evening she wanted to hear all about the lottery win. "Come on, Cleo, did you go into work and tell them where to stick their job?" she asked as she came through the door.

"Let me tell you later, love. Coffee or a drink?"

She wanted a beer, which I didn't have (can't stand the stuff), so she settled for a gin and tonic. I poured my usual Glenfiddich and water.

183

As I handed over her drink she peered closely at me. "Hey, what's up, Cleo?"

I sat down in the chair across from her and we ignored the view from the window. "There's been another murder in Trewith Green."

"What on earth is going on down there? Wait a minute." She paused to think. "That sly bastard!" I raised an eyebrow. "One of the blokes in the department. I'd already switched off the computer and was ready to leave when he said something about 'another one'. When I asked him 'another one what?' he shook his head and said, 'nothing'. I bet that was what he had picked up. Damn!"

"Calm down, Prim, you've got the inside track, remember," I reminded her.

"True." She took a sip then gave me a remorseful look. "I'm sorry, Cleo, I'm so wrapped up in myself and it's you that's suffering."

"Not exactly suffering. Just mad and puzzled."

"Want to talk?"

"Want to take notes? Mind you, I'm not sure how much Steaming wants publicized so you'll have to ask him."

"That's okay. I've got his numbers," she added with a grin.

I told her as much as I knew and she jotted down the bits she needed. When I'd finished she asked, "So do you really think they are all connected?"

"Bit of a coincidence if they're not."

"Supposing someone else in the village or one of her family members wanted to off her and thought this a good time to do it?"

"Wow, I hadn't thought of that."

"You would have, in time. At the moment you're too close to it."

"Steaming probably thought of it."

"I'm sure. Tell me more about the lady. What did she look like?"

"I think she was in her mid-60s. When going to town or WI meetings she wore Hyacinth Bucket type dresses."

Prim frowned, then grinned. "Drop waisted, florals. Kind of 'Mother of the Bride' sort of thing."

I grinned back at her and nodded. "Exactly. And she was the world's worst gossip."

"Made up."

"And not really understanding situations." I told her about the younger women going to Southampton and added, "One of my favourites was about one couple whom she called alcoholics. Turns out they would have a glass of wine with their evening meal and maybe a drink in front of the telly."

"How did you find out?"

"My cleaning lady. Mrs. Walsh. Yes, she's a bit of a gossip, but talks fact, not fiction. I think the couple concerned are friends of hers."

"And word does get out!" Prim put her pad and pen into her bag, then said, "Now, before I grab a cab back to the office to work on this, how about telling me about this lottery win? Did you tell them where to stick their job?"

"No, because I didn't want anyone knowing I'd come into money. I worked out my month's notice."

"Don't think I could have done that," she confessed.

"You do have an interesting job. Let's face it, working as a secretary in public relations isn't that interesting. The people I worked for have bigger egos than the Millennium Dome (now known as the O2 Arena) at Greenwich. What

185

surprised them was that I actually handed in my notice. They assumed I was there for the long haul – until my retirement. It didn't occur to them to wonder why one of their secretaries suddenly began to wear more expensive clothes. They'd never bothered to inquire into my private life, not even to ask about my holidays or weekends."

"Miserable buggers."

"Yeah, but I had a good laugh when I saw my 'farewell' cards which wished me good luck in my new position. No one had asked, but I think a few other secretaries and junior ranks were speculating.

"The bosses gave me a check for what they thought was an adequate return for over twenty years of devoted service. If I'd been at retirement age and officially retiring I would have been insulted. Instead of which, it was hilarious. My colleagues had a collection and bought me a gift they thought was suitable for a middle-aged lady - a pottery vase. To be perfectly honest, it isn't something I would have gone out and purchased for myself."

She grimaced, "Me either. What did you do with it?"

"Gave it to someone who appreciates it more than me."

"Gor blimey, as they say down my way! Talk about a load of stingy whats-its."

"Never mind. Let's face it, I have the last laugh."

"True."

We then thrashed around the problem of the murders and she gave me some Internet tips and web sites. And approved what I'd done so far.

Well, you see, I had a brainstorm – must have been the wine with lunch. I called Raoul and left a message asking him to let me have the names and addresses of the people his family had contacted for references for the Spencers.

Also the names and addresses of anyone who had contacted them for a reference.

"Great. That'll give you a good start. If you can't get hold of those people at least you'll have an idea which direction to look in. Check the obits in the local papers and also try the Registry of Births, Marriages and Deaths. Then you'll be able to pick up on next of kin."

"Should keep me going for a few weeks." I smiled ruefully at her. "Thanks, Prim, I appreciate this."

"I'll catch my reward one weekend."

"Hi," I greeted the answerphone at the other end of the line (like stepping backwards in a dress shop, treading on the toe of a dummy and then apologizing!). "Paula, its Cleo. Just to let you know I'm back. Give me a call later."

Yes, back home. After talking with Primrose last night and in view of Mrs. Cheetham's death I thought I ought to come back. The only problem is that the police tape is across the garage doors so the next call was, of course, to Steaming.

"Wotcher, Steaming, I'm back in Trewith."

"I suspected you'd hot foot it back, but didn't think you'd be back this early."

"I was awake a bit early and thought it wasn't worth hanging around up in town for the day. Got a problem though."

"Oh?"

"Yeah. Oh. I can't get the cars out because of the blue and white decorations."

"Oops, sorry about that. I'll check the SOCOs to see if it can be removed."

"Or at least taken off the doors."

Having got that sorted out I had a sandwich, then decided to get stuck into some of that research work. And, of course, wait for Raoul to call. I also began browsing on the computer wondering where to begin. It seems an awful lot of work and at the moment I have no idea what to say to any of these people if I do contact them.

And, of course, there is the possibility that one of them might be a murderer. Am I about to play a dangerous game?

Chapter 26

Well, I haven't got very far yet with the research. It was flaming boring going through the obit columns of some local newspapers, all of which was a bit pot luck anyway. Knowing where Raoul's grandmother had lived in Hertfordshire I'd been looking at local papers not too far from that town, round about before and after she'd died. I reckon it's a dead end anyway. How would I know who to look for? There are so many widows it would take me forever to contact all their next of kin to find out if the Spencers had worked for them.

Talk about saved by the bell! Obviously I thought it was a young uniform come to tell me he'd moved the decorations. When I opened the kitchen door (being a townie I always keep the doors locked), I found Steaming and Jenny Dixon. What a good job I'd switched off the computer! Wouldn't want them to know what I was up to. At least, not yet.

"Just in time for an afternoon cuppa," I said as I ushered them inside. "Does it take two of you to undo the parcel?"

Steaming grinned. "No. Just one, but we need to talk about Mrs. Cheetham."

"Okay. Sit down while I put the kettle on." Go on, groan at the pun. It was totally unintentional.

Steaming relieved the moment. "You'll look lovely wearing it," which gave Jenny the excuse to giggle. I'm sure she'd wanted to when I made my Freudian slip.

Okay, kettle filled, switched on, teapot, caddy, cups and saucers at the ready and I sat down at the table with them.

189

"So, what do you want to know about Mrs. Cheetham?"

Jenny had notebook and pen out so I told them about my first meeting with the woman. "To be perfectly honest, I didn't like her," I finished, then got up to make the tea.

"What happened when you found her in the garden?" Steaming asked.

"That was the last time I saw her," I reminded him before launching into that story.

"Do you think Janet gave her permission?"

"I doubt it. The more I've thought about it the more unlikely it seems. Janet wasn't exactly the most forthcoming person I've met so I don't think she would have opened up to Mrs. C, who was a really pushy person.

"So you don't think she was friendly with the Spencers?"

"Certainly not Janet, but Dan did get around a bit. Either she knew what he was up to or didn't and used to make it up."

"We'll never know now," Steaming commented. "Had you met her many times?"

"She waylaid me once on the way to the village and again in Lymington. After I'd bought Land Rover."

"Tell us about those meetings."

So I did and finished by asking, "How was she killed?" Well, the papers hadn't said so I assume the police wanted to keep quiet about it.

"Strangled with, we presume, her own scarf."

"Let me think. I can't remember whether she ever wore scarves. For the WI and Lymington she was in one of her 'posh' frocks. On the way to the village she had on a skirt and blouse and when she was in the garden she was

190

wearing trousers and a blouse. Nope, don't think I've ever seen her in a scarf."

"So the murderer could have had the scarf with him or her?" Jenny asked.

"What do you think? I've noticed that women either wear scarves or they don't, other than in winter to keep the neck warm," I added.

Steaming looked from one to the other of us and nodded. "I think I would agree with that. Which means we might be looking for a woman."

"Which means that it might not be connected with the Spencers' murders," I summed up. "Incidentally, I've got some floaty scarves I sometimes use. Killing her in my garden with a scarf might have been intentional."

"To point the finger at you," Steaming put in.

"Exactly," I agreed, "but if that was the case, whoever did it didn't know I was away."

He groaned. "Back to the drawing board." He then turned to Jenny, "You'd better remove the police tape before we forget. We'll never hear the end of it." He turned to me and grinned.

Why did he send her out? They could take the tape down on their way out.

"Have a good time in London?"

"Not bad. Paula came up one day."

"See any old friends?"

Uh-oh, "Went for dinner with Raoul."

"Anyone else?"

"What is this? The third degree? One of the things I do when I go to London is to meet up with friends and, sometimes, relatives."

"Why didn't you tell me you know Primrose Day?"

191

"For what it is worth, I knew her when I worked in PR and she was a dogs-body reporter. Oh!" Light dawned and I grinned. "Sorry, mate. I didn't know until we met for lunch that she is now a crime reporter and it just didn't occur to me to mention it yesterday when we were on the phone."

"She called me last night. Did you give her my phone numbers?"

"I offered to but she told me she already had them."

"So you did discuss the Spencers with her?"

"I really didn't have much choice as she'd seen it in the papers. Anyway, we only discussed it peripherally. I've promised her the inside story once its all over."

He looked a real sourpuss over that.

"Come on, love, we girls have got to stick together. It's what friends are for."

"I hate all these revelation articles."

"Tell you what, before I dish the dirt with her, we'll discuss what I can tell her and what I can't."

He sighed. "I suppose you can't be fairer than that. Thanks."

As there wasn't anything else to say on the subject, he left.

Back to the computer from which I was again interrupted (thankfully) by the doorbell. This time the front one.

With the chain on I opened the door a couple of inches.

"Who are you?" I asked the man and woman standing there, she a couple of inches taller. When I looked down I saw the heels. They didn't look as if they were collecting for anything.

The man spoke. "Rob and Ros Cheetham."

Cheetham? Related to Mrs. Cheetham, obviously. "One of Mrs. Cheetham's sons and his wife?"

"No, son and daughter," Ros smiled. "We came down today and have been sorting out at the house."

Gawd, they were quick off the mark! "The police let you?"

"Yes. They finished there this morning. Can we come in?" she asked.

The only problem with the door chain is having to close the door before you can release it. Pain in the neck.

They came in and I took them into the living room. "Can I get you a drink?" I could see they were going to refuse so I went to the booze cupboard and took out the Glenfiddich to show them. "There's also gin, vodka, sherry and port."

Needless to say they opted for the good stuff – Glenfiddich and soda - and sat side by side on the sofa. I took an armchair and studied them. "Twins." No, they are fraternal so they don't look much alike. I judged it from their age.

"Of course. Didn't Mum tell you?" Rob asked.

Another penny dropped. He is Robert and his dad was "Bertie".

I raised an eyebrow, "She told me lots of things but, I'm afraid, I wasn't always listening. So, what do you want?"

"Nothing. It's just that we thought we ought to call on you as you were Mum's best friend," Ros told me, her deep set grey eyes regarded me. Was it my imagination or did she look sly?

"Where did you get that idea? I only met her four times." I held up a hand. "Okay, I do know. She told you."

"Yes, when we spoke on the phone last Sunday," she pushed a strand of mousey hair behind an ear. His hair is the same colour but as it's short he can't push it behind an ear, although I did notice him running a hand over it occasionally. Nervous habit?

"Incidentally, aren't there three of you? I seem to remember someone telling me that."

"Tony, our younger brother, lives in Australia," Rob confirmed. The one that really got away!

"And where do you two live?"

"Croydon. Just outside London," Ros explained. And I don't sound like a Londoner, so I don't know where the town is?

"Know it well. Easy to get here then to visit your Mum."

They had the grace to look embarrassed.

Rob cleared his throat. "Well, you see, Miss Banks….."

"Marjoribanks."

"Sorry?"

"It's spelt M-A-R-J-O-R-I-B-A-N-K-S, but pronounced Marchbanks."

"Sorry, we thought you were Miss Margery Banks."

I grinned to show no hard feelings. "I suppose you weren't listening very well to your Mum." I held up a hand again as Ros opened her mouth to protest. "Don't worry. Remember, I had met her and I know how she would waffle on. So, when exactly did you last visit your Mum?"

So long ago they had to work it out.

"About a year ago," Ros admitted. "You see, we both work in the City which means lots of overtime and weekend work."

"And we have our friends and hobbies," Rob added.

194

I think they were surprised when I didn't reprove them or anything. If she'd been my Mum I would have skeddadled as soon as I was old enough.

"So we've cleared the air as to why you came to see me, but what was the real reason? And don't say because she was killed here," I glared at them.

"Well, no, but…." Ros couldn't finish.

"We wondered if you had any idea why she was killed? We've been trying to work it out."

"As you haven't been back to the village recently and thought I was her best friend you assume I would have an idea."

"Exactly," Rob confirmed.

"You won't mind my being very blunt?" They shook their heads. "The palette is wide. She told so many lies about people, almost anyone in the village could have dunnit. Then, of course, it might be related to the deaths of Janet and Dan Spencer."

Light dawned on the fraternal faces. "We didn't think of that!"

I beg your pardon? I thought. The most obvious and they didn't think of it? Nah, don't believe them.

"She did tell me she knew them and knew all about them."

"So they weren't her friends?" Rob asked.

"Doubt it. She might have known Dan as he got around a bit, but Janet wasn't the sociable sort."

"What did she know about them?" Ros sat forward eagerly.

"If she had known anything and had told me we'd probably have a good idea who killed them."

Ros sank back on the sofa, a mass of disappointment.

195

Another penny dropped. They were already cleaning the house, ergo they want to sell it, but can't until Probate has been granted. If their memories of Trewith Green aren't very good you can't blame them, but why the urgency?

Eventually I got rid of them and put a frozen meal in the microwave. Time to settle down for an evening of playing with the telly.

And wondering exactly what the Cheetham twins real motive was in coming to see me. Where had they been when their mother was killed?

Chapter 27

It was a couple of days before Raoul came through with the information I'd asked him for – the names and telephone numbers of the people who had employed the Spencers before and after his grandmother.

Now I'm trying to work out what to say to these people when I ring them. I can't say I'm the police – that's illegal. Perhaps it's just best to tell the truth. But what reason can I give for calling them?

Oh well, trust to luck.

Got more or less the same response from both of them. The first one I called was the people who were next-of-kin to the old girl the Spencers had worked for before they came to me. Daft cow that I am, I should have called them for a reference. Anyway, the woman I spoke to was dead snooty. You know, all posh and speaking with the likes of me just "wasn't on" so it was tough going.

All she would tell me was that the Spencers had worked for Raoul's grandmother before working for her mother-in-law. "My mother-in-law employed them herself so I know nothing about them."

"But you met them?"

"I saw her whenever we visited, yes."

"And?"

"I beg your pardon?" Forgive me for breathing.

"I wondered what your opinion was."

"I didn't have an opinion. She was my mother-in-law's housekeeper." Oops, don't get friendly with the help.

"I see. Did your mother-in-law ever comment on their work? You know, like was Mrs. Spencer efficient?"

"My mother-in-law was a very private person. We did not discuss such matters."

Guess there's no point in asking about the Will. Never mind I can get that as it's in the public domain.

I rang off from her and called the people of the old girl before Raoul's grandmother. Talk about a ditto response. I'm not surprised the Spencers' were able to rip them off. Wouldn't surprise me if they'd forged the Wills. Wonder why they'd come to me? After all, they did meet me first and I've got to be loads different from the old girls. I don't think they were stupid so perhaps they suspected I had won the Lottery. I can guess that Dan probably thought I was a gambler and would be a soft touch. But Janet? Did she think I didn't have friends or relatives and might make a Will in their favour?

Oh, ugh. Keep me alive until that Will is made then…. I went cold at the thought.

And I wonder where that money is that went missing from the savings account? If Janet took it out and put into another account presumably her brother has that account book, especially as it hasn't yet been found. I would have thought he'd have taken the money and scarpered. Interesting thought. Wonder what Steaming thinks of that?

I dialed his number and, as he sounded fraught when he answered, I said, "Just a quickie, chum. Does Janet's brother have a savings account book with the money they presumably took from the Spencers' account?"

"I have no idea. We don't have enough for a search warrant. Why?"

"Well, if he's got that why hasn't he taken the money and run?"

Steaming thought about that then came up with a probable answer. "Because the account is in both names and needs both signatures?"

"Right. And they met in Lymington regularly so the account could be with one of the banks or building societies there."

"Hmm. Wonder if Wiles has chased that up? I'll have to check with him but that's a good thought, Cleo. Thanks. Wonder why I hadn't thought about it?"

"Maybe because it's too obvious. I only thought about it when I wondered why he hadn't disappeared."

"We'd better keep an eye on him."

"Good idea. Meanwhile I'm following something up as well."

"You're what?" The tone sounded ominous. Perhaps I shouldn't say anything more.

"It's probably nothing. I'll let you know if I find out anything."

"You'll let me know now."

"What will you do if I don't?"

He slammed down the receiver. Some people.

I'd no sooner replaced the phone than it rang again.

"Hi, Cleo! How's it going?"

No doubt about that boisterous voice. "Hi, Prim. Don't you have no work to do?"

"Sure. That's why I'm calling. I'm getting the exclusive, right?"

"Oh, I get it. Singing for your supper."

"That's right. So, how's it going?" she repeated.

I told her about the two females I'd spoken to, finishing, "Definitely of the snooty brigade, but I'm surprised they didn't just ring off."

199

"You caught 'em by surprise and they were probably brought up not to be rude."

"To the staff?"

She giggled. "Yup, even to the staff, even if they didn't get friendly with them. So, what's next on the agenda?"

"Jacuzzi," I responded succinctly.

"Yeah, that's what else I was ringing about. This weekend okay?"

"Of course. But don't you want to know what else I've got lined up?"

"Sure."

"Wills."

"Eh?"

"Wills. At least the ones of those two old girls?"

"Give me the names and I'll look them up. Save you a trip."

I gave her the details and she promised to bring the results with her.

We rang off and would you believe the damn thing rang again? All of a sudden I'm popular?

"Hello, Cleo, how are you? Your phone has been busy."

"Hi, Paula. Yeah, it stays silent for hours then everyone calls, but that's normal, innit?"

She chuckled and agreed, going on to ask, "Are you doing anything tonight? I thought you might like to come over for dinner. Margaret's in London staying with Edward and his wife for a few days."

"I'd love to. Ta very much. What time?"

"Any time after six then we can relax with drinks first."

I don't know whether it was my imagination but there was something in her tone of voice that piqued my interest. Even if I had had something else planned, I would be going to the Linley's to find out what was up.

Chapter 28

When I got there Gerard was nowhere to be seen, but Paula quickly handed me my tipple – scotch and water, of course - and a small notebook and we went to sit on the terrace overlooking the formal garden.

"Don't give me much time to sit and admire the garden do you?" I grinned. "What's this?" I held up the pastel blue notebook – with silver hearts dotted all over it would you believe? "Your love diary?"

"Not mine. Margaret's."

"She know you've got it?"

"No way. She dropped it at the stables and one of the girls picked it up. As I was up there today exercising Star she gave it to me."

"You've read it I presume?"

"Guiltily, yes. Gerard doesn't think I should have done so which is why he's indoors preparing dinner."

"Wow! One talented man. Can I borrow him some time?"

She laughed, which is what I'd intended.

"What d'you want me to do with this?" I waved the book at her. "Return it to Margaret?"

"No. Read the pages I've flagged."

"Sure?"

"Definitely."

Not much liking the idea of reading someone's unpublished diary I gingerly opened it at the first book mark.

Dan must really like me. Today he gave me back all the money he borrowed. Said he'd had a win on the lottery. He's put the rest into a savings account for the future.

(Ours? Hope so.) And as he doesn't want Janet to know he asked me if I'd look after the account book. Now that's really trusting me! I've put it in my secret safe place so Mum won't find it….

"More like he had a win on the horses," I commented dryly, then asked, "Obviously you didn't find it?"

"I don't even know about the secret safe place!"

"Very secret. Wonder why she never told us or the police about this money?"

"Read on."

It's a shame the book is sealed in an envelope. I've no idea how much is in the account. But to think he trusts me to keep his secret – NO MATTER WHAT HAPPENS. I wonder what he expects to happen?

I looked at Paula, "Not to be murdered, anyway."

"You've reached the 'no matter what bit'?"

"Yeah. Should I read on? Or do we go and find this savings account book?"

"Try the other bit I've marked."

I flipped to the other tab.

I gave Dan back his account book today. He said that as his brother is now back in England from abroad, he would give it to him to care for. He didn't like the idea of my keeping secrets from parents.

"Back in England? Nah. Out of clink I reckon," while thinking what about the secret of Maggie knowing Dan?

"Do you think so?"

"Yeah. Steaming said he was a con. I wonder if his brother did get the book or whether that's what he wanted to find when he came to the house that time?"

"Could be. But, Cleo, I want your advice. Should I give this book to your nice policeman?"

"My what? He's not mine and I'm not sure about the nice bit! I reckon he could get pretty nasty. Especially about withheld info."

"So I should give it to him?"

Difficult this one. I mused for a bit. "How about photocopying those pages and giving the book to Margaret? See if she gives it to him?"

"If she hasn't up to now…."

"Yeah. Why don't you give him the photocopies and explain the situation to him? He's got kids so he knows how to handle them." I paused. "At least, I suppose he does."

"The book?"

"What about it? Drop it under Margaret's bed. She'll find it."

Paula smiled with relief. Gawd, am I glad I don't have kids. Must soften the brain.

Chapter 29

I didn't get to talk to Prim before Saturday. When she called to let me know what time to expect her, I was out walking in the forest, getting used to the new guise and thoroughly enjoying it. Got quite close to some ponies and even saw a couple of deer. Anyway, Prim left a message but only the time to expect her. So, of course, I was pretty edgy by the time she arrived – in time for elevenses.

"Oh, wow, Cleo, this is smashing!" she exclaimed as she got out of her primrose yellow Mini then stood and looked at the house and garden. "Can't wait to see the rest. Just a mo." She dived back into the car and came out with a holdall and a dress on a hanger.

I took her up to the best spare room so she could sort herself out, "The bath is a spa so you've got it to yourself."

"I want to see the house first," she demanded, dropping the dress on the bed. I picked it up and hung it in the wardrobe all by its lonesome. "Thanks, Mum," she grinned.

Following the tour we sat out in the garden with coffee and doughnuts. I had to laugh as Prim insisted on putting up the sunshade over the table. "Anyone would think you were afraid of getting sunburnt," I teased.

"I am," she retorted. "And there is such a thing as skin cancer, don't forget. I hope you remember to put on lotion when you're in the forest or wherever you're taking a walk."

"Yes, Mum," I grinned and she chuckled. "Anyway, did you find out about them Wills?"

"Yup. I'll give you the copies I made a bit later. Let's just relax now."

What a tease. As she'd done me a favour I couldn't very well push her on that point. So we sat and I told her what I'd done about the house and garden. Once she felt she'd digested the doughnut Prim decided it was time to jump in the pool and get some healthful exercise. So we put on swim suits – how I envy her lithe figure! – and went to the pool room. For me it was time to lay the ghosts properly and with a companion to help…. Huh! While I did my dog paddle around the shallow end, she powered up and down the pool like a demented Olympic champ. Made me tired just watching her. Eventually she slowed down, rolled onto her back and just lay there barely moving.

"Better?" I asked.

"Much. I needed that. It's a great way to get rid of the strains and stresses. Wish I had a pool I could jump into every day."

"Funnily enough I don't use it every day."

She looked at me, suddenly serious. "I guess not. I forgot. Sorry."

"Don't be. I need to start using it more. I also need to learn how to swim properly."

"Let's have a lesson now. Come on, Cleo. Show me what you do, then I'll show you how to do a stately breast stroke."

It was fabulous! At the end of half-an-hour I could breast stroke a width without turning it into a dog paddle or touching the bottom of the pool.

Prim eventually decided we'd had enough so we showered off, I got some cokes from the fridge and we relaxed in the Jacuzzi.

My patience was finally rewarded when my crime reporter relented and, after showering and changing into shorts and tops then munching up some salad she gave me the papers to read while we ate.

They didn't take much reading. "Hmm. They weren't left all that much money. £25,000 and £10,000."

"Yeah, but add that and maybe some larger sums up and it begins to make a nice nest egg."

"True. And if they finagled it, clever. Not enough to sue over."

"But enough to stir resentment, maybe."

We mused over that, but it didn't really help the situation. "I reckon the police have already seen this so I won't need to mention it, will I?" I asked.

"Quite honestly, Cleo, I don't reckon those two families would have thought it worthwhile. I checked them out and they're rolling in it. Why didn't you want me to check on the one in between?"

"Personal."

"Know them, do you?"

"Not exactly," I prevaricated. I hadn't wanted her checking up on Raoul and his family for two reasons. One, it's too personal and the other – I'm scared what I might find out.

"I'll put your mind at rest, love. They're not exactly rolling in it and the Spencers did get a cut, but I doubt they had anything to do with the murders."

Whew!

Primrose finished champing her apple, put the core on the empty salad plate and, while wiping her sticky fingers on a paper serviette asked, "So, what's happening now?"

I didn't need a full explanation. She wanted the low down on Mrs. Cheetham.

"Nothing that you don't already know police-wise. Even though Steaming is in charge he doesn't confide in me," I grinned at her.

"Anything else he does do?" She quirked an eyebrow.

"No way. I don't play with married men. There are way too many problems in the world without my adding to them." She nodded understandingly. "There is one thing though. I had a visit from two of her kids." And related the event.

When I had finished, she mused, "Wonder where the scarf came from?"

"No idea."

"You didn't recognise it?"

"I haven't seen it."

"Oh. Be interesting to know what it is like. Is it a long floaty one, or a square?"

"Probably a long one. You'd have difficulty strangling someone with a square," I pointed out tartly.

"True, unless you'd done it manually then put the scarf around the neck to make it look that way."

"Fingerprints. There'd be bruising."

"Sure, but suppose that is what happened but the police aren't releasing that information hoping that the culprit will slip up."

"My dear Holmes, you could be so right." We laughed. "I think I know how we can find out something about the scarf. Hang on."

I went indoors to make a phone call. "Hello, Jenny, it's Cleo. Can you talk?"

"I'm just going off duty."

"Good. Go and get a swimsuit and come over here. I've got a girlfriend staying so we're having a girls get together."

"Mmm."

It was tempting for her so I added a bit more sugar. "I'm sure you're in need of time in the Jacuzzi. Just think, time in it and a nice glass of cold, white wine."

"See you when I see you."

Notice she hadn't used my name? I reckon either Steaming or Blondie was nearby.

Back on the patio with Primrose I repeated that conversation. Prim laughed. "You are naughty! But clever. Yes, she is just the person we need. We might not find out too much about the actual crime but we might learn the colour or make of the scarf."

"Which will get us where?"

"Finding out where it came from."

"The police are probably already doing that and they have the man power."

"Sure, but what about the Croydon connection?"

"That's a bit of a leap."

"Not really. It isn't difficult to find people's addresses. Finding out where the twins live will give us an idea where they clothes shop."

"Probably in the City."

"Not too many clothes shops in the City and the ones selling scarves are usually the chain shops."

"All selling the same which will prove nothing."

That deflated her, but she wasn't down for long. "So we find out where Ros works and I get to know some of her mates."

"Still a long shot and how would you have time?"

"All part of my job. It would also be on expenses."

That's right, she could find out who was close to Ros Cheetham and which of those was willing to talk to the press. Clever.

209

"We'd better get off the subject now," I suggested. "Jenny might arrive some time soon and we wouldn't want to make any slip ups."

"So tell me about her."

"In her twenties and, as Paula once put it, far too pretty for the job."

Primrose laughed. "A lady of the old school obviously."

"Definitely, but she does actually have a good sense of humor and I realized afterwards that the comment may have been tongue in cheek."

"Anyone around!" Jenny called.

"Round here on the patio!" we chorused.

She joined us – in shorts and tee shirt and toting a canvas carryall.

I introduced them. "Oh yeah. St.... the Boss mentioned you," Jenny greeted Prim.

"You can call him Steaming. We do," I told her and she grinned.

"Ta. Actually, when you called him," she looked at Prim, "he seemed about to live up to his name."

"You were there then?"

"Yup. Overtime's a wonderful thing, which is why I was anxious to get off now. Time off in lieu of pay," she added dryly.

"Makes sense when you're in the middle of a triple murder enquiry," was my tart response.

"No comment," was Prim's contribution. "It's happening all over. And the general public wonders why crimes don't get solved quicker. Anyway, I'm ready for another swim." So saying she got up, went indoors and disappeared. Jenny? Stripped off. Her swimsuit was under the shorts and tee.

"Coming?"

"I'll go in the Jacuzzi after I've dumped these things in the dishwasher," I indicated out lunch plates and glasses.

Jenny went into the pool room and dived straight in, quickly followed by Prim. Then they were racing each other up and down. Such energy.

They were still at it when I returned clad in another swimsuit and switched on the Jacuzzi. That tempted them so they left the pool and dripped over to join me. "Prim, before you get in, the wine is in the fridge." Yup, I have a fridge handy.

She poured out the wine, handed them around, then joined us.

"So, Jenny, what did Steaming say about me?" I don't think Prim wanted to know from vanity, but from curiosity.

Jenny shook her head. "No idea. I took one look at his face, indicated I would go and start the job he had been giving me and left. I fired up the computer, got started, then skedaddled to the loo."

We laughed. "Ah the joys of being a woman."

"Nice to know that most men can still be embarrassed by the 'woman thing'," Jenny agreed.

"What sticks in my craw is when they start going on about something not being a woman's job." Both Prim and Jenny were in that unenviable position. As a humble secretary I hadn't been in competition with the opposite sex.

To calm the waters (as it were!) I put in my tuppence-worth. "What makes me laugh are these men who bitch when we aren't in the mood or say we have a headache." They murmured their agreements and exchanged a smile. They knew what was coming next. "Who is dying of pneumonia after one sneeze?"

211

"Men!!!" we chorused, then toasted them.

Jenny decided against coming out for dinner with us. Well, I didn't blame her. It wouldn't do to be seen socialising with me or with Prim. We bade her farewell with promises to get together again some time.

The scarf? Primrose got that out of her. Chiffon in lime green and purple. Obviously a long one and I'm sure I'd seen one like it somewhere, but couldn't for the life of me remember where.

We had a great weekend. Lymington for dinner that evening and on Sunday we went for a ramble and had a pub lunch then, before she left to go back to London, I let Prim drive the Roller through the village. It gave her a laugh seeing me togged out like Dame Edna, and the few villagers about seeing this gorgeous black girl driving my car had something new to gossip about.

Of course, after she'd left I had time to think: about the money left to the Spencers and about the savings book Dan had placed in Maggie's keeping.

How much money had been in that account? Where had it come from? Which and whose account was it? Dan's and Janet's? Janet's? or Dan's brother's? Someone still unknown? And how could I find out?

And who had I seen with a scarf like the one that had been found around Mrs. Cheetham's neck?

Chapter 30

Well, I didn't have to worry about that for too long. No prizes for guessing who turned up on my doorstep on Monday – in time for lunch. That's right. Steaming.

It was a typical English summer's day – wet and humid, so as I opened the front door he was living up to his name – steaming.

"Why on earth are you wearing a jacket?" I asked.

"Been working, of course," he said pithily as he took it off and draped it over the knob of the newel post. I sighed, removed it and put it on a hanger which I keep conveniently on the clothes rack behind the door.

"Come on. I suppose you know you're in time for lunch." I led the way to the kitchen.

I was going to put a couple of frozen meals in the microwave but he stopped me, "I'll do a trade."

"Okay." Obviously I had an idea what he wanted but wasn't going to give him the satisfaction by asking. Anyway, if he wanted to cook a meal who was I to stop him? Save me organizing something in the evening.

What did he cook? Pork chops and spuds and I did a salad to go with it. We had to finish up with ice-cream – that's all I had for dessert. Of course it brought forth a sarky comment which I refuse to repeat.

And, of course it was me that had to make the coffee and it was then he decided to surprise me – should say that until now our conversation had been mostly about London. Sort of what had I done there which led to a discussion on theater, films and whatnot.

The surprise? He took some papers from his pocket, opened them up and laid them on the table in front of me. Photocopies of Maggie's diary. As I didn't know what I was supposed to know – or not know if it came to it – I just looked at them. Then keeping me face in neutral asked, "Well?"

"Come on, Cleo, I know you didn't send them to me anonymously. Not your style. I'm pretty sure they're copies from Margaret Linley's diary." He paused. "Aren't they?"

"What makes you think I know?"

He sighed. "Cleo, stop ballsing about. They are, aren't they?"

"Yup. But I'm sure Paula wouldn't have sent them. She was going to call you on Friday about them. At least, that's what she said."

"Yeah, well I wasn't around then."

"She still wouldn't have sent them anonymously."

"I agree. But I think Margaret might have."

"That's possible. But I don't understand it. Paula was going to take copies, drop the diary under Margaret's bed and call you. And leave you to sort it out with Margaret," I added with a grin.

"But I wasn't around so perhaps she changed her mind." He then realised what I had said. "Me sort what out?"

"She would give you the photocopies and leave you to get the truth and the diary out of Margaret."

"How does she think I would do that?"

"Dunno, but you told Gerard you've got daughters so presumably she thinks you know how to get around teenagers."

"Humph." I always wondered what that word sounded like – now I know.

"I assume you want to go and see Paula?"

"Of course.

"Want me to give her a bell?"

"Don't bother. I'll go and see her in a minute." He changed tack. "What d'you reckon was really in that envelope?" He nodded at the copies.

"Building Society or bank book," I told him succinctly.

"No proof."

"Come on, love." Wow, did I call him that? "Maggie not stupid. She'll have felt it to make sure. Like we did Christmas presents when we were kids."

"Could have been something that shape and feel but not be a savings book."

"Let's do a 'frinstance'. Say it was. I'm wondering whether it was the one you've already found. The one they found in the flour bin. Say he found it and took it. Janet would know who had it when she couldn't find it."

"How would she get it back?"

"Threaten to tell me about his gambling."

"But they'd both have lost their jobs," he pointed out reasonably but, if I may say for a cop, dumbly.

"She had lots of dosh in another account somewhere. The job didn't matter to her. That's why she broke rules like using my pool at night."

He conceded my point then carried on the 'frinstance'. "Suppose it wasn't that book and was, say, his brother's?"

"His brother was in clink, though, wasn't he?"

"Yeah, but Dan could have had the book and got worried Janet might find it."

"So gave it to Maggie and took it back when his brother came out."

"Which means another session with Brian Spencer." He grimaced.

"Shouldn't be difficult."

He looked grim. "He's skipped."

215

"Gawd give me strength! What on earth do we pay the police for?" I got up and started pacing. "You had him and let him go…"

"We didn't have any reason to hold him longer."

"He's a criminal! Surely you could have found something else to question him about."

When I finished my tirade which, I confess, got a bit lurid, Steaming asked, "D'you think I haven't been thinking those same things? Cleo, we can't hold people indefinitely on suspicion alone. We have to have proof."

I sat down again. "I know. I'm sorry but it just makes me mad. All this pussy-footing around the guilty in case their human rights are violated. Don't matter about the human rights of those they've violated."

"Don't get worked up again, love. It's not worth it. There's nothing we can do about it. Can we get back to the 'frinstance' of the money being Brian's? What I've done is get the team searching his record to see if he was involved in any heists. If he was then the chances are that Margaret could have had his savings book. What I reckon is he could have opened an account before the job and put the money in before he was caught and given the book the Dan."

"Bit stupid that, don't you think?"

"Criminals often are. There is an alternative. He did a big job with a gang and gave the book to whoever was the boss. Once the money was laundered, his share was put in the account and the book sent to Dan for safe keeping."

"I like that one best," I told him.

"Me too. We'll just have to see what the researchers find."

I then reminded him about my call before I went up to town. About Janet's brother, Jack Smith, staying at a B&B in Lymington.

"I left that to Sergeant Wiles to chase up. They went to the B&B and checked the records. Your car salesman was right. He had stayed there several times. I checked it against the dates you gave me of when you were away. They match."

"So she took time off, I guess."

He shrugged. "Possibly."

"Why didn't the owner of the B&B come forward when you put out an appeal?"

"Said Jack Smith wasn't exactly an unusual name and didn't recognize him from the pictures we showed."

I snorted. "More likely didn't want to get involved."

"True. Like your car salesman," he added dryly.

"What does Jack Smith have to say?"

"He was staying there to visit with his sister as Dan and he didn't get on."

"What about the money missing from the building society account?"

"Says he doesn't know anything about that, but that they opened a joint account some time ago when she had a small win on the lottery and didn't want Dan to get his sticky paws on it." He grinned. "I guess the win is the cash out of Dan's and Janet's account. The dates match."

"Hmm. I suppose the other bits and pieces were more lottery wins?"

"His and hers apparently," he said dryly.

"Likely story. Strange a brother and sister having a joint account though."

"You would have thought she'd have put the money into an account in her name only, wouldn't you?"

"She never struck me as being the kind of woman who could be coerced into sharing her money. Brother or no brother," I told him.

217

"I guess we'll just have to believe him when he says they were very close and that she said she wanted his name on the account so that Dan couldn't get to it."

"Almost like a premonition, innit? Except he can't get his hands on it. I suppose all that dosh is now Jack's? If he's innocent," I finished, then asked. "What joy with the village ladies?"

He pursed his lips. "Small bets, nothing worth blackmailing them for."

Damn.

"What about Mrs. Cheetham?"

"What about her?"

"Have you found out about the scarf? Fr'instance," I added with a grin.

He shook his head. "Still no luck."

"I suppose she could have blackmailed it from someone. Or stolen it."

"Back up. How do you know she didn't buy it?"

"As Jenny and I agreed, if you remember, women are either scarf people or not. I'd never seen Mrs. C in a scarf so I'm assuming she didn't buy it."

"Certainly not locally."

"And she never went anywhere else."

"How do you know?"

"She told me she only ever went to Southampton with Bertie. She didn't like it 'cos its big, dirty and noisy."

"You never told me that before."

I shrugged. "Didn't seem relevant. So, how did she get it? And I do wish I knew why she was in my garden."

"Picking the flowers again," he responded sharply.

"I know that, but why? No one knew I was away and the gates were open."

"Maybe someone saw you leave."

218

"Like this is a busy road!"

"You never know. Perhaps Mrs. C had been in the area and hid behind a tree or something and realised you were going away."

"Then what?"

"Hot footed it home to get her gardening things and came back."

"That doesn't work. She wasn't killed the day I left."

"True."

"Anyway, why would she be wearing a dressy scarf?"

"How do you know that?"

"Guesswork. The weather wasn't cold so it wouldn't have been a practical scarf." Oh, well saved, Cleo, I mentally patted myself on the back.

He gave me a suspicious look, then continued with this theory. "Suppose she had been blackmailing someone and they followed her."

"Knowing I was away?"

"Nope. Just followed her out of curiosity and in the hope they could talk to her in private."

"But strangled her instead? Surely she'd have seen that coming."

"Okay so she was picking flowers and didn't hear whoever had followed her."

"Better. But who?" He shrugged. "Anyway, I still want to know why her twins really came to see me and how they knew where I live. Especially as they didn't have the name right. Unless," I added thoughtfully, "the slip up with my name was deliberate."

"We're still following them up."

That told me one thing. They hadn't been at work that day. So where had they been?

Chapter 31

Steaming looked at his watch. "I'd better get moving. Go and see your mate Paula."

"You'd better check she's at home," I warned – too late as he took his mobile out and keyed in her number. Gawd, what a memory! Bet that's helped him get to be Chief Detective Inspector.

Fortunately for Steaming, Paula was in so he took off, but not before inviting me out for dinner that evening. "One proviso, though, it's only on if I don't get called away on an emergency."

"I bet you say that to all the girls!" I retorted before accepting. If he wants to tell his wife he's working that's his affair. I was still trying to find a way to tell him what I'd been up to and suggest the police follow it through. I reckon it'll be easier telling him in public. He'll have to keep his voice down!

After he'd left I got back to thinking about the account Janet opened with her brother. Why on earth did Jack mention it to the police? If he'd kept his mouth shut... Ah. Light dawns. If the police went around the banks and building societies in Lymington they'd have found out anyway. Maybe her brother wasn't so daft after all.

Yes, alright, I'll admit it. I quite fancy Steaming. Don't ask me why 'cos I don't know. When we were kids at Junior School he was as bad as the rest of the boys for teasing the girls – horrible brat. Then in the Seniors, when we were in our teens, he'd sometimes stick up for me. But I never went out with him.

I left school before he did, then his father's firm moved so they left London. I occasionally saw him before his gran died – she wouldn't leave Plaistow. Once she died that was it. Never saw or heard about him until he turned up here.

Yeah, I guess we've both changed a lot. I might never have been married but that doesn't mean I don't know nothing. You know. I'm "experienced" as they say. Before AIDs that is. I've kind of gone celibate now. Actually it isn't so bad as my hormones don't screw up the rest of my life.

I remember shocking the other secretaries at work once when I said I'd rather have an affair with a happily married man.

Think about it. Less chance of infections, no man hanging around the place and none of his laundry. Just the fun without ties or worry.

Actually I was only kidding anyway. No way would I want to be the reason a marriage breaks up.

Which brings me back to Steaming. His real name? George. We also called him Georgie-Porgy.

Over dinner at a pub in the depths of the forest – I couldn't have found it in daylight with a map! – I discovered how much Steaming had changed.

"George…"

He pointed his empty fork at me, "David."

"Eh?"

"When we moved and I went to another school I decided to use my second name. Nothing I can do to stop the Steaming, but it did stop Georgie-Porgy."

"Okay. I can live with that. When you come to think about it, kids are cruel buggers, aren't they?"

"Not 'arf. So, what were you going to say?" He turned back to his venison.

"I was going to ask what happened at Paula's. Did she know that Maggie had sent you the photocopies?"

"Nope. She's still got the copies she took so we think Maggie took copies and sent them."

"Good kid. Trouble in the teens is that you don't fit your hormones."

"Tell me about it! Remember my kid sister Lynette?"

"Yeah."

"Pregnant at sixteen."

"No! What did your parents do?"

"Dad had his usual rant and rave, Mum cried, but they came through. She got married in her twenties to a good chap who adopted Marina."

"And it's all worked?"

"Sure. He's in insurance. Not a cop."

I digested that last comment. It made me wonder. I decided to test the water, "How many daughters you got?"

That stopped him stuffing his face. "How d'you know about them?"

"Paula. You told Gerard, remember?"

"Oh, yeah. Two." He took out his wallet and showed me a picture of them. One dark like her Dad. The other one had gingery hair, freckles and teeth. Not pretty – yet. She might grow into those teeth.

"Nice." I pointed to freckles. "Like her Mum?"

"A bit."

Why did I feel let down? I'd already known he was married. He must have seen something in my face because he reached over and took my hand. "I'm divorced. Few police marriages seem to work these days."

I turned my hand and clasped his, "I'm sorry, David."

He shrugged. "It happens and it's better for the children not to have to witness rows and take sides. Chris

222

and I are still friends so I get to see the girls whenever I want."

"What are their names?"

"Tony – short for Antonia. She's fourteen. And Helena. She's eleven."

We chatted about the girls for a while. He obviously adores them. Eventually the meal finished and, coffee drunk, we left.

As we drew up outside my place I asked (feeling like a stupid teenager), "Nightcap or more coffee?"

He gave me his lopsided grin, eyes twinkling. "I thought you'd never ask."

Inside as I was taking off my jacket he helped, hung it up then, before I could walk away, put his hands on my shoulders and turned me towards him.

Yeah, we kissed. It was a bit tentative at first – was he as nervous as me? You betcher!

Well, one thing led to another and we never did make it to the kitchen or the living room.

Was I glad I'd tidied up the bedroom before going out! Mind you it didn't stay tidy for long as various bits of clothing were dropped or went flying across the room.

Amazingly for a first time it was wonderful, as if we'd been made for each other. He knew exactly what turns me on and I seemed to know what he likes. And he has my dream body – firm, not too muscle-y and not too hairy.

As we were both hot for each other the first time was passionate and quick, but later we were able to take it nice and slowly and enjoy each other's bodies.

Needless to say, I did not get around to telling him about my researches into the old ladies the Spencers had worked for. It wasn't exactly pillow talk so I'd have to find another

223

opportunity. I did not look forward to it, but then men can be like teenagers and surprise you, can't they?

Chapter 32

Why are men so stupid and go and spoil everything? There we were in the kitchen after a great night and he goes and gets all unreasonable.

All I was trying to do was help.

Oh yeah, and confess before he found out. Well, I thought (like you do) that after a night of my company he'd be in a good mood.

What had surprised me – slopping about in a wrap – was that he turned up in the kitchen showered, shaved and dressed!

"Wow, I am honoured. Don't often have brekkers with a well-dressed man!"

"Don't often have brekkers with a man. Full stop!" he retorted and I batted him on the head as I passed behind him. He was already sitting at the table that's how I reached. "Ow! Lucky for me I keep razor etcetera and a change of clothes in the car."

"For instances such as this," I retorted.

"No, for nights when I get called out. Don't have to go home before going to the office."

"Don't you keep spares in the office?"

"As well."

"Right little boy scout, you are."

Eventually I got around to it. Being brave. "David, have you thought about an old lady's relative offing Janet? Or having her offed. You know, the oldies they've worked for in the past."

"Uh-huh." Well? How uncommunicative. Did he mean yes or no?

"Well, what I thought…"

He finished crunching the toast. "I know what you think, Cleo." He leaned across the table and stared deep into my eyes. I felt myself go red. (I used to do that at school whenever teacher asked a culprit to own up. Guess who got punished for doing nothing?) "What have you been up to? Come on."

"Well,…" I gulped then told him, omitting Prim's name.

I certainly wasn't prepared for the explosion that followed.

"You stupid cow!" He stood up, pushing back the chair. "Don't you realise you could ruin the investigation? Even ruin a case for the prosecution!" He'd now reached the back door where he turned and pointed a finger at me. "Don't you dare do anything else like that. Now or in the future. You hear?" I nodded, he opened the door and steamed out.

I'll keep my mouth shut in future. He can sort out his own crimes. Miserable bastard.

Of course, by the time I had had a soak, played the piano and chatted on the phone to Paula, I felt a bit better. Not enough to forgive him. No way. And I came to a decision.

Go away for a holiday. He could like it or lump it. I decided to take a cruise, then he couldn't get hold of me. And I had a one of my brainstorms. I called Prim to see if she could get time off to join me. We get on well and it would be nice to have company for a change. And I thought she deserved a decent holiday.

"If you can get time off how long d'you think you can be gone for?"

"Slow down, Cleo. You call me up out of the blue and ask about my holiday allowance. Why? Thinking of inviting me to spend it in the New Forest?"

"Nope. Fancy a Caribbean cruise?"

"A what? Are you out of your mind? You've got to be joking. I'd love to go on a Caribbean cruise but there's no way I can afford it."

"You don't have to. My treat."

"Oh, now, come on, Cleo..."

"No arguments. I want to go on a Caribbean cruise and I want company. I like you. We get on okay. And I can afford it. If you want you can look on it as my lottery gift."

That silenced her. I could picture her frowning as she persuaded herself to accept. "Okay. You're on."

"Great! So, how long can we be gone for?"

"Let's check my diary. Nothing I can't put off. The dentist can wait. I've got sixteen days left this year. I'll try to get them, if not it'll have to be fourteen."

"Allowing for flight times I guess we'll look for a ten night cruise."

"No, listen. Its number of days not counting weekends," she reminded me. "Even if I can only get fourteen days we still have time for a fourteen night cruise."

"You're right. When can you let me know? I'd like to go as soon as and need to call the travel agent."

"I'll try to get back to you today. Okay?"

"Okay!"

"Yer ready fer tea?" Mrs. Walsh popped her head around the door. I'd been so wrapped up in dreams of a cruise that I hadn't heard her arrive.

"Always. I'll come and have it with you in the kitchen." Mind you, I'd have to put up with the smell of bleach, which makes the tea taste ghastly. She always does the kitchen and bathrooms first using a ton of bleach. Makes me wonder whether she's got shares in the company!

"Should tell you," I began as I sat down and she poured out, "I'm hoping to go away for a couple of weeks."

"Will the perlice letcha?"

"How can they stop me? I'm not a suspect or anything."

"True." She pursed her lips. "Reckon as how yer need a 'oliday. Where're yer goin'?"

"Caribbean cruise, if I can. I've just been talking to a friend to see if she wants to come."

"The young lady what was 'ere at the weekend?"

Told you she knows all the news even though she didn't, to my knowledge, see Primrose.

"That's right. She works for a national newspaper."

"Seckertary?"

"No, reporter. I've known her for some years." Before she went into cross-examination mode, I changed the subject. "It would be nice if, before I go away, the police would solve the crimes."

"I bin thinking about Mrs. Cheetham."

Was this two minds thinking alike? I'd deliberately joined her in the kitchen because I wanted to talk about Mrs. C. Mrs. Walsh obviously knows a lot about the village and, I hope, would let me know which ladies are into scarves.

"Me too. I'm puzzled about the scarf. She didn't seem the sort to wear one."

"In the winter she did."

I grinned, "Don't we all! When I found her picking flowers she wasn't wearing one, just that floppy cotton hat.

228

Let's face it, a long scarf would get in the way." Knowing Mrs. Walsh wasn't daft, I assumed she had already guessed it had been a long scarf.

"That's what I've bin thinking. Even if someone give 'er a scarf I can't see 'er wearing it in your garding. Going to the shops, maybe."

"I don't recall seeing any of the ladies wearing scarves. Not when I've been to the shops or at the WI meeting I went to."

She thoughtfully sipped her coffee. "Well, there's a thing. The only ones I c'n think of are Mrs. Jessop and Mzz Henderson. She insists on using 'er own name instead of 'er 'usband's," she added disgustedly, from which I gathered they are young women. "They both work in hotels and wear suits and them funny little scarf things."

"Cravats." Obviously a pair of receptionists.

"That what they call 'em?" Sniff. "Either give 'em a tie or a proper bow."

Oops, shades of Maggie Thatcher blouses. You know, those ones with the extended collar that tied into a floppy bow.

"So no one in the village is big on scarves?"

"I didn't say that. I think when some of them go to town," I assume she means Southampton, "they posh up in suits and sometimes use a scarf. Fer decoration."

I decided I'd need to ask Paula. Which, when you think about it is a good idea. She can get talking to them more easily than me and find out if anyone has or had a green and purple scarf.

Coffee finished I left Mrs. Walsh to get on with her job and shut myself in the office to call Paula.

Having told her about the possibility of going on the cruise I then broached the subject of the scarf.

229

"I probably shouldn't tell you this so don't let it go any further, it was a green and purple one."

"Oh. How did you find that out? Have the police shown it to you?"

"No. Primrose and I got a bit sneaky at the weekend and invited Jenny Dixon over for a swim.

Paula laughed. "I only hope your detective friend doesn't find out."

Me too! Actually I liked the detective-friend bit. She should know! I'm not going to tell her yet as it might now turn out that that was a one night stand.

"Hopefully he won't. I've been trying to work out where the scarf came from. Mrs. Walsh tells me Mrs. Cheetham didn't wear fancy scarves."

"No, she didn't. I presume you want me to do a bit of gossiping to find out who has lost a scarf?"

"Please, but do be careful and discreet as I'm sure the police have been asking around."

"Which gives me the perfect sympathetic 'Lady of the Manor' approach," she pointed out.

Our conversation then turned to generalities before we finally rang off. And, of course, Mrs. Walsh wanted to clean the study.

Prim eventually called back to say she could get the time off so I contacted my travel agent and we're leaving on Thursday for Miami. I managed to get two decent sized state rooms with balconies (you don't think I do my sunbathing in public do you?). What Prim doesn't know is that we're flying first class. I know I can rely on her to be properly dressed.

With luck, by the time we get back David will have solved the murders, but I don't think my luck is that good at the moment.

The cruise was fabulous. The food, entertainment and crew were superb. We took tours at all of the islands wherever the ship docked. Sometimes together, but often separately so we could compare notes. Of course Prim chose some scuba diving and I picked the lazier ones.

In Jamaica we had a fantastic time as some of Prim's relatives met us at the ship, showed us around and threw a party.

And, yes, of course, we did discuss the murders. A bit difficult not to really.

One afternoon when we were shade-bathing on my balcony Prim brought up the subject of my research into the old ladies.

"You know, Cleo, I really think Steaming went over the top."

"Not really. Once I'd calmed down and thought about it I could see his point of view."

"You didn't do anything to compromise the case, as he said," she insisted. "What you did was what most people would have done in the circumstances."

"You think?"

"Of course. Your housekeeper and her husband are murdered so, of course, you want to know more about them."

"That's stretching it a bit," I smiled ruefully.

"Yeah, well. Do you want to know what I really think?"

"No, but I'm sure you're going to tell me."

"He was scared that you might get hurt."

No, I haven't told Prim either. As I didn't have an answer to that I merely shrugged.

My mistake. Prim isn't stupid.

She sat up and turned to look at me. "You haven't! You have!"

"What?"

"I thought you didn't get involved with married men."

"I don't." I hoped that would shut her up.

"He's divorced." She grinned. "I'm thrilled you've got it together."

"Can I remind you why we've come away?"

Of course she wasn't going to leave it at that and teased me periodically about David.

It seemed we'd hardly had time to bat our eyelids at all of the officers before we were heading home.

There I found the red light on the answerphone was doing its nut. The first message was from Steaming. Of course. Well, what I'd done was leave a message for him – from the airport – to tell him I was going on the cruise. But not which one or when I'd be back.

The second message was from Steaming. The third message was from Steaming. You get the idea. Not a happy man. Good.

It wasn't until I was in my bedroom unpacking that I realised something. Something that scared the hell out of me. The room had been searched! Very carefully – but searched. Like things on the dressing table not quite where I'd put them. A drawer not quite shut. Oh I knew Mrs. Walsh would have been in to clean up but she's always very precise about everything.

I went down to the kitchen and got a pair of rubber gloves then walked through all of the rooms. Yes.

232

Definitely. I shuddered. Then I went to check the alarm –
I'd turned it off as soon as I came in, of course. I did all the
things you do – it wasn't working. Some bastard had
disabled it.

Chapter 33

Good job it had been an overnight flight and that I'd slept. First of all I called the alarm company to get someone out ASAP, then I rang Paula. She wasn't in but Mrs. Walsh was there.

"Mrs. Walsh. It's Miss Marjoribanks."

"Oh, hello. Didja have a nice time?"

"Lovely, thanks. Don't get offended because I don't mean no harm, but when did you last do my place?"

"Why? Did I miss something?"

"No. Nothing like that. I just need to know." I didn't want to tell her. Not a case of not frightening the horses but I didn't want the news all over the village. At least, not yet.

"I come in on Wednesday morning like we agreed."

"That's fine, Mrs. Walsh. Thanks. Can you ask Mrs. Linley to ring me when she gets back?"

We rang off. Oh well, get it over with, Cleo, I thought. Yeah, I rang Steaming who thought I was calling to apologize.

"Cleo, where the hell have you been?"

"Like my message said. On a Caribbean cruise. I'm back now," I hurried on, scarcely pausing for breath, "and my place has been gone through."

"Do what?"

"Someone's disabled the alarm and been in here since Wednesday when the cleaning lady came in."

"My God! What's been taken?"

"Far as I can tell, nothing."

"They vandalised it?"

"Nope. Just someone very careful. Like a criminal what knows what he's doing."

"Brian Spencer," he responded flatly.

234

"Don't you think?"

"Don't touch anything. I'll be there as soon as I can with a team."

He thinks I'm stoopid?

Of course there weren't any fingerprints. While SOCOs did the necessary (again) Steaming and I went for lunch – at a pub of course. And after chatting in his car I apologized. So did he. No, we didn't kiss – with all them eyes around?

With autumn upon us the sun was shining and it was just like mid-summer's supposed to be. Just as well as it meant we could sit outside in the pub garden and get more privacy for our chat.

"Any ideas what Brian would have been looking for?" David asked, taking a draught of his beer.

"His bank book, I reckon." And took a sip of wine.

"Or something of Dan's."

"But why turn over the house?"

"Couldn't find it in the flat."

That stopped me chewing. "Oh Gawd. I never thought of that."

He smiled reassuringly. "I did and they'll check it out."

I heaved a sigh of relief. "At least it'll make sure he's not set up camp there."

"Yeah, but it'd be nice to know where he's hiding out."

"Come on! You're the cop. With all this forest around? Can't be difficult to find somewhere to camp."

"True. And even if he didn't know the forest before, he's now had time to get to know it pretty well."

"D'you reckon Jack Smith might have chummed up with him?"

"Thought about it but nah, don't think so. After all they're probably both after the same thing."

"All the more reason to get together I would have thought."

"My guess is Jack wants to guard what he's already legally got. He won't want to share it with his sister's brother-in-law."

I ruminated on that for a bit. "Perhaps you're right. So, say, Brian's looking for that book."

"Yeah." He gave me a questioning look.

"It's not in the flat – you've searched that pretty thoroughly." I said tactfully. "So maybe it was in the house."

"And if it wasn't?"

"Then it's somewhere else. Where did Dan sometimes go?"

"Bookmakers."

Saints preserve me! Why are men so dense? "No, dummy. He used to meet Maggie in that copse where I found her when she fell off Star. Want me to take you?"

"Before or after coffee?"

"Before. Hopefully before Brian Spencer thinks of it."

"He may not even know about Maggie. At least, I hope not otherwise he might try and get at her."

"Don't put ideas in my head. Anyway, she's at boarding school through the week."

"What about weekends?"

"If she's out she's usually on the horse so if he approached her she could get away," I pointed out. I was just glad he didn't say anything about Brian Spencer possibly having a gun. Thinking about it was bad enough.

But to get back to our search of the copse. Although David had laughed when I appeared in a gaudy top, khaki

236

knee-length shorts, knee high socks and walking shoes (don't care what I look like do I?), now he saw why. At least once we reached the pub I had removed the top and he could see the shirt. It would have been no good trying to tramp through the woods in a caftan now would it?

We searched high and low – literally – looking for a hiding place. Would you believe I even hoisted David up so he could look and feel around in a hole in a tree? That was the only way we could do it. Mind you, he did manage to grab a branch once we'd got him high enough, which helped. But we must have looked a right silly sight!

Nothing nowhere. Oh well, it was a thought.

"Sorry, David," I apologized as we made our way back to his car. "I'm afraid you've messed up your shirt and shoes a bit."

"Not for the first time," he confessed. "As Gran used to say, it'll all come out in the wash."

"Popular saying in Plaistow."

"Yeah. Now let's get back to your place and see how SOCOs have done."

"If they've finished one of the bathrooms you can get cleaned up."

"Ta."

And, as I said, they found nothing. Niente. But Steaming did arrange for regular patrols at night. And the burglar alarm was working again.

Eventually I was left in peace to do the unpacking and get some laundry started. I then poured out a large Scotch and headed for my bathroom. Bliss.

Having eaten at lunchtime I only wanted a salad in the evening so before getting that ready I called Prim.

"Just wanted to make sure you got home okay."

"Of course. I was probably home before you."

"You never know with public transport. Can't understand why you didn't use a cab."

"To cross London?" she reminded me.

"Yeah. I suppose you've got your laundry done and everything?"

"Yup. All ready for work tomorrow, and I've been out for lunch with one of my contacts."

"Contacts?"

"Yup. One of Ros's work-mates. Seems like Ros is into scarves and, wait for this…," she paused.

"Waiting."

"She wasn't at work the day her mother was killed. Supposedly they went to their grandmother's funeral." She paused again.

"There's more, isn't there?"

"You bet. They don't have any grandmothers. Apparently they both died some years ago."

"So where was Ros?"

"Exactly. Did she come down to Hampshire?"

"She could easily have done so, followed her mother to my place and, Bob's-your-uncle."

"Be interesting to find out."

"Have you called Steaming to tell him?"

"Nope. I thought you might like to tell him."

"Coward!"

"Not really. It's just that I thought you might want an excuse to call him."

"With the number of messages on the machine from him I didn't need an excuse."

"So you've spoken to him already?"

"Had lunch with him."

"Oh good, you've made up."

238

"You could say that." I then gave her a run down – without naming names – on what had happened.

"Oh, Cleo. You must come up to town and stay here until the police find whoever did that."

"Have to confess that was my first reaction but why should I be scared out of my home?"

"Cleo! Listen, love, no one's going to think you're a wimp."

"I know. Not that I care if they do…"

She chuckled. "No, I guess not. Well, you be careful and make sure that alarm is on."

No sooner had I put the phone down than it rang. Paula.

"What were the police doing out at your place, Cleo?" Before I could answer she rushed on, "Mrs. Walsh left your message and one of her own."

Repeat performance. I managed to divert her from inviting me to stay with them by telling her about the cruise and finished, "I don't suppose you've had any luck over the business of the scarves, have you?"

"Oh yes, it worked. One of the WI ladies has lost a green and purple scarf. She told me a little while ago so I've given her your detective's telephone number and told her to call and tell him. I told her I thought she ought to in case it was important, but probably wasn't relevant to the case."

Clever Paula. Don't want to frighten the natives.

By which time jet lag was beginning to come over me. Eat, drink and bed was the order of the evening.

I can't believe I overslept! Good job my time's my own. Mind you, there was no problem with filling the time. Both cars needed washing. Yeah, I know I could have taken

239

them to the car wash, but would you have put my Roller through one of them drive through things? Used to scare the hell out of me when that drier bar came down and towards the windscreen. I was always afraid it'd forget to go back up and was ready to throw myself down across the front seats!

I got my babies out of the garage, found the hose and the car cleaning bits and set to work. To be perfectly honest, I enjoyed it. As it was an Indian Summer I put on shorts and tee-shirt, got thoroughly soaked but it didn't matter. Once I'd done the outsides I took a break to dry off and change into dry clothes before tackling the insides which were quite easy – duster and vacuum.

Now, don't ask me why I did it but I decided to check the glove box in the Roller. I suppose my subconscious reminded me that as Dan had acted as chauffeur he might have put a couple of bits of his in there.

Of course he had. And you'll never guess what I found under the maps and other bits of junk!

Chapter 34

"What do you mean, calm down?" I was only a little excited. "I'm okay, but aren't you just a little bit excited that we've found another piece of the puzzle?"

David sighed. "Yes, I'm pleased. But, Cleo, it doesn't solve the whole crime."

We were in his office and on the desk between us was a bank book in the name of Brian Spencer. Yup. What I found in the Roller. If I'd looked properly before instead of just the usual rummaging or grabbing packets of tissues out of it we might have found the answer sooner. Needless to say I'd put the car away, showered, changed, and belted up to Southampton in the Land Rover to deliver the book. I could have phoned him from home but I'd wanted to see the expression on his face when I handed it over. Nothing. What a disappointment.

"Go on, open it up."

He did. "Three hundred and forty-two thousand and twenty-eight pence. Hmm. Obviously proceeds of a crime."

"And why he's searched my place looking for it."

"Yeah. We'll definitely be keeping a close eye on your place. In fact, I think Jenny ought to come and stay with you again. Better still, Jenny stays there and you go up to town."

"David! I can look after myself."

"Cleo, I don't want you in any danger. Gawd, if anything 'appened I'd never forgive meself." Oops he must be worried he's going cockney.

I sat and looked at him. I don't want to miss out on any excitement. And I might actually miss him!

"Please, Cleo."

"Oh, alright, but I've got to go back to the house to get some things."

"Promise me you'll go up to town?"

"Yeah. When I know what train I'm on I'll call you. Will that do?"

He smiled and I have to confess when he does that it knocks me socks off. I'd give him anything.

"Want the spare keys?" I grinned as I delved into me bag searching for them.

"If you can find them," he teased.

I did and held them up. He reached for them and I tweaked them away. "I want a reward first."

He thought he knew what I meant. "Not in the office, Cleo, someone might come in." He was horrified. Trust a man to get it all wrong.

"A kiss, stoopid."

That was okay. He came around the desk as I stood up. Yes, very nice and no one came in so we didn't have to jump apart looking guilty. Before letting me go he murmured, "I reckon I'll have to come up to town as well."

"You better."

I managed to persuade myself to leave and headed back to Trewith Green.

Did I say I wanted excitement? No, I'm not talking about me and David. It began when I got home.

As I turned into the drive I saw a battered BMW on the driveway. Never seen it before and didn't think any more of it. I pulled up behind it. By the way, it's a double driveway that circles round in front of the house. Important point that.

Anyway, I opened the door of the Rover and heard someone coming from round by the garages. I quickly shut and locked the door with me inside, of course, which was just as well. It was Brian Spencer. He came charging round the corner of the house, got into the BMW and bombed off down the drive. Well, not exactly sped, but you know what I mean.

Took me by surprise so it was a few seconds before I switched on the engine and got started again. As I followed him out of the gate and to the left a flash of yellow passed me, braked, turned into the driveway and eventually caught up with me – Prim on a surprise visit. Wonder what she wants?

No time to think about that. Having led us on a bit of a dance the BMW did an about face (clever clogs isn't he with a handbrake turn?). As he passed me Brian gave me a vee sign which I returned. Prim followed me up and she later told me, also gave him the finger and apologised for not trying to stop him. "His car would have made mine a heap of scrap metal." Not to say endangered her life.

We made our turns using a convenient lay-by and were again in pursuit. I think Brian must have forgotten he'd have to slow down going through the village because of the bumps in the road (called "sleeping policemen" of all daft names) so we caught up with him. Once through the village we put our feet down and, would you believe that Paula (in her Toyota) was just coming out of her driveway? Yup, she followed Prim.

We must have been a funny sight. A worse-for-wear BMW, a new Land Rover, a yellow Mini, and a staid Toyota.

He led us a merry dance up and down narrow twisty country lanes, across open moorland, down through Lymington – that slowed us a bit – along the coast road towards Christchurch then back up into the forest.

Lymington was an obstacle course with pedestrian crossings, traffic lights, buses, jay walkers, other drivers. Sometimes Brian got ahead, only to be caught by one of the hazards and I'd catch up to him only to have the hazard clear and away he went. Sometimes he and I would be well ahead of the others. Talk about nerve-wracking. And can you tell me where the police are when you need them? Not a sign, not a sniff. Ironically it didn't seem as if the bystanders even realised what was happening.

So here we were with more twisty lanes but no slow traffic such as a tractor. No flocks of sheep, no ponies, donkeys, deer or cattle. Has Mother Nature given them radar to keep them out of the way I ask myself?

As we come up onto moorland again I notice a figure on horseback. Maggie on Star? Then, in the rear view mirror, I see we've lost Paula – we're going uphill at this stage. Perhaps she's just stopped to call the cops or given up or run out of petrol.

I was wrong. She'd found another route. As we rounded a bend I could see her drive straight out of a side road in front of the BMW which swerved across the road, hit a log which stove in the wing – straight into a wheel. Bingo!

Brian dove out of the car and started running but Maggie had that bit under control. She headed Star towards him.

By this time we were all out of our cars and giving chase. As Star closed up on him I realised he had a knife in his hand. Everything then happened at once.

Paula and I yelled, "Watch out!" Star reared and Prim made a flying tackle and brought him down (did I tell you she plays rugby?). I sat on him – obvious choice. Paula kicked the knife out of reach and sat on his head. Prim sat on his legs. Maggie and Star circled. Brian Spencer knew he couldn't get away.

And that's when the police arrived. Prim and Paula had both called.

What a day! After the police had finished with us we stopped off in Lymington for afternoon tea. Maggie had a friend living nearby who looked after Star for her.

"Who's going first?" I asked looking at my gang. I'm sure my eyes were glittering as much as theirs. They chorused "You!" Prim adding, "You started it."

"Okay." So I told them what had happened right from my return from the cruise. When I got to the bit about Brian's bank book Maggie said, "So Dan lied. That bank book he gave me to look after was probably Brian's."

"Yup," I agreed, thinking, but not about whose money it was, and Paula kept her mouth shut. After all, we weren't supposed to know what she was talking about, but Maggie gave me a knowing look. I ignored it and continued to where Prim had joined the chase. "What are you doing down here?" I looked at her over the top of my glasses.

"A rumour. We got a tip off at work that an ex-con who had been in on a big job was in this area. I put two and two together and managed to get the job."

"Good timing. A crime reporter catching the criminal. Paula, your turn."

"I was going to go to the village but just joined the chase. I called the police at that last hold-up in Lymington but didn't realise we were going back into the forest. I think the police looked for us along the Christchurch Road."

We all giggled. "Margaret?" I even remembered she didn't like being called Maggie.

245

"I was out riding and Mum called me from the car so I came over that way."

"And did we all enjoy ourselves?" I asked, smiling at them. We raised our cups and agreed it had been fun and, as we'd caught Brian Spencer, rewarding.

The police might be a bit miffed but we didn't care.

Prim stayed the night and made use of my computer to e-mail her report to the paper. I don't know how she did it, but all the while she was driving in the chase she had dictated what was happening. Apparently she's got a voice-activated tape recorder. Oh, alright, audiotape. Or whatever.

And David steamed up – of course. Wanting the story first hand. Once Prim and me had finished he said to her, "Thanks for the info from the paper."

"S'alright," she shrugged. "Just doing my job."

"No point in asking you not to tell your paper what's happened?"

"Right. As they say, too late!"

He sighed - what no steaming? "I thought as much. The sergeant who interviewed you should have told you not to report it yet."

"Sorry, St….., David," she apologised, trying to look innocent. We all knew she'd known that but what's a working girl to do? And she did manage to stop herself from calling him Steaming.

"At least you've now got an handle on where that money come from," I pointed out to him.

"And I've stopped the paper mentioning the bank book," he admitted with a grin.

Prim stood up and stretched. "I'm going for a swim to get the kinks out. Anyone else?"

We decided not to. Once we knew she was in the pool David and I headed for my bathroom Jacuzzi – so what's new?

"Sorry I can't spend the night, old love, but I've got to get back to work," he whispered in my ear before getting out of bed later that night.

"Okay," I mumbled and went back to sleep thinking it was a good job the guess suite was some distance away as we had been quite noisy!

Prim persuaded her boss that she ought to stay in Trewith Green as it looked like things might be hotting up. I think what swung it was the fact that the paper wouldn't have to pay for hotel accommodation!

Chapter 35

The next morning we strolled down to the village, ostensibly to do some shopping.

"By the way, Cleo, I'm bringing this with me," Prim held out the voice-activated recorder as we turned out onto the road.

I grinned, "Don't trust your memory?"

"It's easier than trying to make notes as we walk along," she retorted and switched on the recorder. "Where did you first meet Mrs. Cheetham?"

"As Paula and I were walking to a WI meeting, the day after I found Janet. She came up to us and introduced herself."

"Nothing more?"

"Nope. I didn't encourage her and managed to avoid her when we were in the hall."

"When was the next time you saw her?"

"One day when I was walking to the village she appeared out of this turning on the left."

"What's down there?"

"Houses, so she could have been visiting someone."

"Or waiting for you and just pretending to have visited."

"Right, but what still puzzles me about that is why she was waiting for me. How did she know I was going to the shops?"

"Guesswork. She may have waited other times and just got lucky this time. What was your conversation about?"

"To be perfectly honest, I really don't know. After she had commiserated with me about Janet and about living alone, she waffled on about things in the village, but I wasn't listening."

"How far did she walk with you?"

"To just past The Crescent. That's coming up on the right. We'd crossed over onto the pavement and two ladies were chatting outside the General Store. She said she had something to do, turned around and went down The Crescent."

"Why would she go down there?"

"She lives down there, but I didn't know that at the time."

"Do you know the house?"

"Yup. I dropped her off there once when I gave her a lift from Lymington."

"Can we go and look?"

"Of course." Being interviewed by the press was as hard as by the police! And I hadn't remembered anything else, which had actually been the reason for the exercise.

Talk about a surprise as we approached the Cheetham residence. Ros was tidying up the front garden.

"Good morning, Miss Cheetham," I greeted her cheerily as Prim tucked the recorder into the pocket of her jeans. I did wonder if she had left it on.

"Good morning, Miss Marjoribanks," Ros said as she stood up and came to the front gate. "Did you want something?"

"No, dear, just passing. My friend and I are out for a walk. How is everything?" I had no intention of introducing Prim in case any of Ros's friends had mentioned her.

"Slowly. I'm on some holiday time at the moment and thought I'd come and try to start cleaning this place up. As we don't yet have Probate we can't put it on the market."

"Difficult for you, especially when you have your own place to look after," I sympathized. "Is you brother coming down at the weekend to give you a hand?"

"Hopefully, yes. I'm also hoping his girlfriend will come with him. Mum really let this place go. Everything needs a coat of paint."

"Sounds like a case of all hands on deck. Well, I'll wish you luck. Bye."

We wandered off in silence which Prim eventually broke. "That answers one question."

"What's that?"

"They aren't a Greek tragedy."

It took a moment for the penny to drop. Rob has a girlfriend who isn't his sister. I had to stop and laugh. That was something that hadn't occurred to me. Prim soon joined in the laughter and any neighbours peeping through the net curtains must have thought we were crazy. Two grown women hanging onto a garden wall and laughing until tears poured down our cheeks.

"Come on," I panted, "before they call the men in white coats to lock us up."

We started our ramble again, punctuated with bouts of giggles. I wonder why it is that sometimes a fairly innocuous comment can set one off like that?

"Incidentally, Cleo, did you notice that none of the neighbours has flowers in their front gardens?"

"D'you reckon Mrs. C. used to help herself so they stopped growing them?"

"That would be my guess."

Mine too.

As we came out of the other end of The Crescent Prim asked, "Where does Paula live?"

I pointed down to the right, "About half a mile down there."

"So the first time you met Mrs. C. you were walking along here and the second time was at the other side of the village."

"Right, and as I didn't know she lived in The Crescent...."

"Would have been a puzzle. Can we go over and stroll through the graveyard? I love reading some of those old stones. They can be quite funny."

That's what we did and I told her about the church, the school and the War Memorial.

Eventually we reached the General Store and if I had thought it was going to be a quick in and out job I was mistaken.

There were several ladies in there and they had heard about our car chase and wanted to hear first hand. So we told them, which gave them a good laugh.

"I saw you all drive by but didn't think anything of it," Mrs. Lawrence told us. (In case I haven't mentioned it before, she's one of the owners and sometimes works the till). "You weren't exactly speeding by," she explained.

"Can you imagine trying to speed through the village, what with the speed bumps, the corner and the memorial?" I asked generally and there was a nodding of heads.

"Mind you, drunks and teenagers try it," someone pointed out.

I will leave it to your imagination as to some of the results.

As nothing seemed to be happening, the next day Prim went back to London. Probably as well as I don't think she could have persuaded her boss otherwise.

For something to do I then joined the Women's Institute, which is a good way to get accepted in the village.

At my first visit as a member I got talking to a pair of delightful old ladies whose memories of the village as it used to be are fabulous. I'll definitely be chatting some more with them, but something they said that day got my brain working.

"You'd think that now things are better in the Country that services would be better, wouldn't you?" Mrs. Chandler said rhetorically. Mrs. Paine nodded in agreement. "They're worse than they was after the war."

"When you would expect them to be bad," was my contribution.

"Yerse, but they're not. Them politicians don't know ordinary life," Mrs. Chandler confirmed one of my beliefs. "Fancy the post office leaving the village."

I didn't think it was worthwhile pointing out that that wasn't he fault of the politicians.

"That's right," agreed her friend. "We have to go to Lyndhurst to get our pensions now."

"Does someone give you a life?" I asked.

"No. We gets the early but there and if we don't see someone for a lift back we gets a taxi."

Oh, wow, I thought. Old age pensions are stingy enough without having the old things pay for taxis to get their pittance!

"What we needs is a bus. Even a small one," Mrs. Chandler told me.

Was it my imagination or was she giving me a meaningful look? Maybe she's a White Witch because I had the right thought.

"If the village had a mini-bus it could get people to and from the other towns as well."

"S'right, Mrs. M. That's what we need."

Later at home I planned out something along the lines of getting a mini-bus and giving it to the village. Driver? Maybe someone currently unemployed could take the PSV (Public Service Vehicle) test and be the driver.

I'll need to discuss it first with Paula and Gerard as this is their "Manor", then chat with my solicitor and financial chap. Perhaps we can set up a Trust. Or something.

Oh yeah, David and I had a weekend in London.

Apart from the obvious, we got in a concert and on Sunday morning strolled the deserted streets of the City admiring architecture, criticizing the glass and concrete monstrosities, laughing at the 'gherkin' (a glass edifice supposedly shaped like that vegetable but frequently called something else!) and finding hidden corners. We ended up having a late lunch at St. Katharine's Dock - at the Dickens Inn, an old, old brewery that was moved from its original site when St. Katharine's was turned from proper docks and warehouses into a tourist area.

During the weekend we tried not to discuss the murders. Any time one of us began to say something the other did or said something distracting. Not too difficult when you are indoors with your lover! The problem was when we were out. Especially when David realised that, whenever there were other women about, I was checking out what they were wearing. Of course I was doing it deliberately in an attempt to goad him into telling me about the scarf!

"Good try, love," he smiled at me fondly. "Nope, not telling."

"Sure your Gran wouldn't want you to tell me?"

"Positive sure, cross me 'eart and 'ope ter die, as we used to say."

"Oh well," I sighed. "What're we goin' to do now?"

"I could throw you across the table and have my way with you," he grinned evilly.

As we were in a posh restaurant I knew my answer, "Garn! Dare you!"

He suddenly stood up and for a moment I really thought he was going to. He took one look at the expression on my fact, sat down and laughed. I did too.

"Cleo, my love, you really did think for a few seconds that I'd do it."

"Daft, innit?" I agreed. "Taxi?"

"Best idea." No, not for sex, but to get us back to the flat. Then sex.

Later I played the piano for bit while David relaxed on the sofa. When I played the last chord he said, "I remember that."

"Fur Elise, by Beethoven."

He grinned, "That's right. Didn't your Mum call it 'Furry Knees'?"

"Yeah. Right punster she was," I grinned at this fond memory of Mum and joined him on the sofa. He put an arm around my shoulders and I snuggled up to him.

"I'm surprised you ended up working as a secretary, love. I can remember you playing at the school concerts. We all thought you were going to be a concert pianist."

"Don't I wish! Dunno as how I would have been good enough for that. No, I always knew I was going to be a secretary."

"That keen, eh?" he quirked a disbelieving brow and I poked my tongue out at him.

"Brain-washed, more like. Mum and Dad were a bit old-fashioned. You know, working class girls don't need a higher education because they're going to get married and have a family."

"Usual for the East End in those days," he agreed.

"Yup. Even as late as the early 1960s there wasn't much choice for girls even if they did go to High School. Teaching or nursing. No ta!" Even now I go cold at the thought of that choice. You've really got to want to do them. "At least Mum and Dad had their own ideas for me. Not a shop girl or a factory hand, but a secretary. Fortunately we learned shorthand and typing in the last year at school."

"But surely you kept on with the piano lessons after that?"

I hooted. "David, darling, I was a teenager. I no longer had to spend hours practicing at the piano!" He looked puzzled. "My wages weren't that fantastic and for Mum and Dad it wasn't important that I kept up the piano. After all, I could play tunes they recognised, and that was enough for them."

He took my face in his hands, his thumbs gently stroking my cheeks. "Poor darling," he murmured before our lips met in a deeply satisfying kiss.

Sometime later when we were lying on the floor, relaxed in each other's arms and various bits of clothing scattered about the room, I returned to the subject of careers.

255

"David," he hummed as he nibbled my ear, "when did you join the police?"

He propped himself on an elbow to give me a quizzical look. And a view of his hard body, fortunately not too hairy. I almost forgot what I had asked him!

"More or less right out of school. I'd always wanted to be a Bobby."

"You joined at fifteen?"

"No. Eighteen. I had a second shot at the eleven-plus or whatever it was called, and got to grammar school."

Clink, clink, clink, the pennies dropped. "Of course. I'd forgotten that. Yeah, your Gran was so proud."

"Like these?" he asked as he teased my nipples.

Late Sunday afternoon we were on the train going back to Hampshire. As it pulled out of Waterloo Station I asked, "Can we talk police biz now?"

He sighed, looked at me and smiled. Wish he wouldn't do that in a public place. It makes me want to ravish him. "Go on."

"Paula phoned and told me one of the village ladies had lost a scarf and that she'd told the woman to call you."

"She did and, no, it wasn't right one. Sorry, love, I'm not telling you. I don't want every crank calling."

"Well, I guess its got to be a long one." I didn't get any further. He kissed me. "Anyway," I tried to get my thoughts in order once I'd surfaced, "I'm wondering about Mrs. Cheetham's twins. It was odd the way they visited me and, as for getting me name wrong, that sounded rehearsed."

"I agree, but I can't find anything that relates."

256

"What about if one of them wants to get married?" He raised his eyebrows. "The other one would have to do a buy out. They'd need the money for that."

"True, but do you know if one is going to get married?"

"Rob has a girlfriend."

"Doesn't mean 'e wants to marry 'er."

"No, but it's a thought."

"Anyway, how do you know?"

I told him about Prim and me meeting Ros.

When I'd finished he merely commented, "Interesting."

Oh, ta, leave me in the dark, why don't you.

As they say, all good things come to an end and for the next few weeks life was a bit flat (apart from the few times David and I got together, of course). I got on with learning Portuguese and practicing the piano. Maggie took to coming over to use the pool at weekends and although I suggested she bring some friends, she didn't. I did notice when Prim was down one weekend that the pair of them got on like the proverbial house fire. Not a bad role model for a teenager. I guess I've become the favorite "aunt", although I don't feel like one.

Of course Brian Spencer got away with it - again.

"As he wouldn't confess to killing either Janet or Dan or both, and we don't have anything to tie him to the murders there wasn't anything we could do," David told me as we were sitting cosily on the sofa in the living room after dinner one evening.

"What about the money?"

"Withheld until the experts can trace it back to its source."

"But what about the info from Prim's paper?"

"Not our Manor. If that force is successful then Brian could find himself in Court again on another charge."

"But in the meantime he's free and clear?"

"Yup. And nothing we can do about it."

"What about Jack Smith?"

"Presumably enjoying his new found wealth. He's moved out of his digs, bought a bungalow in the suburbs and got an improved car."

"Would you call it the perfect crime?"

"What? The murders?"

"What else d'you think I'm talking about?" I dug an elbow in his ribs.

"Ouch." Needless to say a tussle ensued that put an end to the conversation and led to a more interesting activity.

Of course I still haven't done anything about the pool room. Actually, what with Prim, Maggie, Paula, Gerard and David all using it (even Jenny Dixon on a couple of occasions) there hasn't exactly been time to get it redecorated. Anyway, the ghost was laid. Might as well just leave it.

And I've got another problem. What to do with the flat over the garage. If I'm not going to have a live-in couple it's going spare.

David's got his own place nearer his office. It's too far away for Prim. In any case when she stays she likes the guest suite and its Jacuzzi. Maggie's too young and it definitely wouldn't be tactful to have Jenny Dixon live there. Not with her boss visiting.

Oh well, leave it empty. Never know, I might one day get around to having a couple again – when I'm in my dotage and too decrepit to travel.

258

And that's where we were at. The double murder still unsolved and that satisfying occurrence looking more unlikely by the day.

With a bit of luck, we can all settle down and just get on with our lives. Or so it seemed, but I should have remembered that these days my life never runs smoothly.

Chapter 36

So there I was pottering about with a duster – well I was expecting David and didn't want the place to look too bad. Mrs. W isn't due until tomorrow. Yes, of course, he's going to cook dinner. Only problem is he's not sure what time he'll be here.

Of course, when the doorbell rings I assume it's him. Bit earlier than expected but who's counting? I shoved the duster behind a cushion on one of the chairs and toddled out to the hall. The bell pealed again.

"I'm coming. I'm coming. I suppose you forgot your key again." I warbled and felt right embarrassed when I opened the door without checking – not David, but Jack Smith, Janet's brother. Well, what could I do? I invited him into the kitchen and offered him a cup of tea.

"Yeah, that'll go down a treat."

No please or ta. I made it and left it to draw before asking what I could do for him. "I want the bank book."

"Eh?"

"Brian's bank book. He ain't got it so I reckon as how you must have it."

"Not me." Alarm bells started ringing. Better tell him where it is. "The police have got it."

Suddenly I'm looking a gun in the eye. Help!!!

"Siddown, you stupid cow. You don't think I believe that, do you? It's not in the flat."

"How d'you know? I was there when you looked and…."

"Shut the fuck up! I've looked again, ain't I?"

"I see." I try to stop my hands from trembling by holding them tightly in my lap. "Did you look through the house as well?"

"No, but I'm about ter tear it apart if you don't tell me where the book is," he snarled as he leant across the table. Yuck, halitosis. That or his rotten teeth – all yellow. With the money he's now got you'd think he'd do something about them.

"It's with the police," I enunciated clearly and slowly.

"I told you, bitch, I don't believe you." He hit the side of my head with the gun.

"Ouch."

"Shuttup."

Wish he'd make up his mind whether he wants me to tell him where the book isn't or not speak at all. As you can imagine, my mind's now racing. Why does he want Brian's bank book? He can't take the money out. Anyway, how does he know it exists? Come on, Cleo girl, David's coming, if you can keep Jack talking... How?

"Shall I pour out the tea?" I remember it and use it as a stalling tactic.

"Yeah. An' no funny business."

With a gun at my back? Come on, Sunny Jim, I'm not that foolish.

"Milk and sugar?"

"Yeah. Two spoons."

I put the tea – in a mug – in front of him. "Siddown." He waves the gun at me. I do hope the safety catch is on.

"Can I ask you something?" I ask him quietly as he slurps his tea.

"What?"

"How d'you know about Brian's bank book?"

"Janet told me."

"How did she know about it?"

"Found it in Dan's things. Then it disappeared."

To Maggie, then to the Roller.

"So perhaps Dan gave it back to Brian," I suggested.

He shook his head. "That's what they was arguing about."

Eh? Who? When? Lightning struck and I did my best to keep my face plain. You know, expressionless. Dan and Janet fighting by the pool?

"You there then?"

"Nah. I come to see Janet. We was going to meet in the pool room. I was outside and saw 'em through the winder."

"Arguing."

"Yeah, then he pushed 'er."

"Into the pool."

"Yeah." Tears actually came into his eyes. This weasely creature about to cry?

"Why didn't she just swim away?"

"'Cos she banged her head on the side of the pool."

"Didn't he try to get her out?"

"Nah. He just turned and ran out the room."

"Did he realise she wasn't going to surface?"

"Dunno."

"So didn't you try to get in to save her?"

"Couldn't. The doors was locked."

Of course. But I wouldn't have put it past him to break a window if he cared for her that much.

Then the front door bell rang. The cavalry!

"No funny business, you," he threatened me with the gun again.

"I'll have to answer it. Otherwise whoever it is'll come round the back."

"Alright, but no funny business, you hear?"

262

"Okay." As the side of my face was throbbing I was pretty sure it was at least red so David would know something was wrong – hopefully.

"Come on, get moving," Jack ordered as the bell sounded again.

He walked me down the hall then stood so that he'd be behind the door training the gun on me. Stupid idiot – right by a window!

I opened the door part way and blocked David, "Sorry, George, I've got a dreadful headache so I'm going to bed. Can you come back another day?" While I'm talking David's eyebrows nearly disappear into his hair and I manage to point to the door hoping he'll get the message. He did. He stepped quietly back and leaned to his left so he could look at the stained-glass window and saw Jack's shape through it.

"Sorry to hear that, Cleo. Of course I'll come some other time." Then all hell broke loose as, with both hands, he shoved the door right back, squashing Jack, I yelled, "Watch the gun!" and threw myself on the floor. If it hadn't been so serious it would've been laughable.

Anyway, Jack dropped the gun in surprise, David kicked it in my direction and I kicked it towards the kitchen before getting up to get my duster and pick up the deadly instrument.

Good job them leaded windows are strong – didn't break.

Meanwhile David had Jack in a very firm grip with his arm up his back. And, of course, Jack was whining that "it hurt".

So back to the kitchen where David plonked Jack on a chair and, still holding him whipped out his ID card. Jack crumpled not only at sight of the police card but also because, as he looked at David, he recognised him.

"While I'm still holding him, Cleo, would check the back door is locked, give me the key, then close the kitchen door and lean up against it."

I obeyed (guess he thinks I'm heavy enough to make it difficult for Jack to force his way past me!), then David relaxed his hold slightly. "So, Jack, are you going to be sensible?"

"Yeah. Ain't got nothing left now."

Still standing guard, David let him go. Jack collapsed on the table and cried. Wimp! Feeling sorry for himself.

Keeping his eye on Jack, David made his way to the worktop where I'd laid down the gun. Carefully, using the duster, he checked the safety catch then opened it. Glanced at me, held it up and tipped it. Empty.

Putting it down carefully he told me, "Cleo, come here and wrap this for me."

Yes, master! Of course I didn't argue. Well, in the circs what would you do? He guarded the door while I did that then I went back to the door and he – at last – got out his phone and called Sergeant Wiles. His orders were to get a local cop car to pick up Jack Smith and take him to Southampton.

And Jack snuffled on. I pointed to the roll of kitchen paper and David took the hint, pulling off several sheets and handing them to the weeper.

As soon as we heard the cop car – yeah, all sirens on (just like little boys, aren't they?), David manhandled our prisoner out into the hall and handed him over to the uniforms.

"Whew!" he exclaimed. "Are you okay?"

"Think so." He opened his arms and I walked into them for the obligatory cuddle. By now I was feeling a bit weepy myself.

"Come on, love." He led me into the living room and sat us on the sofa. Then I felt a hanky in my hand and realised I was crying.

After a good unladylike blow (good job he's known me since we was kids) and a wipe of the eyes I sat up. "Sorry about that."

"Shock."

"Yeah, I know." Then I remembered what Jack had been telling me when David arrived and passed it on. Needless to say he got "Steaming" again! Out came the mobile and orders went out that no one was to interview Jack Smith until the boss got there.

"Will you be okay, love?" he asked anxiously. Wow – he is improving. I thought he'd just go charging out of the door.

"I suspect I've got to be. Go on. You know you're dying to go speeding up to Southampton with the siren going."

"I take it that lump coming up on the side of your face is where he hit you?" I nodded. "With the gun?" Again I nodded and he kissed it better. "Put some ice on it, take some aspirin or something and go to bed."

"Yes, bossy." Now that he'd reminded me I could feel my head beginning to throb. Hope I don't get a black eye! "Oh go on! Go and put your siren on and break the speed limit!"

He grinned, kissed me (most satisfactorily) then almost ran out of the room. He certainly ran to his car and, as I'd surmised, put on the siren. Small boys.

265

You notice he wasn't bothered about my safety? And there was Brian Spencer somewhere out there.

Chapter 37

There are times when this place is like Piccadilly Circus with people in and out. I'd only just gone into the downstairs loo to check my face and see whether it needed an ice-pack when the front door bell rang. No peace for the wicked, as my Mum used to say.

I looked through the ripple window at the side of the front door. No cars, police or otherwise, but it looked like two shapes.

Of course, the twins. I undid the chain and ushered them into the living room.

"We just saw the police drive off," Rob told me.

This can't be mere curiosity, they had to have been outside waiting. It's not like this house is surrounded by others and the neighbours can see what's going on.

"We thought they'd come to arrest you," Was Ros's contribution.

"Why me? I haven't done anything wrong. They just arrested the man who murdered the Spencers."

"You killed our mother, didn't you?" Rob accused me.

"I – do what? You're crazy. Why would I?"

"You found her picking your flowers and got mad at her. You used one of your scarves."

That reminded me where I'd seen such a scarf before. Idiot that I am – I used to own one like it – donkey's years ago!

"Why don't you sit down and we'll talk this through," I suggested, indicating the sofa.

"Sit if you want to, we'll stand."

For a quick get away? While they were standing, so was I.

"We've worked it out," Ros told me. "I've seen you about the village in your caftans. You like floaty things so I think you've got a collection of floaty scarves.

What do they know about the scarf? Even I don't know whether or not it is 'floaty'.

"Do you know what I think?" I looked from one to the other, "I think you read too many mystery novels."

Rob stepped forward threateningly, but Ros said, quietly, "No, Rob, let's hear her opinion. Be interesting."

"Thanks. I think that when your mother telephoned that last time she told you I'd told her off for stealing my flowers and you thought you would take advantage of that. It doesn't take that long to drive down from Croydon and you don't have to go through the village to get here. I think once you were here you telephoned your mother, said you'd made it alright with me and that she could come and pick some flowers. If she'd said anything about my being here you would have told her that you'd take me to Lyndhurst for coffee so that she wouldn't be embarrassed. Or something like that.

"I think you've tried to set me up, but it won't work because I wasn't here."

They exchanged a look and I wondered whether I had imagined the alarm in their eyes. Although I'd put forward this theory because it was possible, I don't think I seriously thought it was the truth. I was still, sort of, thinking that Mrs. C. had been killed by either Jack Smith or Brian Spencer because they had overheard her telling me she knew something about the Spencers.

I went on, "I was in London and with other people that day. What's the problem? You need money quickly so one of you can buy out the other?"

268

At that Rob lunged at me, the door opened and in walked Mrs. Walsh with an aerosol that she directed in Ros's face. Don't know what it was but it must have stung like hell. She yelled!

Rob had grabbed my shoulders and pulled me in front of him – so I'd get the next squirt? I felt a prick on my neck.

Gerard then entered, complete with one of his hunting rifles and aimed it at Rob. Paula and Maggie came in and helped Mrs. Walsh with Ros. They must have had it planned as Paula had a bottle of water and a cloth.

"Mr. Cheetham, as an Officer of the Court, I am arresting you and your sister for the murder of your mother. You will drop that knife," Knife! "and let Miss Marjoribanks go."

He did, thank goodness. I wonder how many people have been threatened by two murderers in one day? Am I ready for the Guinness Book of Records?

Paula sat me on the sofa and held my hand. "Alright?"

"Bit shaken up. That's twice my life's been saved by the bell this morning. Ta." She looked surprised so I added, "David has just arrested Jack Smith for the Spencer murders. He was here threatening me with a gun." She put an arm about my shoulders and gave me a hug.

In the meantime Gerard was on the phone, presumably to the nearest police station for transportation to take the twins to Southampton. I should add that he still had the rifle trained on Rob and Mrs. Walsh and Maggie were standing guard over Ros.

I can just imagine the chaos at the Southampton Police Station when David gets two more to interview and charge!

I took advantage of the wait to find out more and asked, "How did you know I wasn't at home?"

269

"Mum told me," Ros said sulkily.

"How did she know?"

"You don't keep your gates shut," Rob pointed out.

I sighed. "Okay, so she came to the house and saw I was away. How did she know how long I would be away?"

"Dunno," Ros shrugged.

"Let's get this straight. You called your Mum the day before you killed her and she told you I was away."

"Yes."

"Did she tell you she was stealing my flowers?"

"Yeah. She was gloating about getting one over on you," Rob sneered.

I shrugged. "Didn't do her much good, did it? So you knew she was coming here the next day, took the day off from work and drove down. If your car was here your Mum would have known you were here."

"We didn't park it here."

"No, we put it in one of the car parks and came through the woods."

"Then waited until she arrived?"

"Hid behind the garage," Rob elucidated.

"Then we waited until she was cutting the flowers and come up behind her," Ros finished gleefully.

"I don't think we need the details," Gerard interrupted the terrible twosome and I snuck a look at Maggie. Big round eyes at eager for the grue. "Why did you do it?"

"She wouldn't sell the house."

"She didn't need a big house any more for just her," Ros pointed out reasonably. Well, for her it was reasonable.

"Where would she have lived?" Paula asked gently.

"We were going to sell our place and with the money from the two places buy our own places. Rob and Mary

270

would have their place and Mum could have lived with me."

Tell that to the Marines! "In Croydon?"

"Or somewhere near."

So with a mother they couldn't wait to get away from and who didn't even like Southampton they expect us to believe that?

Eventually two police cars had arrived and taken off the culprits and I had spoken with David. At first he was angry at being called away from interrogating Jack Smith then, when he heard the story and had had a quick word with Gerard, was all commiseration. Of course he finished by telling me he was sending Jenny to take our statements. All heart.

So, how had my posse known I needed saving?

Mrs. Walsh made some tea and we all adjourned to the kitchen. With cups of fragrant brew in front of us we told her to begin.

"I was cycling up the road and passed them walking up 'ere. Thought there was only one place they was coming to so I cycled past, to give 'em time to come up the drive, then I come back.

"Once they was inside I went round the other side," away from the living room windows, "and come in the kitchen. Crept up the 'all and listened at the door. Went back to the kitchen and called Mr. and Mrs. Linley."

Gerard took up the story. "I got the rifle, told Paula I was coming, so she came, too."

"So did I," Maggie pointed out. As if we hadn't noticed her!

"What made you suspicious of the twins, Mrs. Walsh?" I asked.

271

"Well, they was always in trouble when they was young. You remember, madam." She looked at Paula who nodded, "They stole from the shops but because no one liked their mother and thought they were only doing it to get attention, no one took 'em to Court."

"More's the pity," Gerard commented dryly. "You have no idea how many times I told people not to let them off with a slap on the wrist."

"Yes, dear, I remember," Paula smiled fondly at him. She'd obviously heard the story more times than she'd needed to. He smiled back. And he does have a lovely smile; it takes the grimness from his face. "Sorry, Mrs. Walsh, carry on. We're dying to know what really happened."

"I wasn't in this part of the village when their Mum was killed so the penny didn't drop. That day I was out in the back garden and I saw a couple in the woods." Her garden backs onto the forest and there's nothing unusual with seeing ramblers. "Anyway, when I was cycling along today I realised it had been them."

"Wow!" Maggie exclaimed, her eyes glowing. So much excitement for a teen.

"Exactly, Miss Margaret."

It was then my turn and I related what had happened before their arrival.

"I know Ros is into scarves because Primrose got to know some of her workmates."

"Dad, do you think I could become a journalist?"

"We'll see. It depends on your grades, doesn't it?" The eternal parental response.

Then Jenny arrived to take our statements. Then Primrose called. It had come up on the wire so we did a telephone interview and she promised to clear it with David. And I promised not to talk to any other journalists.

Then they were all gone and I sat down with a glass of whisky to try and recover.

Then remembered Brian Spencer.   Not three times in one day. Oh, per-lease, no.

Chapter 38

Sometimes over the next couple of days I got quite nervous wondering if Brian had killed Dan and would he do the same as Jack and come here looking for his bank book? Then I reversed the thought. After all, why would he kill his own brother. It wasn't as if Dan had money. If he'd trusted Dan with the bank book he surely didn't have to kill him to get it back.

Eventually of course I did hear the story but had to contain my curiosity for a few days. Until David finally got an evening off and came and cooked that meal.

"Come on, David, tell me before you start cooking. Don't leave me in suspense," I pleaded.

"But you know what's happened. Even if I hadn't telephoned it's been on telly and in the papers."

"I know that, but what's the inside story as it were? I shan't be able to eat me dinner."

He gave in and told me exactly what had happened the night Janet Spencer was murdered. Well, we'd got to the bit where Dan pushed her in the pool.

"Apparently Jack ran around the outside hoping to get into the house and save his sister."

"D'you believe that?"

He shrugged. "Either way. Of course he couldn't get in but Dan saw him and jumped into your Volvo and sped off. Jack's car was outside on the road and, if you remember, it wasn't a very good one."

"Virtually knackered," I agreed.

He nodded and continued, "Dan headed off up onto the moors with Jack struggling to keep up. Unfortunately the Volvo didn't have much fuel and in a deserted area chugged to a stop so Dan left it and ran into the woods to hide.

"Although Jack knows the forest pretty well he couldn't find Dan so had to leave it until daylight. Dan met up with Margaret Linley the next morning and asked her for money."

"Which she asked me for."

"Right. The reason Margaret didn't meet him the following day is because he didn't turn up."

"Jack had found him?"

"Uh-huh. He'd been hiding out in the woods and Jack found him."

"But what about me car? Why wasn't that found sooner?"

"Jack siphoned petrol from his own car and into yours. He then took his car to a car park in Southampton and came back by public transport and on foot. Then he used your car. As he couldn't look for his bother-in-law in the dark he went back to Southampton for the night."

"With my car?"

"Yup. That's why it couldn't be found. When he caught up with Dan he shot him. Then, using a blanket, he took the body in the Volvo and dumped it in the river Beaulieu where it went out on the tide. He then drove your car to where it was found, before going off to collect his own car, hide the gun and laying low."

"Presumably the gun I found?"

"That's right."

"So where did he get the gun he had when he came here?"

David shrugged. He wasn't bothered with the nitty gritty.

"What I don't understand is why Jack came to the house that evening. I thought he'd never been here before."

"According to Jack, Janet had called him to say she and Dan had had a row about the bank books. Janet had found Brian's and wanted to know why Dan had it, and Dan wanted to know about the missing money from their savings account."

"We'll never know what she told him but obviously she had changed the hiding places for that one and hers and Jack's account book. She was, possibly, going to give the books to Jack that evening."

"Or maybe they were going to do a flit."

"Maybe."

"Greed's a nasty thing."

"Sure it is."

"Do we know which bank book Margaret had?"

"The assumption is that it was Brian's book. After Janet found it Dan had to find somewhere else to hide it. Don't you want to know about Brian Spencer?"

"Yeah. Where is he?"

"Apparently scarpered. Last heard of heading for Spain."

"You'll get him back though?"

"Not me. The other lot will – if necessary. Don't know where he got the money from but as he hasn't got his money they may decide it isn't worth the expense."

"At least he hasn't got away with murder."

"Nope. He may be a crook but he's not a murderer.

So, there we were, two murders all for the sake of three bank books: one belonging to Janet and Dan, one belonging to Janet and Jack, and Brian's – all containing ill-gotten gains.

My curiosity satisfied, David prepared a luscious dinner which we were able to eat in peace and quiet in the dining room where I'd made an effort with the table. Right down to candles and soft music.

The End

Printed in Great Britain
by Amazon